Under the Redbud Tree

E Dee Merriken Monnen

Robert D. Reed Publishers
P.O. Box 1992
Bandon, OR 97411
Phone: (541) 347-9882 or 541-999-6125
Email: cleonelreed@gmail.com
Website: www.rdrpublishers.com

Cover: Authors Hike: https://authorshike.com/

Editor and Book Formatting: Cleone Lyvonne Reed, MSE

SOFTCOVER ISBN: 978-0-9858907-2-8

EBOOK ISBN: 978-0-9858907-3-5

Library of Congress Control Number: 2024935258

Designed and formatted in the United States of America

Dedication

In memory

of my parents,

Lyal and Marilla.

Acknowledgments

Mary Waltenberger

Jeanne Robinson

Eric Monnen

Pastor Jake Reid and his wife Valerie

Shannon P. Dill, University of Maryland Extension Educator, Agriculture & Resources

Robyn Hall

Helen Christensen

Rachel Ames, Atlantic Tractor

Rebecca Stefanski

Garvin Oneil, Manager of the Menger Hotel, San Antonio

Contents

FOREWORD

Delaware and the Eastern Shore of Maryland are two separate states, but culturally they are like Siamese twins connected along a common boundary. Residents dart across the border as if it were one state, and if you could lop off the northern area “above the canal,” Delaware and the Eastern Shore of Maryland would be of one mindset, conservative and neighborly.

Ask any Marylander on the Delmarva Peninsula if they’ve ever been to the Maryland State Fair near Baltimore and most likely the answer will be no. Ask them if they’ve ever been to the Delaware State Fair, and they’ll probably tell you what concert or special events they plan to see. That’s because the Chesapeake Bay represents more than a geographical divide to many longtime residents of the Eastern Shore.

Unfortunately, Delmarva’s moral compass isn’t pointing north as much as it once did due to a local and national paradigm shift in God consciousness. And although much of America’s strong moral values have eroded over the decades, it has a bulwark in believing farmers who know their lives and livelihoods are dependent on God. They are the ones who feed America and plow out the driveways of the elderly after a heavy snowfall. They are members of the volunteer fire company, the school board, and the church board. They are the last protectors of a wholesome, traditional lifestyle which most Americans hold dear. We tip our hat to the Farmers.

– James W. Phillips
Sheriff of Dorchester County, Maryland
Grain and Poultry Farmer

David (Dave) Johnson Family Tree

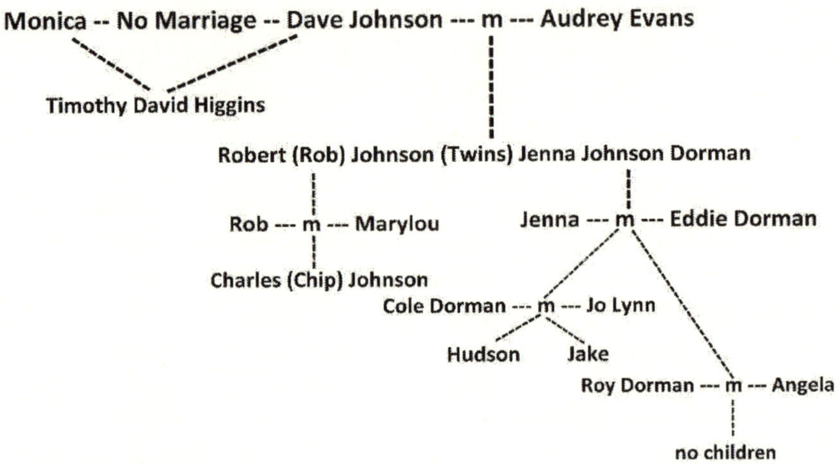

PROLOGUE

St. Louis, Missouri
Spring 1962

"Okay, that's a wrap!" A man's angry voice roared over the intercom. Monica removed her headphones, and the jazz ensemble stopped playing. There was a brief silence inside the recording studio before the furious voice sounded again. "Monica, you can't hold your jaw while singing. It changes your embouchure and timing."

"I'm sorry, but my toothache has been getting worse all day. Can you find another singer?"

"Monica! We can't use another singer because the customer specifically asked for you. I tell you what. Musicians, you can all go home. Monica needs to see a dentist before they all close for the day, and then maybe we can start again tomorrow."

Monica let out a sigh of relief. "Thank you, and don't worry. I'll find a dentist, and I'll be back singing like a bird in the morning."

Grace, the receptionist at St. Louis's newest dental office tucked her novel and a magazine into the desk drawer and grabbed her purse. "Doctor Tim, it's nearly five o'clock. Should we lock up or wait one more hour?"

Dr. Timothy Higgins stared out the window. "No not yet, Gracie. We may have our very first dental patient. There's a young man getting out of his car, and he's coming this way. I'll wait in the exam room." Tim disappeared, and Grace rolled her *here-we-go-again* eyes.

A few moments later the front door swung open, and the potential patient entered. "I'm so glad you're still here. It's my last stop of the day." He plopped a large phone book on Grace's desk. "Cheers!" He turned on his heel and left without another word.

While thumbing through the yellow pages, Grace walked back to the exam room where her boss sat slouched down on the dental chair. "Well, Doctor Tim, the bad news is that the young man was not a patient, but he did deliver some good news." She placed the open phone book in Timothy's hands and pointed. "Your very first yellow page ad."

"Gracie, this is more than good news. It's great news. We're now officially listed!"

"Oh dear, I guess I'll have to start answering the phone."

Tim jumped out of his chair. "You bet you will! Oh, you just watch, Gracie. Our phones will soon be ringing off the hook! As of today, we may not be in the money, but at least we're in the phone book!" He took Grace's hands and began to dance around the exam room, and while they continued their frolicking, the phone rang. "Ah ha, Gracie! What did I just say?"

"I'll take it back here." Grace picked up the extension line. "Good afternoon, Dr. Higgins dental office, how may we help you? ...Yes, we're still open. ...Oh, that sounds like you need immediate help. May I have your name, please? ...Monica Dawson, and do you know where our office is located? ...That's right. ...Don't worry. We understand. You're having terrible pain, so no doubt we'll be seeing you shortly, and don't you worry. We'll be here waiting for you. Just come on over now. Bye."

"Hallelujah," Tim shouted. "How do you like that? Dad told me not to expect my practice to grow until my ad appeared in the yellow pages, and now we have our first patient!" He abruptly wiped the smile off his face. "Oh, but I'm so sorry. My dear Gracie, from now on, you'll be working for your paychecks. For that matter," Tim laughed out loud, "me, too!"

Anxious to see their very first customer, they waited impatiently—Tim in his exam room, staring out the window and Grace stationed behind her desk. Both watched the clock in nervous anticipation until Monica Dawson, a young, refined looking woman entered the office. She had thick auburn hair that was coiffed in a trendy bouffant hairdo underneath a smart pillbox hat. Her understated makeup framed her attractive face, which was accessorized by aquamarine earrings that matched the color of her sparkly eyes.

"Hello. I'm Monica Dawson," she said as she waddled up to the receptionist desk wearing a stylish maternity outfit. Monica couldn't help but notice the receptionist's bulging eyeballs staring at her very pregnant waistline and how she managed to pull them politely back into position.

Grace extended her open hand. "Why don't you have a seat? You'll be more comfortable."

"I'll say. My ankles are so swollen." Monica sat on the padded armchair next to Grace's desk, removed her white gloves, and then reached in her purse for a compact to powder the damp sheen from her face. As Monica looked around the spacious waiting room, the strong odor of fresh paint and new fabrics made her feel a bit queasy. "Say, this place seems brand new."

"It is—very new—and we're glad you found us. Pardon me for saying, but your hairdo and stunning outfit make you look like Jackie Kennedy when she was with child."

"Thank you. A friend of mine bought the dress pattern from *Advance Patterns* and sewed this outfit for me as a maternity gift. Except for a different fabric, I think it's a perfect copy of a Jackie Kennedy dress."

Grace handed Monica a paper attached to a clipboard. "Do you mind filling out this form? We'd like your full name, address, and phone number." Monica pulled a pen from her purse just as Grace began to talk about herself, not bothering to address Monica's throbbing jaw.

"You know, I was a registered nurse at St. Louis General Hospital, but it was too much for my sixty-plus-year-old body. Fortunately, this job is a piece of cake."

While massaging her jaw, Monica looked up from her paperwork. "I can see how a dental office would be easier employment. Excuse me, ma'am, how soon can I see Dr. Higgins?"

"Oh, you'll love Dr. Higgins. I think he looks like James Garner, and he's always so cheerful and has a great sense of humor. It makes me wonder why he doesn't have a steady stream of eligible ladies asking for checkups, but you happen to be our very first patient."

While she continued to fill out the form, Monica began to worry whether she had made the correct choice of dentist. "Are you telling me the dentist is inexperienced?"

"Oh, not at all. Dr. Higgins worked across town with his father for three years. …Say, are you okay? You look a bit tired."

"I've had an exhausting day, and my sore tooth interfered with my work."

"I assume Mr. Dawson knows you're here."

"There's no Mr. Dawson, but the father of this child wanted to marry me. …Oh, but he didn't know about the baby. We met last July at the Delaware State Fair and fell passionately in love."

"Anyone can see there was passion."

"It was only a one-week romance, and before week's end, we were engaged." Monica held out her left hand. "He gave me this diamond."

Taking the clipboard from Monica, "It's beautiful—looks like more than a karat."

"It is, and it does the trick for a single woman in my condition. Dave asked me to quit my job, elope, and live with him on the family farm. Unfortunately, I realized—obviously too late—that this city gal has no business being a farmer's wife." Admiring her long, polished nails, "I simply couldn't picture myself canning tomatoes and feeding chickens for the rest of my life."

"Neither can I."

While holding her jaw, Monica stood up and looked around at random places on the ceiling with dreamy eyes. "Dave Johnson was a wonderful guy—kind, sensitive, tall, and *very* handsome. His hair color was dark like mine. After I said I couldn't marry him, he told me I could keep the ring. I think my refusal angered him a bit."

"After buying a ring like that, I'd say you probably angered him a lot."

"But strangely, he never showed it. The fact that he allowed me to keep this beautiful diamond demonstrated his generous nature. When we broke up, neither one of us knew about the baby. How could we after knowing each other for only one week?"

Monica winced in pain as beads of sweat began to displace her foundation makeup. She let out a soft moan as she grabbed a tissue from Grace's desk to dab her face.

"Is your discomfort from your tooth or the baby? Well, in either case, Dr. Higgins is waiting for you in the exam room. Let me help you get situated in there. This way, please."

With her hand still pressed against her right jaw, Monica followed Grace into the next room, and used Grace's shoulder for balance as she stepped up onto the chair.

"May I take your hat, Monica?" Grace said. "I wouldn't want you to crush it when you lean back against the headrest."

Dr. Higgins stood nearby staring at Monica's beautiful face and eyes, so much that he could barely get his name off his lips. "Hello, I'm Dr. Higgins." He politely ignored her fully extended belly. "I assume the trouble is on your right side."

"Yes, sir." Monica tried hard to get comfortable in the chair, but no matter what position she took, her baby decided it wasn't good enough. "Dr. Higgins, thank you for waiting. Getting a cab during rush hour is so unpredictable, and there is no way I could work tomorrow with this sore tooth."

"It's okay, just open wide and let me get a good look." He adjusted the light strapped to his head.

Monica could feel the metal instrument tapping on her suspect tooth. "Ouch!"

"Yep, that's the one. Your wisdom tooth needs to be extracted."

"How soon?"

"Right now. I can give you a local anesthetic, and it won't take long to remove it, that is, once your jaw is numb. You probably should come back and have your other wisdom teeth removed before they become sore as well—at least that's what my father would recommend. He's also a dentist."

Monica watched with a nervous stare as Grace filled a syringe and handed it to the doctor. She then closed her eyes as tight as possible and squeezed the arms of the chair until her knuckles turned white.

Tim expelled a few drops from the needle, leaned over Monica and looked for a specific spot in her mouth. "Okay. Open as wide as you can, Monica, and don't worry. This needle won't hurt me. It never does."

As Dr. Higgins administered the anesthetic, Monica realized that Grace was right. *This doctor does have a sense of humor and Hollywood good looks. His strong face, dark wavy hair, and tall masculine build are quite attractive.*

"In a few minutes, that should do it," the doctor said. "I'm hesitant to give you much more in your condition, but if you need more, let me know."

"I will."

"Good. In the meantime, you mentioned that you wanted to work tomorrow. May I ask what you do for a living?"

"Normally, I'd sell JJ Weatherby microphones and speakers. During the season, I worked with two other singers doing three-part harmony routines at State Fairs all over the country. Our music attracted dozens of buyers to our booth using JJ Weatherby mics and speaker systems. On good days, we'd make several sales."

"What would you do during the winter months?" Tim asked.

Monica's speech was garbled. "I'd perform at indoor gigs—mostly electronics shows in big cities. Two years ago, the JJ Weatherby Company sent us to Germany, but today in my condition I'm limited to singing jingles for a commercial ad agency here in St. Louis." Patting her tummy, "With no husband and two mouths to feed, I'm hoping Mr. Weatherby will rehire me, because in sales you can earn a good living—with jingles I barely get by."

"That means you must be a very good singer."

Grace noticed that Monica's face appeared droopy. "Do you think she's ready, Doctor?"

"Maybe. Let me check. Open wide. Can you feel this, Monica?"

"Uh-uh."

"I believe that's a no," Dr. Timothy said. "Okay, I need you to open as wide as you can." He reached in her mouth with a forceps. "You'll feel pressure but no pain. Ah ha! That's it, Monica. Pretty quick, even for me, and the tooth is out in one piece. That bad boy won't give you any more trouble." The tooth pinged as Tim dropped it into the metal cup on his stand.

Monica wanted to commend him for the great job, but before she got the chance, Tim said, "Grace, gauze, please. Monica, I want you to gently bite down on this. That's it, nice and easy. Hold it right there."

Monica felt like gagging. The large wad of gauze filled most of her mouth.

"You're doing great. Just continue biting down." As Tim focused on Monica's face and mouth, he said, "Grace, please check by my feet. The floor seems a bit slippery."

Grace looked down and in a calm and professional voice said, "Monica, your water just broke."

Monica's furrowed brows and widened eyes showed fear and humiliation until she was comforted by Grace's gentle hand on her shoulder. "Don't fret, my dear. Winston Churchill's mother was at a formal dinner party and seated among many dignitaries when her water broke. The hostess sprang into action, quickly tossed all the mink coats off a bed, and that's where Winston was born."

"I never knew that about Churchill," Tim mused.

"Now look at me, Monica," Grace said. "I'm a registered nurse, and we'll call for an ambulance, so relax and take some deep breaths. Everything will be fine; however, do you mind if I check to see how much you're dilated?"

With her numbed jaw and mouth full of gauze, she nodded briskly and watched as Grace washed and dried her hands and donned a clean lab coat.

Monica let out a painful groan, and then said in a loud but garbled voice, "I hink hy hay-hee kuhing!"

"You're in luck, Grace," Tim chimed in. "I have mastered the gauze-mouth language, and Monica just said, she thinks her baby's coming." Tim gasped, "Dear heavens! She said her baby's coming!"

"Doctor, please! Get that gauze out of Monica's mouth so she can breathe and talk, and then give us some privacy. You can help by grabbing lots of towels." She pointed at the linen closet on the opposite wall. The tall, glass doors showed that dozens were available. "Towels, Timothy, now!"

Monica was relieved that Tim had turned away and toward the linen cabinet when Grace lifted her skirt.

"Oh, Monica, you're crowning! And in this situation crowning is not a dental term." Grace returned her attention to Monica, and in a gentle voice said, "Breathe, Monica, breathe, deep breaths, and don't be frightened. I can see the top of baby's head. Your baby wants out now. Most babies take their time, but this one is eager."

Monica could feel beads of sweat rolling down her forehead and cheeks, and the most excruciating pain between her legs, as she clutched the arms of the chair. "Ooh, ooh!"

"Timothy! Where are my towels? I need them now!"

Between punctuated deep breaths, Monica said, "Does this mean you're not calling for an ambulance?"

"Yes, Grace," Tim's shaky voice broke. "You did mention an ambulance."

"Ambulance!" Grace's reactive tone changed from loud to sweetness. "No, the baby has no intention of waiting for an ambulance. Just stay calm, Monica, and remember to breathe. During the Depression, I delivered dozens of babies in many homes, and this delivery looks quite normal."

Tim swallowed hard. "Normal! You think having a baby in a dental office is normal?" Tim's tone abruptly changed to contrite. "...But, but, er, uh, Monica and I are grateful for your vast maternity experience. Isn't that right, Monica?" He turned his attention away from Monica to give her privacy.

Monica never imagined that her baby would be born under such conditions. Her anxiety was high but not as pronounced as Dr. Timothy Higgins, who had finally retrieved a large stack of bright-white towels from the cabinet. He handed several to Grace and dropped a few on the floor to mop with his foot. The remaining ones were placed on the tray next to the metal cup where Grace could reach them.

"Tim, get a cold cloth and dab her face. Then, I need you and Monica to pay close attention to my directions as we deliver this baby."

Tim stammered, "We're going to deliver a baby?"

Monica noticed Grace's stern eyes firmly affixed on Tim as she said, "Yes, Tim, we are going to deliver Monica's baby because we have no choice."

Monica's heavy breathing was dizzying. She turned her head to the right and looked downward at Tim's knees which were shaking underneath his long white pants that were wet above his shoes. She let out a painful wail and grabbed Tim's forearm with a white-knuckle grip.

Tim placed his hand over Monica's. "This is a first for both of us. How are you holding up?"

Monica nodded. "And you, Doctor?" She said as she watched Tim's face turn ashen.

"Uh, I believe Grace wants you to take more regulated deep breaths, and I could use a few deep breaths myself…." He inhaled a deep breath and exhaled with relief. "…but rest assured, I'm okay."

"I'm glad," Monica said with disbelief before letting out an ear-piercing scream.

"That's it, Monica, one final push. Tim, get me something sterile to tie off the umbilical cord," Grace demanded, "and I'll need a pair of scissors from the autoclave. And put on a fresh lab coat because I may need you to hold the baby. Quickly now."

With Grace's guidance, it was a spectacular performance by everyone, just as if they had previously rehearsed the entire event. "Tim, if you would bring your car up to the front door, I believe the three of us can manage to get Monica and the baby to the hospital faster than any ambulance."

The following day, Monica sat up in her hospital bed holding her new little boy. The physical pain that she had endured along with the emotional stress of being an unwed mother had disappeared as she proudly realized that motherhood was her new calling. She sang to her new son in soft tones as she held his little hand, unaware that Tim had entered her room with a bouquet of red, long-stemmed tulips and her pillbox hat.

He stood near the door and listened to the sweet lullaby. Transfixed by the beauty of the scene, he waited until the lullaby ended. “Ahem, hello, Monica. These are for you. New mothers must have flowers.”

Monica looked up at Tim. He was no longer the nervous bystander in the dental office, but rather a strong, handsome visitor. “Goodness, those tulips are beautiful! Oh, and my hat, I was wondering when I could retrieve it. Thank you, Dr. Higgins. How thoughtful!”

“Call me Tim, since we’ve shared a very special event together.”

“We certainly did. And, thanks to you, my jaw feels much better.”

“I’m so glad. May I hold him?”

“Of course. His name is Timothy David Dawson. The Timothy is for you, the attending dentist.”

“Trust me, there were no child birthing classes at dental school. However, the name you’ve selected is a great honor. Thank you.”

“No, I’m the one thanking you, remember?”

Admiring the little one in his arms, “Does David senior know about his son?”

“I guess you figured out that Dave is the biological father, David Johnson, and the answer is, no. He doesn’t know. I called off my engagement to David before I knew I was pregnant. Then in my fifth month and after much anguish and prayer, I telephoned his farm in Maryland. He lives on the Eastern Shore just outside the town of Corinth. I was ready to tell him that I was going to have his baby, except his new bride answered the phone.”

“I bet that was a big surprise.”

“It was. Audrey is her name. I was stunned that he had gotten married so soon. But then, during my conversation, I learned that she was the girl next door. Her family owns the neighboring farm and a large canning factory. If you've ever eaten Evans brand fruits and vegetables, those are her family's products."

"Did you not know that he had another woman in his life when he asked you to get married?"

"Tim, when I see a man as handsome as Dave, I always suspect other ladies. Naturally, my heart sank when I discovered he was married, but only a little. His wife seemed so nice, and she was bursting with joy about their wedding and honeymoon which they had just returned from. So, you see, under that circumstance, I couldn't tell Dave about the baby, and to tell him now would only complicate his life and mine."

"I believe you made the right decision."

"When I hung up the phone, I got down on my knees and begged God to forgive me. It was so wrong of Dave and me, and I had no other choice but to ask God to help me raise my baby. I don't know what I would have done had I been alone in my apartment with a baby so eager to be born, and now I'm convinced that my sore tooth was God's way of making sure I had help."

Tim gazed at Monica with a pleasant smile. "You're even more radiant today. What's more, you were so brave by allowing us to help—not that you had much of a choice—but you showed such courage."

Monica had been paid many compliments from men over the years, but none so sincere. There was something different, something special about Tim, which she couldn't describe. "It was you and Grace who put me at ease. When I walked into your office, only the good Lord knew that little Timothy needed immediate help, and that you had a registered nurse and experienced midwife working in your office. I'm convinced it was divine providence, Tim."

Swaying gently with the baby while admiring his tiny face, "Timothy David, you are a beautiful boy. You may think you had a rough start but know that all things work together for good to them who love God."

"Thank you for those reassuring words."

Tim handed the baby back to Monica. "Timmy, I wish I could stay longer."

"You're not leaving so soon?"

"I'm sorry, but I need to return to the office. Thanks to my new yellow page ad, I have a patient who will be there about the time I get back."

"Well, thank you for coming and for the flowers."

"In a couple of weeks when you're feeling up to it, and if I can convince Grace to babysit, I'd like to take you to dinner."

"Take an unwed mother to dinner?"

"Monica, the world unfairly shames unmarried mothers, but not me. I want to take you to a restaurant that is as beautiful and elegant as you are."

"How can I resist after those compliments. Yes, I'd love to have dinner with you."

CHAPTER ONE

SIXTY YEARS LATER

Corinth, Maryland
April

After a hearty breakfast of biscuits 'n gravy, eggs, and syrup-drenched scrapple, eighty-four-year-old Dave Johnson sat in his rocker on the front porch as he did on most mornings with his old hunting dog Samson next to his feet. It was his time of reflection and relaxation. Dave especially loved the month of April when the verdant shoots of winter-wheat covered his fields as far as he could see. There was nothing more beautiful than a glorious green carpet across his vast property, a sight which always made him mindful of his most deeply held values: the love of the Almighty, the love of family, and the love of the land.

He thought about his hometown of Corinth and how it had lost so much of its vitality since he was a young man. The historic town once boasted of several factories, a bustling downtown, a movie house, a vibrant trucking industry, two automobile dealerships, and a lake for swimming. But over time, the movie house became a struggling house of worship; the government condemned the swimming hole because of elevated bacteria levels; the car dealerships closed when their owners retired; the downtown stores were crowded out by regional malls; nearly all the factories were bought up by international conglomerates; and burdensome taxes and regulations destroyed many local businesses including trucking. All told, the town of Corinth was left with several shuttered factories, two vacant car dealerships, and a nearly abandoned downtown. In addition, its wealthiest citizens moved away in search of more lucrative places to live. Only a few stores survived by specialization and by the good graces of many residents who faithfully patronized the local merchants.

Dave stared at the empty rocker by his side. "Audrey, we were witnesses to these changes in Corinth, but our life together has been so wonderful, my simple few words cannot convey how much you have blessed me and helped me search for the beautiful side in life. For instance, look at our lawn. No, no, not the wheat fields—the front yard. Our *love tree* is in full bloom, the redbud tree your father planted the week before we were married. We decided it would always represent our committed love and devotion to one another. Your father called it the *Passover Tree* because it blooms around Good Friday and sheds its little crimson flowers as if they were tiny droplets of blood. Remember how we'd spread a blanket under that redbud tree when it was in bloom? We'd daydream as if we had hours to watch the little petals flutter down. You'd put your head on my shoulder so I could steal several tender kisses, until our young twins interrupted the magic."

Dave's daughter Jenna opened the screen door and stepped out onto the porch holding a percolator in one hand and a letter in the other. "Who were you talking to, Daddy?"

"Oh, just thinking out loud so Samson and I can hear my morning thoughts."

"More coffee?"

Dave raised his mug, "Yes, please."

"I got a letter from your sister. Aunt Millie says that great-grandchild number four has arrived, a perfect little girl. I had invited her to come for a visit, but I don't think she'll leave her ever-expanding family in Denver."

"I know it may seem illogical, but after your Aunt Millie's husband passed, her travelling days died with him. Maybe one day she'll change her mind and hop on a plane, but she's a real homebody."

"Then, would you consider visiting her?"

"I'd like to see my sister again. You remind me of her—tall and thin. You both look like Johnsons, dark hair and deep blue eyes. Though I would imagine Millie's hair has turned gray like mine. Don't forget, Jenna, I'm not as limber as I once was, which makes long trips more difficult for me."

"You're fit enough to travel with Eddie and me, and think of all the nieces and nephews you've never met."

"I don't know, Jenna. I don't like to travel when it's cold."

"Daddy, you sound somewhere between, *yes*, I'll definitely go, and *maybe* if the weather is warm. What do you say? Cole and Jo Lynn will be here to care for the farm."

"I'd like time to think about it. What did they name the baby?"

"Millie."

"Not Millicent?"

"I like Millie. It's not as old fashioned, and it's quite sweet to name the little girl after her great grandma."

Dave had recently buried his beloved wife Audrey just after the fall harvest of soybeans when the days grew short and the nights chilled. The marriage of Dave Johnson and Audrey Evans not only united them as a couple but also united their two family-farms, which had a long, common border and together boasted over twenty-three hundred acres.

But then spring ushered in a time of renewal and freshness. It allowed the family to forget the darkness of winter and discover new beginnings. Jenna changed the name of the Evans Farm to the Dorman Farm with a new sign at the farm's entrance. The land, house, and buildings would eventually become hers; and she would eventually pass it on to her older son Cole Dorman. Although Dave was agreeable to the new sign and the name change, it conjured up troubling thoughts for him. His grandson Chip Johnson, who lived on the Johnson farm, was single and had no prospects for a wife, so Dave worried that his family farm might one day be renamed, too.

Shortly after Audrey's death, Jenna insisted that her father leave the Johnson farm and move in with her and husband Eddie Dorman, giving her father a fresh start in a new house. At first, Dave balked at the idea. He had lived on the Johnson Farm all his life, and he simply didn't think he was ready to live with so many Dormans—four adults and two great-grandsons—but Jenna persisted, and in the end, won. She wanted to be her father's primary caregiver for his end-of-life years, which seemed fair because her brother Robert and his wife Marylou had taken on that responsibility for their mother Audrey. Dave reflected upon how much his daughter Jenna adored him. She kept him occupied with day trips, dinners, and even an occasional bingo game at the fire hall, so to her, it seemed so natural that he should live out his life at the Dorman Farm.

The screen door banged shut after Jenna's husband stepped outside onto the porch. "I'm leaving now. Dad, do you need anything in town?"

"No, not really. Where 'ya going, Eddie?"

"The parts store. I want to buy a new battery for Old Red and get that '71 dump truck back on the road so I can sell it. It's the last piece of equipment left from the Evans estate that we haven't sold."

"Sounds like a good move to me," Dave said. "It's not good to have vehicles sitting idle and rotting away."

"I sure wish I could figure out why it doesn't start. It always seemed to start fine for Mr. Evans, but it has frustrated me to no end."

"I can't tell you much about Old Red, except I remember when Audrey's dad bought it. He was right proud of that dump truck. In fact, so proud that he never allowed me to drive it. Just let me know if I can help."

Eddie smiled wide. "You're on, mister miracle mechanic!" He looked at his wife. "Jenna, I told Jo Lynn I'm taking the grandsons because they've finished their homeschool assignments." Calling into the house, "Come on Hudson, Jake, let's go."

The two boys, eight and five, ran down the hall and dashed out the front door. "Hey, slow down." Eddie caught them just before they jumped off the porch. "Hug your grandma and great-grandpa, and then hop in the back where Jake's safety seat is. We won't be long, darling." He kissed Jenna's cheek, climbed into his pickup, and headed down the long driveway.

Dave's proud eyes watched until they disappeared down the lane. "Jenna, there's nothing better for an old farmer like me than sons and grandsons. In fact, it was Hudson and Jake who finally convinced me to leave the Johnson Farm and live here. Your grandsons are the future of our farms. I just wish Chip would find himself a wife and have a son so the Johnson Farm can remain the Johnson Farm."

"Really, Daddy, is that all you think about?

"Pretty much."

"But it takes more than men to run a farm. I consider myself a farmer *and* a farmer's wife, and quite grateful to be the next owner of this farm."

"Well, Jenna." He took his daughter's hand. "Any woman who can drive a combine as well as you deserves the title, *farmer*."

"Thank you, Daddy. Say, what are you doing today?"

"I'm going to mosey over to Rob and Marylou's for a while, maybe even cut their grass. I still need to keep a sharp eye on the Johnson Farm. Besides, Marylou has invited me to lunch."

"Oh, Daddy! Marylou has a standing invitation for you, breakfast, lunch, and dinner."

"I know. It's just nice to have an entry in my social calendar—and what do you know? Today, it's lunch at Rob and Marylou's." Dave and Jenna laughed together, as they loved to do.

"I think I'll leave you and Samson to your morning thoughts. I have lots of work to do." Jenna gave her father a kiss on the top of his head and went back into the house.

Alone again, Dave gave a second look at the empty rocker by his side. "Audrey, we did a good job raising our twins. Jenna and Robert turned out to be very fine folks."

CHAPTER TWO

The Johnson Farm

"Chip! Chip, are you around?" Robert Johnson, or Rob as his family called him, searched near the barnyard. "Chip!"

"Yeah, Pop."

Rob heard his son's voice from inside the shop area of the barn, a building that was as large as a high school gymnasium to house all the massive farm equipment and vehicles for both the Dorman and the Johnson Farms.

Chip stepped outside wiping the oil from his right hand with a rag. "I'm in the middle of changing the oil on your pickup."

Rob looked at the smudge on his son's forehead. "Did you wipe your sweat with the wrong rag? Your face sure looks like it."

"No, Dad, it's these darn mosquitos. They're out early this year."

Like his father and grandfather, Chip had a strong, handsome face and a tall, athletic physique, but unlike his father and grandfather, he inherited his mother's medium-blonde hair and his Grandmother Audrey's shy nature.

"Dad, I can get a couple more years out of your truck, but you should be looking for something newer. The rust on your undercarriage and door panels is bad, and it's crazy that you need to sit on a thick cushion to drive so the upholstery springs don't stab you."

Rob removed his work gloves from his leathery hands. "I know, and I'll start looking for something newer. It's just that I love my old reliable pickup. Say, your grandpa will be here soon to spend the day. I think it would be good to ask him a few mechanical questions. It reminds him that he's still important around here. Besides, you'll not get a more professional answer from any other mechanic."

"Will do."

"Good, because he's driving up the lane right now. Mother's fixing a special lunch this afternoon, so make sure you're cleaned up by then."

"What's so special about it?"

"It's all of Dad's family favorites. Marylou is breaking tradition by not inviting Jenna's grandkids, but don't misunderstand your mother. We love those boys. It's just that sometimes we'd like to have a meal without all those youthful commotions."

"I don't mind the boys. They're good kids, and I'm used to them."

"That's good, Chip, because one day you'll appreciate that experience and training when you have your own children, especially boys. At least that's your grandpa's hope, and mine, too."

Looking at the approaching vehicle, "Dad, are you sure that's Grandpa's truck?"

"Sure am, and it's right on time. Say, that's not his truck. It's got a logo on it—*County Extension Service.* I guess the county tightwads finally bought Buddy a new pickup. His old truck was worse than mine."

The shiny white pickup parked about twenty feet from where Rob and Chip were standing, and when the door opened, they were surprised. A shapely brunette stepped out wearing jeans, a plaid flannel shirt, cowboy boots, and a baseball cap with a county logo. "Are you Mr. Johnson?"

"Actually, we both are," Chip replied.

Rob cinched up his overalls and made sure his shirt was tucked. "If you wait a few minutes, another Mr. Johnson should be driving up this lane. That would be my father."

"I'm Sandra Moore, but, please, call me Sandy," handing a business card to both men. "I'm the new County Extension Agent."

"What happened to Buddy?" Chip asked.

"Buddy retired, and I was hired to fill that position. For now, I'm starting out by getting to know all the farmers in the county. I'm visiting as many farms as I can today, introducing myself and letting folks know I'm here and ready to help."

"Well, then, allow me to introduce you to my son Charles Johnson. Everyone calls him Chip. I'm his father Rob, and my dad Dave Johnson is heading this way in that white pickup. Lucky day for you—you get to meet all three Mr. Johnsons."

Chip's oily forehead didn't mask his handsome features when Sandy asked, "Chip, are you entering anything in the State Fair this year?"

"No, I'm working on the Greatest Yield Award."

The $25,000 *Greatest Yield Award* was sponsored by local banks and businesses in the county that did most of their trade with the farming community. It was an award open to all farmers, but normally it went to the farmers who had the latest technical skills and equipment that gave them an edge.

"That's a worthy goal," Sandy replied with an alluring smile. "I'll help any way I can. When I get back to the office, I'll look over your aerials and double check the results of your soil tests and see what I can recommend. The rest will be up to you, and of course, nature will need to provide the perfect weather."

Dave parked his pickup nearby and walked over to his sons. "Well, who's this pretty young lady?"

"Glad you asked," Rob said. "This is Sandy Moore. She's replacing Buddy at the Extension office. Here's her card."

"...Hmm. Impressive, a master's in agriculture from University of Delaware."

"It's just book work and passing tests, but, Mr. Johnson, your farm is truly impressive. All my college education can't hold a candle to your hard work and perfection. I'd say the Johnson Farm is the gold standard for great looking farms."

"Why, thank you, Sandy," Dave said. "My son Rob and grandson Chip take great pride in maintaining this farm, and it shows."

"It truly does," Sandy said. "Your healthy fields, bright white fencing, and well-preserved outbuildings are visible proof. And, Mr. Johnson, your manicured flowerbeds and ornamental trees surrounding your two-story house makes your property fit for a storybook illustration. I must say this is the greatest looking farm I've seen so far in these parts."

"Thank you, Sandy," Dave replied. "Most of the credit goes to my grandpa who built the oldest section of the house and turned the first shovel of soil in the fields. My grandmother started the flowerbeds, and we've since had the pleasure of maintaining them."

Rob put his hand on Dave's shoulder. "It was my dad here who erected the first

Johnson Farm sign out by the road, even though he's the third generation to own the place."

"So, Buddy's finally retired," Dave chuckled. "He's been saying he would for years. I should call him up to go fishing."

Rob tried not to stare as he looked at the new extension agent. "Sandy, I don't believe I've seen you before. Are you from around here?"

"Texas—my family's ranch is there—cowgirl country is where I'm from but landing a job in this county has made Maryland my new home state."

"And we're mighty glad you're here," Rob added. "We need more farm girls in this county. Don't we, Chip?"

Dave noticed Sandy's flirty smile as she looked at Chip. *I wish Chip could recognize her obvious interest in him. Here's a good prospect for a wife, and she can't take her eyes off my grandson.*

Sandy changed her focus to the front pasture. "While driving up your lane, I noticed your beautiful black and white Belted Galloways. What's your plan for such a small herd? I come from a large cattle ranch, so I'm curious to know if this is a profitable venture."

Rob removed his hat and scratched his head. "Well, that's a good question. Right now, our cattle operation only breaks even. Of course, we do have all the finest steaks we can eat. So, if the herd pays for itself, we'll keep 'em."

"If that's the case, then I'd keep them, too," Sandy said, and then hesitated. "Gentlemen, I don't mean to be rude, but I really need to press on so I can meet as many farmers as possible today."

"You're right," Dave said. "But your visit here is too brief, because Rob, Chip and I would like to show you more of our farm operation. We also have poultry and substantial peach orchards."

"Don't worry. I'll come back soon. Just give me a call, and let's set aside some real time."

"Then, you must come back here for lunch, say around noon." Dave said.

Rob piped up, "We're having a very special meal today, and you are most welcome to join us."

"That's right, Sandy, a real special meal," Dave added. She started to turn away. "And we'd be very disappointed if you don't share it with us."

She hopped in her pickup and rolled down the window. "Okay, noon it is."

As Sandy's pickup headed back down the long driveway, Chip said, "Golly, Grandpa, that was fast thinking inviting her to lunch, and did you see how fast she accepted?"

"Yep, I noticed," Dave said. "I also noticed how she smiled at you when you said, hi."

"Oh, Grandpa, you think all the girls are flirting with me. And speaking of flirting, Dad, your flirting was obnoxious and embarrassing."

Dave gave his grandson a scolding look. "Well, Chip, how old are you now?"

"Twenty-seven, but you know that."

"Chip, when the Lord favors you with a chance to meet an intelligent farm girl with the looks and figure of a young Elizabeth Taylor, don't let her get away. I nearly let your grandma get away, and I was a fool to ever think a city girl could replace your beautiful grandma. Audrey was the perfect wife, mother, and grandmother, and I miss her every single day."

"Are you talking about me and Sandy?"

"You bet I am," Dave snapped back.

"But we just met her."

"Chip, that farm gal is pure charm. As your grandpa, what I'm trying to tell you is that you can't be all work all the time. It would break my heart if our Johnson Farm had to change its name because there were no Johnson men to inherit this operation. Why do you think your Aunt Jenna waited until your grandma died before she changed the name of Evans Farm to the Dorman Farm? Jenna didn't want to break her mama's heart even though Audrey knew, as an only child, that sign would eventually change."

"You want me to have a son so our farm can remain the Johnson Farm. See, I get it, Grandpa," Chip said.

"I hope so, and I think you should find out a little more about Sandy Moore before some other farmer puts a ring on her finger."

"Grandpa...who's Elizabeth Taylor?"

CHAPTER THREE

The Last Straw

Eddie and Jenna's younger son, Roy Dorman, and his wife Angela lived on a tree-lined avenue in the rural town of Corinth, where some of the county's oldest homes proudly stood. Their single-story Victorian with its tall roofline displayed fish-scale shakes in the gable while the collars on all the porch posts were adorned with gingerbread corbels. Their home was a wedding present from both sets of parents, who wanted the newlyweds to be able attend college without the stress of a mortgage.

Eddie pulled into their driveway and parked. "Hudson, Jake, I'll just be a second. I gotta leave these papers with your Aunt Angela." He entered the house.

During business hours Angela could be seen working in her home office that was located just off the front hall. The large arched opening allowed her to watch the front door for customers when they didn't use the separate office entrance off the wrap-around porch.

Angela, a petite and shapely young woman with long ginger hair, was once crowned homecoming queen at Corinth High School. Roy always boasted that he married her for her brains and beauty. When she heard the front door open, she looked up from her computer and saw her father-in-law enter.

"Hello, Angela. I'm dropping off a few receipts. I'll just put them here on this side table."

"Thanks, Dad." She stood up and walked into the front hall. "Do you have a minute to talk?"

"Not right now, I've got the grandsons with me, and I'm headed over to Morgan's. How about I give you call later."

“All right,” she said in a saddened tone. She gathered the receipts that Eddie had left and slowly walked back to her desk.

Eddie, a tall and hefty farmer, was somewhat older than his wife Jenna. Since his son Cole was running most of the Dorman Farm operation, it was Eddie’s greatest pleasure to spend as much time as possible with Hudson and Jake and teach them all about farming. He drove to Morgan’s Farm Equipment store, and the three walked up to the counter.

“Well, look-ee here,” Hank Morgan said. “I see you brought two little farmers with you.”

“Hank, you remember my grandsons. Hudson is the older and this is Jake, and, boys, Mr. Morgan is the owner of this store. He takes care of me whenever I need a new part for our farm equipment.”

Hank held out two suckers. “And I always take care of my future customers. Here you are fellas.”

The wide-eyed boys looked up at their grandpa for permission. Eddie nodded. “What do you say?”

“Thank you, Mr. Morgan,” they replied.

“I have several items that I need today.” Eddie placed a list on the counter, “mostly for the old red dump truck. I want to get ‘er working again.”

“I know that vehicle,” Hank said. “I wasn’t much older than your grandkids when Arthur Evans bought it, and that same day he drove it right here to our parking lot to show it off. Mr. Evans was so proud of his new truck that wouldn’t let my dad drive it.”

“Don’t feel bad. He never let me drive it either, and I’m family.”

“I’m surprised you still own that beast,” Hank said.

“Well, if you hear of anyone who might be interested in an old dump truck, let me know, ‘cause I want to sell it.”

“Will do.”

“Say, is my boy Roy working today?”

Hank gave Eddie a *come-follow-me* jerk of his head and walked into the next room out of earshot of the boys. “I had to fire Roy last night just before closing. I caught him drinking on the job. I warned your son if I ever caught him again with a bottle or with alcohol on his breath, I'd fire him on the spot. I'm sorry, but he left me no choice. I had to let him go."

The news hit Eddie like a lead weight, but he understood the truth and wisdom in Hank's words. "Hank, no apologies are necessary. Naturally, I'm very hurt by all of this, but you did the right thing, and I'm so sorry Roy let you down. There are no hard feelings, and I'm glad you told me."

"Eddie, your son just didn't seem cut out to be a store clerk. In fact, he even told some of my men that all he ever wanted was to be a farmer."

"You know darn well that being around dangerous and heavy farm equipment spells trouble for a man who drinks, so neither his Uncle Rob nor I would allow him on a tractor. Besides, there's no future for him on the Dorman Farm. It's tradition that the oldest son inherits the land."

"Well, Eddie, that's hard news for a second son." Hank turned and headed back to the front counter. "Come on, let's look at your list and get you back on the road."

No other words about Roy were exchanged between Hank and Eddie. Mr. Morgan wanted the matter closed, and Eddie was too upset to talk about it.

"Okay, boys, in the truck. It's time to go."

"Grandpa, can we get an ice cream?" Hudson asked.

"Not today. Something has come up, and we need to get home. Besides, you're still working on those suckers Mr. Morgan gave you."

Eddie loaded his purchases in the back of his pickup and closed the tailgate with extra energy. He hopped onto the front seat and gave no mercy to his driver's side door.

Upon returning home, Eddie went straight to Jenna, who was sitting at the kitchen table sobbing. He wrapped his arms around his wife and pressed his cheek against hers.

"Oh, Eddie, Angela called while you were in town. She told me Hank Morgan fired him, and last night he got drunk and destroyed two mailboxes. The police were called, and they paid a visit to their home. Then after the police left, Angela asked Roy to gather his things and leave. She was very upset and told me that he regularly drinks up all their money, and he refuses to go into rehab."

Eddie pulled up a chair and sat next to his distraught wife. "I didn't know about Angela's decision, but Hank told me about Roy. He caught him drinking on the job."

"What should we do?"

"We're going to have a stern talk with that boy. You need to invite him to dinner so we can give it to him straight."

"Eddie! I can't tell him that on the phone."

"No, but you can always entice him here with your fried chicken and mashed potatoes. If Angela has truly tossed him out, Roy can put his things in the barn, and he can sleep with the employees in the bunkhouse, but don't tell him that part. What I really want is for him to go into rehab. Jenna, I will do whatever it takes to see that he gets help, even if I must drag him there by the ear!"

"We can't force him into rehab."

"I know, Jenna, but there's no way he can go on like this!" Eddie clenched his fists and blurted out, "This is the last straw! Our son has fallen in love with liquor and out of love with his wife. On top of that, he's lost three jobs—no doubt due to his drinking." His face reddened as his upset grew. "Angela is a good woman, and we can't stand by while Roy risks losing a wonderful wife."

"The poor girl has been trying to deal with this on her own, and she needs our help. I'm sure she can give us the names of a few quality rehab facilities."

"Good idea. When you ask, please tell Angela not to consider the cost. We want Roy in the best facility. Then when you talk with Roy, make it clear that we want him here for dinner tonight—you know, in your loving sort of way."

CHAPTER FOUR

Heart Flutters

Dave walked into the kitchen and saw his daughter-in-law standing over the stove. "Marylou, I've invited a nice young lady to join us for lunch, and I hope you don't mind sharing my favorite foods with a pretty girl."

"Of course not. It's just another place setting at the table." Marylou prided herself as a quintessential farmer's wife, who was totally committed to farm life. She loved to cook, can, bake, sew, upholster, hang wallpaper, and she could operate every truck and tractor on the farm. Her wedding picture on the wall near the living room bore witness of a glamourous, svelte woman, but now in her early fifties, the added pounds and sun-drenched wrinkles became the trophies of her age and countless hours of outdoor work.

Dave peered into the downstairs bedroom off the kitchen—the one that he and his wife had shared for many years. "Marylou, I know I did the right thing by moving in with Jenna's family. It's been six months since my Audrey died, and it still hurts when I look into this room."

"It still hurts for all of us, Dad, but it gets better each day. Who's this nice young lady you've invited to lunch?"

Dave closed the bedroom door. "The county's new extension agent Sandy Moore. Buddy has retired, and his replacement is charming and smart, so I told Chip that he needs to learn more about this gal."

Marylou smiled. "And that's why you've invited her to lunch today. I'm glad you're encouraging him to find a nice farm girl. I know Rob will be relieved when our son finally settles down. This farm takes lots of work, but it shouldn't keep Chip from dating."

"It's become clear to me that if my grandson won't go out on the town now and then, I guess I'll have to bring the town to him."

"And I'll always be glad to set another plate at the table for your cause."

Sandy brought much joy and laughter to Johnson house. It started when Dave, Chip, Rob, and Marylou welcomed her at the front door. Sandy's smile and personality could warm up any room, making her an immediate hit with the Johnson clan, and especially when she saw the upright piano in the room.

"Do you mind if I play something before lunch, Mrs. Johnson, or would you like help in the kitchen?"

"Go ahead, Sandy, be our guest," Marylou said. "There's very little left to do before we eat. Besides, I can listen from the kitchen."

Dave chimed in. "There you go, Sandy. Marylou insists that you tickle those ivories, and I, too, miss the sound of a piano. My wife loved to play, and we will be grateful to have music in the house again, if only for a little while."

Sandy sat down in front of the upright and began to play a Scott Joplin tune. She then encouraged an old-fashioned sing-along. "This is what I'd do in college to relieve stress before exams—I'd sing silly animal songs, and every now and then a classmate would join in." She played a long and dramatic introduction before she began to sing, "*Mares eat oats, and does eat oats, but little lambs eat ivy...a kid'll eat ivy too, wouldn't you*?" Sandy changed chords and sang, "*Hey diddle diddle the cat and the fiddle, the cow jumped over the moon. The little dog laughed to see such sport, and the dish ran away with the spoon.*"

Everyone enjoyed the youthful silliness as Sandy continued with another overdramatized piano introduction. "How about this one? *Ab-a dab-a dab-a dab-a dab-a dab-a dab said the monkey to the chimp.* Ab-a dab-a dab-a..."

Marylou poked her head into the living room. "I'm sorry to interrupt your fun, but lunch is ready in the dining room."

"We don't want the food to get cold," Dave said, as he stood to usher everyone into the next room. He placed his face above a large bowl in the center of the table and inhaled deeply, "Oh, how I love the smell of chicken drenched in a lovely broth with those buttery slippery dumplings. And look, we have kale and pickled beets, too. Yes, indeed. That's just like my Mama's cooking."

Marylou waved her hand over the table. "Just find a seat. Any seat is fine."

Dave, Marylou, and Rob sat in their usual places, conveniently leaving two adjacent chairs for Sandy and Chip. Before saying grace, Dave said, "Let's hold hands." He winked at Rob as Chip reached for Sandy's hand—an obvious setup.

"That was a beautiful prayer, Mr. Johnson," Sandy said.

"Thank you," Dave replied. "Have you found a local church?"

"Well, not really, but I answered an ad posted on the laundromat bulletin board. The Corinth Methodist Church was looking for a piano player starting this Sunday. I couldn't imagine an Easter service without a piano player, so I volunteered to play and will continue until the church can find a permanent replacement."

"How nice of you," Marylou said. "That's the church where Rob and Chip were baptized."

After an extended pause Rob affirmed, "Of course Chip will be there Sunday." He gently stepped on his son's foot under the table.

"Yes, you'll see me Sunday, and I'm looking forward to hearing you play some hymns."

"Do you think you'll become a member at Corinth Methodist?" Marylou asked.

"I believe that it's more important to have a close relationship with Jesus, than to be a member of a denomination. But don't get me wrong—I do love going to any church that stays faithful to the Word of God."

"That's a mature way of thinking," Dave said, "because it's not about a church or a building. It's about our relationship with the Lord and gathering with others to worship Jesus."

The conversation continued well after lunch, and Marylou reminded everyone, "If Sandy needs to visit other farms this afternoon, we should respect her need to be on her way."

"I'm afraid that's true, but if you'd like me to help with the dishes, I'll be happy to stick around a bit more."

"Oh, that won't be necessary, although you've been such a delight. Do come again soon." Marylou said.

Rob grabbed Sandy's hand and chuckled. "Today was your first time here, so you are our honored guest, but next time you're going to be treated like family. That means Mrs. Johnson will hand you a dishtowel."

"Well, I must say you sure have made me feel welcomed. Next time I'll be delighted to dry all your dishes, and because I've enjoyed everyone's company so much, I'll even wash all the pots and pans."

"That's right," Rob said. "We want you to feel right at home."

"Everything was delicious, Mrs. Johnson, and I now know what a Maryland beaten biscuit is and can appreciated all the work that goes into making them."

"We should have you back for steamed crabs. Now that the redbud trees are in bloom, the crabs should be running," Marylou said.

"You don't need to wait for crabs," Dave said. "Stop in for lunch anytime. Buddy always did."

"Thank you, for the standing invite, and thank you all for a lovely afternoon."

Dave looked at Chip. "Why don't you walk Sandy out to her truck while we do the dishes."

"Ah, sure," he stumbled out of his chair. "Let me grab your hat, Sandy, and we'll go out the front door."

They slowly strolled to Sandy's truck where Chip opened her door then stammered, "Can I see you again? I mean, we need to work on my wheat yields, right?"

"Sure. Give me a call and let me know a good time."

"Uh, right." Chip sheepishly gazed into her eyes as he stammered, "But Sandy, can I take you out sometime, like maybe Saturday?"

"Oh, I'm sorry. I promised a farmer that I'd stop by Rodney's Roadhouse this Saturday."

"Are you sure you want to go to Rodney's? It's a little rough."

"It's not a date. I only promised to stop by the place. How about I save a dance for you, that is, if I see you there." Sandy paused for a response from Chip, who was so excited and nervous about the idea of holding her closely and swaying to the music, that all he could do was smile and nod.

"Well, I really must head out to the next farm."

"Uh, yeah, of course. See ya around."

Chip watched Sandy as she drove away. He wanted to say more to her, even steal a kiss, but good manners and his shy disposition tempered his desires with the attractive woman whom he had met only hours earlier. As Chip walked toward the rear of the house, Dave met him outside by the kitchen door.

"Well, did you land a date with Sandy?"

"Not exactly, Grandpa. But she said I can call her anytime when I need help with my crops. Say, what's this line about you helping Mom with dishes?"

"I heard that, Chip." Marylou defended her father-in-law from the kitchen window. "Your grandfather has helped many times."

Dave opened the screen door for Chip. "Don't worry about Sandy. You'll see her again on Sunday, that is, if you're interested in going to church with your mom and dad, and I'll be there with Jenna and Eddie."

"Yeah, I'll see her Sunday along with every other single guy in the county who knows she'll be playing piano for the congregation."

"I tell you, isn't God just plain brilliant! He made sure a gorgeous single lady would be at the piano so all the young eligible men will go to church and learn about the Bible." Dave picked up a dish towel. "What did you think of Sandy?"

Marylou's eyes lit up. "She's a real catch, and I like her very much!"

Rob gave his wife a gentle squeeze. "I'd say there's a burn pile that won't need much kindling."

Dave handed Chip his dishtowel. "Let's help your Mama."

"Dad, the dishes can wait." Marylou dried her hands and sat down at the kitchen table. "Have a seat, fellas, you too, Rob. There's something I must tell you." Her tone turned solemn. "When I insisted that Dad stay for dinner tonight, you didn't know the whole reason."

"You sound serious. What's up?" Dave asked.

"Angela has given Roy the boot."

"The boot—as in, she wants him to leave, clothes and all, and split up?" Chip asked.

"That's it exactly," Marylou said. "I don't know if it's a permanent split. He's lost his job at Morgan's."

Rob lowered his head. "Not alcohol again?"

"Yes, and his parents are going to have a serious talk with Roy over dinner," Marylou said. "Dad, they would prefer that you not be present. In fact, Cole, Jo Lynn and the boys will also be dining with us tonight. Eddie is going to insist that Roy get treatment immediately, and he won't give in on this. He has had it with Roy's drinking."

"I sure am disappointed in my grandson," Dave said, "but I know Jenna and Eddie will do what's best for Roy."

CHAPTER FIVE

The Wayward Lamb

Parked on the side of a dark road and acting as if he hadn't a care in the world, Roy Dorman uncapped his last fifth of whiskey, drank directly from the bottle. He stared at its label and said, "Mr. Barleycorn, if you were in trouble—I mean real trouble—would you want to face your angry parents? No, of course not. Although, my mom is a good cook, and I really love her… *belch*…I think it would be better if you and me skip dinner and forget about our troubles. Oops, Mr. Barleycorn, I think I'm going to be sick."

Headlights of an approaching vehicle lit up the interior of Roy's truck. He could see in his rear-view mirror that it looked like a cop. "I can't get sick now." He crouched down in his seat, hoping that the vehicle would continue down the road, but it didn't. He wrapped the bottle in an old shirt and jammed it under his seat.

Sheriff Ken Stewart turned on his police lights and pulled up behind Roy. He knew who was in the truck because he had gotten a call from Eddie who was riding around looking for his son.

Roy's cab was filled to the brim with odd pieces of paper, books, tools and gaming equipment. The bed of his truck was mounded with furniture, a television, and several untied trash bags filled with clothing. Many items had already flown out the back and littered long sections of the road.

After Sheriff Stewart got an initial look at Roy's pickup, his first concern was the truck's lack of visibility. He tapped on Roy's window with his flashlight, and as Roy rolled down his window, a beer can fell out. The strong stench of old sweat and stale liquor told the sheriff everything he needed to know about Roy's condition.

"Good evening, Stewy. Would you like me to step out and take a sobriety test?"

"It's Sheriff Stewart, and from now on, it will always be Sheriff Stewart to you. Hand me your keys, Roy."

"You mean, I'm not going to take a test?"

"Not when your pickup smells like a sewer, and that tee-shirt on your dash looks like you used it for toilet paper."

The Sheriff took the keys and went back to his SUV to call Roy's father. "Hello, Eddie, what's your current location? …Good. You're not too far from here. I'm parked near the entrance of the Whitfield Farm. …Yeah, I got Roy. …Good, I'm glad Cole is with you, 'cause somebody's gotta drive Roy's truck back to your farm. …Don't worry, I'll wait for you."

Eddie Dorman and his family had a stellar reputation. In addition, the Sheriff and Eddie were high school classmates, so he knew Eddie's word was his bond. When Eddie assured the sheriff that Roy would be placed immediately in rehab, Roy was spared a night in jail and an appearance before a judge. "Thanks for not booking him. This is a tough situation for our whole family." He walked over to Roy's truck and could see that his son was passed out cold and had thrown up all over the steering wheel. "Whew, son! What that heck have you done?"

"Yeah, that's pretty bad," Sheriff said. "He must have just puked, 'cause that vomit wasn't there a few minutes ago. If Cole can drive this truck home, he deserves a medal."

Cole approached Roy's pickup and gagged. "Dad! You want me to drive this filthy truck home? I hate the smell of vomit."

"Cole, it's only a few miles away. Just keep the windows rolled down." Eddie got another whiff of the cab. "I tell you what. Your mother always keeps a tube of perfumy hand cream in my glove box. Rub that on your face and a little extra under your nose."

Sheriff Stewart, laughed. "Perfume! Don't worry, Cole. I won't tell a soul."

"Gee, thanks."

"Think nothing of it," Sheriff grinned. "Say, Eddie, while you're here, I want to tell you about a problem in the Corinth area with homeless camps popping up, and some unsavory folks have been wandering these parts for food and stealing whatever they can."

"Well, we haven't had that trouble or seen any vagrants, but thanks for the heads-up. Well, keep an eye out for strangers and let you know if we have any trouble."

"Good."

Cole looked at Roy slumped over his steering wheel. "This is a disaster, Dad."

"Yes, I know. There are some clean clothes in Roy's truck-bed inside those trash bags. That'll give you something to wipe up the puke. It's all over his seat and floor, too. You'll want to wear my work gloves. They're under my front seat."

"Dad, why is there no *we* in your order?"

"That's right, there is no *we*. I only have one pair of gloves with me."

"Well, Dad, you better get mom's hand cream, because this won't be easy. Sheriff, I'm sorry you had to see my brother when he's at his very worst, and I will forever be grateful for your help."

"That's why I'm here, Cole. So, what's the plan here, fellas?"

"I've got a couple of blankets in my truck," Eddie said. "I think we can wrap one around Roy and another over my rear seat, and if all my windows are down, I think I can tolerate driving him home. But first, we need to figure out how we can get Roy out of his truck." Eddie opened Roy's driver's side door and yelled, "Son, wake up! You need to get out of your truck."

"It's no use, Dad. He's out cold."

"Keep trying to rouse him," Sheriff Stewart insisted. "When I first pulled up, I was having a conversation with him, so he can't be that far gone."

"Yes, he can," Cole said. "Just look at him."

Roy's head was sandwiched between the headrest and the door. His hair and clothes were wet with emesis, and his occasionally opened eyes were blood red.

"As long as we can get him out of there, we'll be fine. Here, grab this." Eddie handed Cole the edge of the blanket. "Let's lay it out on the ground and see if we can maneuver him onto the blanket. The first step is to get him out of his truck."

"Okay, Dad. But the next problem will be getting him onto your back seat."

"I think the three of us can handle this," Sheriff said.

"This is well beyond the call of duty, and it's much appreciated," Eddie said.

Back at the Dorman house, Dave was roused out of bed by noises in the kitchen. He donned his robe and slippers and saw Jenna looking in the drawers for a flashlight. "What's going on, Jenna?"

"Dad, Eddie and I are having a problem with Roy. I'm going to walk over to the bunkhouse to alert the workmen. Roy's going to sleep out there tonight."

"Let me change my shoes, and I'll walk with you. A woman ought not enter the bunkhouse at this hour, not knowing how much the men are dressed."

Dave and Jenna didn't have to wake anyone in the bunkhouse since their two hired hands Darcy and Walter were fully clothed and playing cards. The men stood as Dave and Jenna entered. Both men were in their mid-fifties, had average builds and an overall rough appearance—scruffy beards and fingers so dirty they could almost grow something under their nails. However, they never allowed their unkempt looks to overshadow their jolly natures, as they regularly sported broad smiles and *summer teeth*—some are in, and some are out.

Darcy and Walter had a common past as ex-cons. It was the chaplain at the penitentiary who recommended them for work and who convinced Dave, Rob, and Jenna to give them a chance. Rob and Jenna were leery at first but hired the men on a probationary basis due to their renewed faith in God, the chaplain's recommendation, and their good behavior in prison. After a few years on the job, the farm had become their permanent home, and they were given their own separate bedrooms inside the bunkhouse.

"Fellas, I'm sorry to interrupt your game," Dave said, "but I want you to know that Roy will be sleeping off his unfortunate drunken stupor in the bunkroom tonight."

"That's right, and I'm sorry to trouble you." Jenna said.

"No trouble, Mrs. Dorman," Darcy said.

"Thank you. May I ask a favor? Would one of you please help me put a plastic tarp over one of the bunks? I'm not going to allow my son to ruin a perfectly good mattress."

Walter offered a suggestion, "Mrs. Dorman, if he's that plastered, maybe we should set up that old cot that's stored in the barn. When it's open, it sits very near the floor. That way you won't need to worry about a mattress, and if he rolls out of bed, he won't fall far."

"Good idea, Walter, but let's set it up outside by the backdoor."

"It might rain, Mrs. Dorman."

"I don't think Roy will notice. He's really drunk. Besides, my husband said that Roy smells very bad, so no sense stinking up the bunkroom."

"Will he need a blanket and pillow?" Darcy asked.

"He might, but he'll not get them from me. Just find me a sheet that we can fold up and put under his head. A sheet is easy to clean. In fact, if you have a dirty one in the laundry, I'll use that."

"I'll be right back with that cot, Ma'am."

"Thank you, Walter. Mr. Dave and I will be at the house if you need us."

With flashlight in hand Jenna and her father walked back up the driveway. "You're a tough one," Dave said, "but you handled it well."

"Daddy, wait until you see Roy's condition, then you'll have no doubt that I did the right thing."

When Cole and Eddie returned home, Jo Lynn, Jenna and Dave met them in the driveway.

"He's pretty messed up, Mom," Cole said.

"I know, your father warned me," Jenna said.

The commotion had roused Hudson out of bed. He stepped out onto the porch and saw Roy sprawled out on the back seat of his grandfather's truck.

Cole struggled to move Roy. "He's dead weight, Dad."

Hudson stepped forward to get a better look. "Is Uncle Roy really dead?"

"No, Hudson," Cole said.

Jo Lynn stepped up onto the porch. "Ah, sweetie, Mommy's right here, and I'll help you back to bed."

"Don't worry, Hudson. Daddy will be up soon to say good night," Cole reassured.

Once Jo Lynn and Hudson left, Cole and Eddie looked at Roy and contemplated how to move him.

"Mom, can we use your downstairs bathroom to clean him up?" Cole asked.

"Absolutely not!" Jenna snapped. "I want you and your father to take him directly to the bunkhouse. There's a cot waiting for him outside by the rear door. Put him there just as he is, boots too. When Roy wakes up in the morning, I want him to see the horrible condition you and your father found him in. When he wakes up, he can shower in the bunkhouse."

Cole looked at his brother. "Dad, I know how we got him in your truck, but how in the world are we going to get him out?"

"Not here," Dave said. "Why don't you drive the truck to the bunkhouse and get as close to that cot as possible. Then use the blankets he's lying on as a stretcher and cover."

"Good idea." Eddie checked on Roy's condition.

"Is he breathing?" Cole asked.

"Yeah, but you wouldn't want to smell his breath."

After Roy was settled, Cole showered and went up to Hudson's room. He sat next to him on the bed that was dimly illuminated by the hall light.

"Daddy, why does Uncle Roy drink so much? Doesn't he know we don't like that?"

"Of course, he knows but sometimes humans get lost. When we sit in church, there's a big stained-glass window above the altar. It's a picture of Jesus with a lamb over His shoulder. There's a special meaning to that picture."

"What does it mean?"

"Well, remember when we had a few sheep, and the sheep would have lambs? What did those lamb like to do?"

"They liked to wander off and get lost."

"Exactly. We'd hear the little lambs cry for help, and when we heard that bleating, we'd rescue them. Well, sometimes humans wander off and get lost just like those lambs, but we have Jesus who is our good shepherd. He looks for people when they are lost, so He can make sure they get home safely. Tonight, I believe Jesus made sure Roy made it home. So, before you fall asleep, let's pray. We should thank Jesus for being your Uncle Roy's good shepherd."

CHAPTER SIX

A New Beginning

The following morning Roy skipped breakfast and sat on his grandmother's old rocker on the front porch next to Dave. "I guess you're disappointed in me, Grandpa, but at least you're not lecturing me like Mom and Dad."

"Lecturing is your parents' job because they will worry about your well-being for the rest of their lives. But, Roy, as your grandfather, it's my job to love, teach, and help you, which leads me to this one observation. Your shirt is inside out."

Roy removed his shirt and put it on correctly. "Guess I'm a bit hungover."

"It appears so, son. Roy, just because you're in your twenties doesn't mean your parents no longer care about you. Take me for instance. I love your Uncle Rob, and I love your mother Jenna, and because I'm their father, I'll always worry about them. The fact that they won't tie one on and get lost on a country road after midnight, makes my worrying days much easier."

"Yeah, but Mom shouldn't-uh made me sleep outside and use the bunkhouse shower, and I won't go into rehab, Grandpa. I told Dad that it's my life not his."

"Son, it's not just your life. You need to think about how your drinking habit adversely affects others. Do you think your father was in a happy mood as he drove all over the county looking for you last night? He was worried sick, your mother, too. And let's not forget about your brother. Poor Cole had to drive your filthy car home. I got a whiff of the inside, and it couldn't have been easy for him. I tell you what. I'll go with you and your parents today—for moral support."

"But I don't want to go, Grandpa!"

"I'd like to say, *then don't go,* because you're old enough to make your own decisions, but I love my daughter. That's why it's impossible for me to give you advice that would hurt my dear Jenna. Men in their twenties—myself included—tend to make regrettable mistakes. It's a part of life, but an honest man will own up to his wrongs and ask God for forgiveness. Roy, maybe not today, but soon you'll see that rehab is the right thing for you."

It was late morning when Eddie, Jenna and Dave escorted Roy to the Mapledale Rehab Center. The facility felt it was important that Angela be present when Roy was admitted, to let him know how much his drinking had harmed his family relationships. Though Angela seemed to have no more room in her heart for Roy, she had agreed to meet the family at the clinic out of respect for her in-laws.

Everyone sat quietly in the admitting room which looked more like a small den. The anticipation and the unknown kept everyone in suspense. Roy perspired heavily as he sat next to Angela on the loveseat. The practice manager and head Counselor Dr. Wanda Weir entered and sat near the door. Dave, Eddie and Jenna sat opposite the loveseat on overstuffed chairs.

Roy's gaunt and anemic appearance was a far cry from his once handsome form. His unhealthiness destroyed the physical qualities he had when they married, and although Angela's dark circles tattled on her worried soul and sleepless nights, she kept her youthful figure.

Dr. Weir began the session with a question, "Roy, why are you here?"

"I dunno. It wasn't my idea." His gruff response was not uncommon among new patients.

"Angela," Dr. Weir continued, "I understand that after the town police came to your house to inform you that three mailboxes were knocked down by your husband's truck, you asked Roy to leave. Can you talk a little about that?"

Angela squirmed to adjust her skirt to cover her knees. "After the mailbox incident, I was at the end of my rope. How can I go on when Roy's drinking has made me feel guilty and ashamed for falling out of love?" She paused, took a deep breath and grabbed a tissue from her purse to dab her nose. "When Roy and I were in high school, Roy always sat behind me in class. I'd turn around and see his smiling face, and he'd pass love notes to me. We were happy back then, going to proms and football games. We married in the fall after graduation and honeymooned in Charleston. Roy was sober then. We only drank one time on our honeymoon. That was when the hotel gave us each a complimentary glass of champagne with our first dinner. Those were precious memories."

"And are they memories you'd like to relive?" Dr. Weir asked.

Angela scooted away from Roy. "Honestly, I don't believe my good memories with Roy are powerful enough to overcome the bad."

"So, you're feeling a great loss. Am I correct?" Dr. Weir asked.

She held back her tears and her short gasps of breath made it difficult for Angela to speak. "Yes, very much so, and I have no hope of making new fond memories with Roy. We both attended college after we were married. I went on to get a degree in accounting and a C.P.A. But Roy dropped out because he couldn't keep up his grades due to partying and drinking. That's how quickly our marriage went off the tracks."

"Angela, I understand that you are the primary breadwinner," Dr. Weir said.

"We have a small home in Corinth. It has a separate entrance for my accounting business. I can do fine on my own, but Roy has been an anchor around my neck. He can't keep a job. He gave me all sorts of excuses, but I knew it was his drinking. The yelling and physical threats became more frequent, and he'd spend our money on bar tabs and bottles faster than I could earn it. He simply became unbearable to live with, and that's when I had to say, *leave*."

"Angela, what do you hope Mapledale can do for Roy?"

"Dr. Weir, I hope you can stop Roy's drinking. At this moment, he smells of last night's whiskey. There is no way a person can shower away those bad boozy odors oozing from every pore in his body. They're putrid. It's uncomfortable for me to sit here now."

"Can you give us of an example where Roy's drinking embarrassed you?"

"Yes, in church after one of Roy's drunken Saturdays. I could see by the looks on many congregants that they knew I was married to a drunk."

"Angela, it sounds like you have been wanting to share your pain for a long time."

"That's true, Doctor."

"Angela, you don't have to deal with this alone. This room is a safe space, and I want you to feel comfortable releasing your pain in front of Roy and his family, because you have their love and support."

Grabbing another tissue from her purse, "And I thank all of you for that."

"Now, Angela, what would you like Mapledale to do for you?"

"I want to see Roy's smiling sober face again. I miss his tenderness. I miss our togetherness. Roy has forgotten how to love me and his family, and I fear our love is gone forever."

"Do you still love him?"

Angela looked at her lap. "I'm afraid I don't—not this man here."

Huge tears dripped down Roy's cheeks as he listened to Angela.

"Here," Dr. Weir handed him a box of tissues. "Roy what are you thinking at this moment. Everyone can see that you're upset, but can you put those feelings into words?"

"No, I can't." His shaky hand took Angela's. "I love you, baby."

She jerked her hand from his. "You may say those words," Angela fumed, "but I want you to prove it by staying sober. You have more respect and desire for a bottle of booze than you do for me and your family. Where is that man I fell in love with?"

“Let me explain the process here,” Dr. Weir continued. “First, our staff physician will give Roy a thorough physical examination including bloodwork. And, Roy, we’ll want you to stay in our medical clinic for the first couple of nights where nurses can keep an eye on your condition. Soon, you’ll be shown your room, and I’ll introduce you to your roommate. You’ll be expected to attend all classes and complete all chores assigned to you. Angela, I want you all to know that everything we do here for Roy will be focused on his recovery.”

“Dr. Weir, how long will my son be in Mapledale?” Eddie asked.

“More than half our residents stay about sixty days. Others will need more time. It all depends on Roy and how long it takes him to detox and learn how to become a sober and functioning member of society. And, Roy, at the end of your stay, you will feel better physically, emotionally, and mentally.”

“Could his stay be less than sixty days?” Jenna asked.

“By the time a person needs Mapledale for recovery, they require a minimum of two months. And one other thing. There are no visitation rights during this time. Today, while Roy is being admitted, all of you may tour the grounds and even talk with our staff, but the next time you come, it will be to take Roy home.”

Roy looked at Angela, “Will you take me back then?”

Dr. Weir focused her gaze on the two of them. “If marriages haven’t already broken up, they often break up after recovery. It's because alcohol abuse frequently does irreparable damage to a relationship. Staying sober is a daily duty, and our treatment will give Roy the tools to do so. I will, however, make this promise to all of you. When Roy leaves here, he will understand just what he had put you through, and he’ll have the ability to put his most personal feelings, thoughts, regrets, and apologies into words. Hopefully, those words will also include love notes to you, Angela.”

Eddie spoke up, “Jenna and I are hoping this rehab will bring our son back to us sober and cheerful.”

“Mr. and Mrs. Dorman, it’s a difficult and painful time for parents when they are put in a position of demanding treatment for a son or daughter. Mr. Johnson, we also realize that grandparents suffer a similar pain, not just for their grandson or daughter, but also for their adult children who are dealing with an addicted child. So, let me assure all of you that when Roy leaves here, you will be satisfied that you made the right tough-love decision."

"May I say something before we leave?" Dave said.

"Absolutely," Dr. Weir replied.

"Son, it's obvious that I love my children and grandchildren unconditionally, and I consider Angela as one of my grandchildren. It was painful to listen, but I just heard a small piece of the torment that she has endured, and that hurts me to my core. I also know how much Jenna and Eddie have suffered. That's why I'm asking you today to do your very best to beat this drinking habit for Angela, for your parents, for yourself, and for my sake. I want you and Angela to know that I'll always be your loving grandfather, because there is nothing in this world more important than family."

CHAPTER SEVEN

First Steps of Romance

Located just over the Maryland line in Delaware was Rodney's Roadhouse. It had never been a place for fights, probably because Rodney would threaten any rowdies with his shotgun, which never stopped lowlifes from hanging out at his bar. Rodney's business did okay. It paid the bills and gave him a livable income from Tuesday through Saturday. That was when many locals from college hung out to eat the only food on his menu—barbeque, fries and slaw, served on waxed-paper inside a plastic basket. He closed his place on Sundays and Mondays but made up for the lost revenue with his two pool tables and a modern jukebox. For fifty cents a tune, his computerized system played any country song you desired. It never brought in much during the week, but on Fridays and Saturdays the pool tables were in constant use, and the music never stopped. Once the dancing began, the songs flowed into the night.

This Saturday was no different. The crowd was dense, so Rodney opened all the windows, but the slightly stuffy room didn't keep the crowd from the dance floor. Many couples swayed to the music including Sandy, who was dancing with Todd Bennett. One would never know that Todd came from a Mainline Philadelphia family because his mannerisms were rough and uncouth. Local folks surmised that he was the family's troublemaker, and that's why they sent him to Maryland to tend a rundown, hundred-acre farm they bought for him.

Chip entered the room and saw Sandy dancing with Todd. As the dance turned his way, Sandy and Chip exchanged glances.

"Are you interested in that farmer?" Todd asked.

"I'm interested in all farmers. I'm a county extension agent, remember?"

Chip sat at a table with two other men he knew from years back, Frank and Don. Cindy, the waitress, immediately spotted him as he sat down.

"I haven't seen you in here before," Frank said.

"That's right." Chip looked up at the waitress. "Hi, Cindy."

"Hello, Chip. It's good to see you. What will you have? I guess I can't ask you if you want the usual when you're not a regular."

"I'll take a Coca-Cola."

"A soda?" Don laughed.

Cindy defended Chip's choice. "Pardon me, but we are happy to serve coke to our customers."

"Yeah, he's not a drinker like his cousin Roy," Frank's tone cut right into Chip's heart.

"What did you mean by that?"

"I heard Roy's a real drunk. Next thing we'll hear is he's in rehab."

"Are you saying rehab is a bad thing? Or are you just wanting to make fun of Roy to make yourself feel better?"

Don added to the slight, "Everyone knows he can't hold his liquor, and he can't hold a job."

"And I know you guys have had a few drunk driving citations, so if you ever get a nudge from a judge, sixty days in jail or sixty days in rehab, you'll understand that alcohol can get out of hand quickly for some folks, including you."

"Here's your Coke." Cindy placed a frosty can in front of Chip.

"Here's five dollars. Keep the change."

"Thank you, Chip! Are you going to our reunion this fall?"

"I'm planning on it." Chip stood up and walked over to Sandy who was still dancing with Todd Bennett. As the song ended and a new one was about to begin, he took her arm and swung her around. "This dance is mine."

Todd reacted immediately by shoving Chip against a table, causing a chair to overturn. All dancing stopped. “Pardon me, but Sandy is my date tonight.”

Chip looked Todd square in the eyes. “I’ll not pardon you for this, until you apologize to me and Sandy.”

“What gives you the right to steal my girl? Sandy, tell him you’re my date.”

“I’m nobody’s date tonight,” she snapped back. “I came by myself, and I’m leaving by myself, right now!”

Rodney hollered, “Hey!” as he brandished his shotgun. It wasn’t loaded and it didn’t need to be. “Todd, you heard the lady. She’s not your date.”

Sandy grabbed Chips arm. “Come on, Chip. Please walk me to my truck.”

Although Chip was thrilled to hear Sandy’s request, he didn’t want to appear overly excited as they left the bar.

“I’m sorry, Chip. Getting to know a new area and its people isn’t always easy. I think I owe you for saving me from this place and especially for saving me from that creep.”

“I came here tonight because I was concerned that a nice lady like you didn’t know what you were getting into.”

“And I thank you for that. Texas has many roadside hangouts that are decent and fun, but this place is not that at all. I try to be neighborly and not to show favoritism among farmers, because they depend on me for their livelihood. I wanted to be kind, polite and professional.”

“That’s a quality Todd Bennett will never appreciate. He wasn’t cut out to be a farmer and neither were his parents. His fancy city family thought they could buy a dilapidated farm and turn it into something wonderful overnight without even living there.”

“It’s kind of funny,” giggling, “but I found out tonight that Todd didn’t even know that there are dark and light kidney beans. He mixed the two together and planted them as one crop.”

“But he can’t sell mixed beans. Nobody will buy that crop.”

“His Philadelphia parents took quite a loss, but it sounds like they could afford it.”

"Ya know, Sandy, I can tell you grew up learning to love the land and how a farmer passes that love onto his children. You can't buy that sort of love. That's something the Bennett family doesn't understand."

"At least I won't have to deal with Todd in the future. He won't be a farmer much longer, not that he ever was one."

"Yeah, my dad also believes the Bennetts have had their fill of farming, because their land is going up for auction. Look, Sandy, this is not a place where I hang out. I came here tonight not only because I was concerned for your safety, but because you promised me a dance."

"That's quite sweet of you to tell me. Well, Chip, since the music is quite loud, please allow me to keep my promise."

"Right here in the parking lot?"

She reached up and put her hands on Chips shoulders, and he put his hands on her waist.

"Yes, Chip, right here in the parking lot."

They swayed slowly to the music for about six bars of music, and then the song ended.

Sandy pulled away. They barely knew each other, but their attraction to one another was obvious to both.

"I need to go now. I want to be fresh and alert for church service."

"I understand, but I want you to know how much I like being with you."

Sandy smiled, climbed up into her truck, and lowered her window. "Will you be sitting in the pews tomorrow?"

"Yes, indeed."

"Good, then I'll look forward to seeing you."

"Uh, before you go, Sandy, I'd kinda like to take you out on a real date. You know, a nice restaurant or someplace fun."

"Chip, before I start on my personal life, I've got to prove to the county that I'm a top-notch extension agent. I'm not saying *no* to you. I'm just saying for now, I need to focus on my new job. So, see you tomorrow, okay?"

"Yeah, tomorrow." Chip watched Sandy drive away and then kicked up some dirt to express his frustration.

CHAPTER EIGHT

Easter Sunday

Dave and the Dormans gathered on their front porch before leaving for church. Eddie made a humble request. "As we sit silently in the pews, please remember to lift up Roy in your prayers. He's ill, and he needs all of us to pray for him."

Dave concluded by reminding everyone, "We are a family, which means we look out for one another with love and understanding. So, I would like for all of you to think about how you can not only help Roy but help all our family members in the coming days, months, and years."

"I will," Hudson said with enthusiasm. He bumped his younger brother. "Say, okay, Jake, promise that you'll pray for Uncle Roy and our family."

"I promise," Jake affirmed.

When Dave and all the Dormans arrived at the Corinth Methodist Church, they saw Rob, Marylou and Chip in front of the church within earshot of the choir and Sandy's piano accompaniment. *What a friend we have in Jesus...* The music echoed out the front doors and down the arched brick colonnade that provided cover across the front of the church, and where Rob, Marylou and Chip met the Dormans.

Rob leaned over and whispered to his sister Jenna. "Have you heard anything from Roy?"

"Not yet. I'll let you know when I do."

~ ~ ~

The headaches and shakes Roy experienced during his first forty-eight hours of detox in the clinic were severe. His d.t.'s were unbearable at first, but slowly they subsided, and a few days later, the physician declared it was time to start Roy's therapy.

Dr. Weir escorted Roy down a long corridor and stopped at a door decorated with a wreath of artificial carrots, beets, Brussels sprouts and a large silver ribbon. "Here's your new room. As you can see, your roommate loves his vegetables. I've asked him to be present so the two of you can meet before breakfast." She knocked and opened the door, "Good morning, Jasper. Please greet your new roommate, Roy. Please, notice for privacy purposes, we only use first names."

"Well, how-dee, Roy!" Jasper offered his hand in greeting along with a wide smile. The gangly young man had a weak chin, a protruding Adams apple, and was slightly taller than Roy. "Yep, that's how we introduce ourselves here at Mapledale, right?"

Up until this moment, Roy hadn't seen his room or his roommate, but he politely shook the odd-looking man's hand. Jasper was about twenty years of age, wore a bright Hawaiian shirt, frayed cut-off jeans, and heavy work boots. He had a lightning bolt tattoo on his cheek, spiked light blue hair, and a nose ring. Any one of which would have distracted Roy, but altogether it was an overwhelming fashion statement.

"Uh, hi, Jasper."

Dr. Weir opened the top drawer of Roy's dresser. "Your clothes have been put away in either your dresser or your closet. This bed is yours, and Jasper can show you how it's to be made each morning. He's a very good instructor." Dr. Weir turned and stood in the doorway. "I'll leave so the two of you to get acquainted."

"I suppose the good Doc told you that our daily job is to tend the vegetable garden."

Roy sighed, "Yeah, that's what she said. It's supposed to keep my mind off drinking."

"Have you been to any classes? That's where they psycho you to death to find out why you're so eager to destroy your mind and body with alcohol. But I don't need those classes if I have my vegetables. Gardening is the universal cure for everything that's wrong."

"I think our job makes us indentured servants."

Gardening wasn't an unknown chore for Roy. As a youngster, he was tasked with weeding, watering and hoeing the garden, jobs he found boring and tedious. When he was old enough to drive a tractor safely, his father excused him from gardening duties and promoted him to the chicken houses over at the Johnson farm. That was when the gardening duties fell to the women and the farmhands.

"Hey, look at the bright side," the ever-cheerful Jasper said. "We could'a been assigned to the dreaded kitchen duties or laundry service. I think the dining hall is the worst. You gotta set the tables three times a day, bus everyone's dirty plates, and just when you think your job is done at the end of the day, you gotta mop the dining hall floors and help clean the kitchen. But we have it good. We're only responsible for all the vegetables folks eat around here. Do you garden?"

"I've had my share of weeding."

"Well, Roy, let me tell you. Knowing how to pull weeds is a good thing because we only grow organic vegetables. I'm getting pretty good at this vegetable gig, because there's this older dude, Gordon. He's my favorite person in all the world. He owns the landscape company Mapledale uses. He also oversees our work. Do you see how good this place is manicured? Gordon's company keeps it looking nice. Gordon is pure perfection!"

"I hadn't noticed, but now that you mentioned it, the grounds do look great."

"Hey, we couldn't have a better teacher. Gordon gives me all sorts of gardening tips. When I first arrived—drunk out of my mind—I had no idea my destiny was growing vegetables until I met Gordon."

"Vegetables, your destiny? What did you do before Mapledale?"

"Nothing. Yep, absolutely nothing."

Roy was astonished by the way Jasper bragged of his sloth.

"I flunked out of high school…but got a GED! Then I got a dishonorable discharge from the Army, but they did teach me how to make a perfect bed," plopping one foot on the bed, "And I got this great pair of boots!"

"How did you support yourself?"

Jasper laughed, "Roy, Roy, Roy, are you kidding? Support myself? My parents are loaded, I mean really loaded. I don't need to support myself."

"Did they give you money for liquor, and if they did, you're not old enough to buy it."

"It's like this. When my parents went to their Telluride cabin for ski season, I'd stay in their Rehoboth Beach house, or I'd go to their Miami penthouse, or their Maryland estate on the Miles River, and I'd drink up their liquor cabinets. When they caught on to my house hopping—ratted out by all the nosy caretakers—they put me in Mapledale."

"You talk about your parents' houses as if they weren't your homes, too."

"Those places are just buildings." Jasper flopped down across his bed and looked up at the ceiling. "A home means a mom and a dad, and that's what I've never had. My parents were too busy being rich, while I was just an inconvenience."

"How long have you been here?" Roy asked.

Jasper sat up on the bed and pulled back his blue hair tight above his forehead. "Three months. You can tell by my dark roots. I want my parents to keep me here until the end of summer."

"Why would you want to stay longer?"

"Well, it's like this. My parents can't stand having me around, so that's in my favor. Besides, I like it here. My sponsor, friend, and instructor Gordon makes me feel like I finally found a family, and I want to stay here until my rutabagas are ready for the Delaware State Fair."

"Rutabagas for the State Fair? They're out of season for that."

Springing to his feet, "Yeeep! But that's why Gordon says I have a great chance for a grand medallion ribbon because my rutabagas will also be certified organic! An out of season tuber will make mine the only rutabaga at the Fair. Gordon has an idea that if we use the greenhouse, we can fool nature."

"I wish you luck with that one."

"How will you convince Dr. Weir that you need more time here?"

"I've been working on that one. Maybe if I keep telling her that I'm worried I'll get drunk again, she'll tell my parents that I need to stay longer."

"If that's what you really want, I hope it works out that way for you."

"Hey, Roy, ol' buddy, time to get our breakfast. It's that nasty schedule they keep around here. Don't be late for anything, especially meals and classes."

"What are you doing after breakfast?" Roy asked.

"I'm going to chapel. This week the visiting minister is Pastor Greg from the *Church of the Who Knows What.* It's gonna be a non-denominational Easter service. That means people of all religions are welcome, and nobody will like the service. Say, Roy, ol' buddy, you should join me."

Roy was a little overwhelmed by Jasper. "I'll let you know on that one, and what's with this ol' buddy stuff? I barely know you."

"It's like this. I don't make friends easily, and the staff asked me to go out of my way to make you feel welcomed." Jasper put his arm around Roy. "How am I doing, ol' buddy?"

Backing away, "Uh, I'll let you know on this one."

~ ~ ~

The Corinth Church had the good fortune of finding a regular pianist, making it Sandy's first and last turn at the piano. When the service was over and before the benediction, the pastor announced that Sandy would join him at the rear of the church to give the congregation an opportunity to thank her for volunteering her talent for the Easter Service.

After the closing prayer, a line formed in the center aisle of the sanctuary, and slowly it advanced toward the narthex where Pastor and Sandy stood shaking hands.

Grandpa Dave led his family down the aisle and through the receiving line, where he was the first to shake the pastor's hand. "Very insightful sermon. I like how you reminded us that there are many degrees of sacrifice that we can do to show our love for others."

"So true, Mr. Johnson, but the greatest love of all is when a man lays down his life for others. Our Savior's brutal death for the salvation of mankind and His glorious resurrection is the Easter Sunday message."

Dave turned to Sandy and took her hand. "Sandy, you never cease to amaze me with your many talents. Your music today was outstanding. I hope you'll visit our home again soon. It's an open invitation, you know."

Chip, standing directly behind his grandfather, "Yeah, Sandy, you were really good," which was all he could think to say with so many folks around him.

In the parking lot, Rob turned to his son, "I see you're not making much progress with Sandy."

"Dad, she doesn't want a relationship until she's settled into her new job."

"Chip," Dave chimed in. "A girl like Sandy could have dozens of proposals by that time."

"Please, let it go, Grandpa?"

CHAPTER NINE

Old Red

Anxious to get started on Old Red after breakfast, Eddie kissed Jenna and headed out the front door. "Dad, I hope you're not too comfortable in that rocker, because I'd like you to look at Old Red with me. Are you up for it?"

"Absolutely. Come on, Samson. We're following Eddie to the barn." As Dave and his loyal dog ambled along, he asked, "Do you have the keys?"

"Yep, right here," patting his pants pocket. "But I've never heard it turn over."

"Well, you can try again while I'm watching." Dave leaned over the open hood.

Eddie thought he had all the spare parts he'd need to fix the old dump truck, but there was a high probability that he'd have to buy more. "It's been at least twenty years since I saw Jenna's grandfather driving this old beast. Last night I put a new battery in 'er—but it wouldn't crank." Dangling the keys, "So, here goes nothing!" He sat in the driver's seat, turned the key and gave it a little gas, but all that could be heard was a faint click of the key in the ignition switch.

"Yep, still nothing." Dave said. "Let's test the start relay and see if it cranks."

Eddie grabbed a screwdriver with a wooden grip. "Dad, take this and bridge it across these two terminals on the start relay."

Bridging the connection caused the starter to turn, so Eddie jumped in the cab and turned the ignition switch to run, but it didn't start.

“You probably need to replace that solenoid,” Dave said, as he grabbed his lower back. “I’m sorry Eddie. As much as I’d like to work side-by-side with you on this project, standing here on the concrete and leaning over the engine hurts my back, and bending over is an essential position for any mechanic. How about I make a check list for you to follow, and let’s see how that works out for you.”

“Thanks, Dad. I like that idea.”

“I’d like to do the actual work with you, but my hands-on time working on engines seems to have passed.” Dave had solved many mechanical problems over his lifetime. His skill and knowledge of older farm trucks and tractors were especially valuable, but advice would be the full extent of his help with Old Red. “Tonight, I’ll work on that list for you, and I’ll put the tasks in the order that I feel they should be performed. After you’ve exhausted all the possible problems on the list, it should run. If not, I’ll have another look.”

CHAPTER TEN

Friends

Part of the therapy at Mapledale was to teach all residents discipline skills. Every resident was assigned daily mundane duties and an instructor to guide them. The chores were basic and repetitive and designed to reprogram them to think of sobriety as a daily task—one day at a time.

When Roy and Jasper awoke Monday morning and made their beds, Roy noticed Jasper's finely tucked corners, smooth surface, and beautifully fluffed pillows—a great contrast to his disheveled bed. The difference didn't bother Roy because the art of bed making was never his concern.

Jasper strutted around Roy's bed like a military sergeant—erect and hands clasped behind him. He grabbed a hairbrush from his dresser and beat the bed repeatedly with a staccato rhythm, as he shouted with a German accent. "Yew call ziss bed perfect?"

"Hey, buddy, calm down. I don't call it anything," Roy replied.

Ripping off all the sheets and blankets, "This is not satisfactory!"

"Jasper! What do you think you're doing?" Roy was stunned by Jasper's absurd antics.

"I am going to make your bed, and you are going to watch very carefully. When the Nazi bed inspectors come here while we are at breakfast, I want them to conclude that you did a very fine job."

"Well, okay, I guess."

Jasper laughed. "You can thank me now or thank me when you get your outstanding grade for bed-making."

"I think I'll thank you now. Do you mind if I shower before you?"

"No, not at all. But first, look in my closet and pick out the shirt I should wear today."

Roy opened Jasper's closet which only housed a large variety of Hawaiian shirts, all nicely hung on the rod, all collars facing left and hangers one inch apart. "How about this one?" Roy held up an all-white Hawaiian shirt that was covered in machine-embroidered palm trees.

"No, that one is for formal affairs and special occasions. Try again."

"This green and orange one?"

"Perfect!"

After breakfast, Jasper led Roy outdoors to the rear of the Mapledale building and walked over to a John Deere Gator, a powerful golf-cart-sized work vehicle loaded with gardening tools. "This is ours," Jasper explained to Roy. "Hop in."

"Where are we going?"

"To work, Roy! It's your first day on the job. Aren't you excited? I sure am!"

Roy soon discovered that he was about to get a demonstration on how to make gardening an exhilarating experience. Once Jasper sat in the driver's seat, he immediately broke out in song, "*Hi ho, hi ho it's off to work we go…*" He jammed the pedal to the floor and the machine lurched into motion, accelerating the cart as fast as it would go. "Hang on, Roy!"

Roy clung to his seat and the roll bar for dear life as they careened around a sharp turn just before the right front wheel smacked a large bump. "Careful, Jasper, or you'll tip us over. Are you trying to hit all the bumps and holes, or don't you see them?"

"Oh, I see 'em, and, yes, I'm trying to hit 'em. That's why all the tools are strapped down."

"How much farther do we have?"

"We're heading for those greenhouses over there. Watch how close I can get without crashing into that one on the right."

"Don't you think you should slow down?"

"And spoil our ride?"

Roy's body whipped to his right as Jasper jerked the wheel to the left, so the vehicle would skid to a sideways stop, inches from the greenhouse. Roy was relieved to be motionless.

Gordon, a short, thin American of Philippine descent in his mid-fifties stood at the greenhouse entrance. "I see you made here again and in one piece."

"Gordon, I want you to meet my new roommate, Roy."

Gordon shook Roy's hand. "Very nice to meet you. I'm Mr. Gordon, your gardening instructor, and I'm glad to see you survived."

"Gordon is more than an instructor! This modest man is a plant genius, and a follower of Jesus, but don't let his size fool you. This sexy Romeo is a father of five! I bet his wife is a real beauty!"

"She is, but you'll never meet her."

"Ah, shucks, Gordon. I was hoping she'd come to my baptism?"

"She'll come for that."

"Great! And you'll be there too, Roy ol' buddy. Have you been baptized?"

"Yes, when I was a baby."

"And that's good enough for God. I never knew there was a God until I met Gordon." Hugging Gordon with one arm, "Isn't that right?"

"For your faith in God, I'm quite pleased," Gordon said. He took a few small tools from the back of the Gator. "Jasper, Roy, if we have time later on, we'll start filling these pots with fresh soil so you can plant the next row of rutabagas tomorrow."

"Roy, this man's soil is like nothing you've ever held in your hands. It's Gordon's special mix, and he sells it at his Delaware nursery."

"I want you both to notice how nicely your first row of rutabaga is coming along. When you pay attention to every stage of plant growth, you will learn to recognize potential problems, but there's one other critical thing needed to grow your rutabagas."

Gordon pulled out his phone and showed Jasper a photo that advertised a cooler.

"A florist's cooler?" Roy said. "Gordon, do you want to sell flowers, or do you want to grow rutabagas?"

"Good question," Gordon said. "A rutabaga is a fall tuber, and the Delaware State Fair is the end of July. That's the problem, and it means we need to fool the rutabaga with light and temperature, so it believes it's fall when it's really summer. The greenhouse will work for now. It's spring and the added heat of a greenhouse will fool the rutabaga into believing it's summer."

"So, what do you suggest we do?"

"I think this florist's cooler can help with the temperature, and I have an idea for managing the light, but there is a big unknown. Our idea is untested, and our plan could be a total flop. What we do know is that a rutabaga takes about a hundred days to mature, so our timing is critical."

"See, Roy ol' buddy, I told you Gordon's a plant genius."

"That's obvious," Roy said. "It's clever to think of a florist's cooler, but it's very expensive, and Mapledale will never pay for that."

Jasper put his hand on Gordon's shoulder. "Like, how much does this thing cost?"

"Between two and three thousand; a bit more to have a computerized cooler component. Jasper, we really need it by the end May, or you'll have to pick another vegetable."

Roy looked at Jasper. "I hope this doesn't mean the end to your rutabaga dream."

"I should say not! I won't compromise on my rutabagas. I'll call my dad's accountant."

"That's fine with me," Gordon said, "but residents are not allowed to use a phone, so I should make the call."

"You can't. Donny boy doesn't know you." He swiftly grabbed Gordon's phone and punched in a number, "Stand by, Gordon. It's ringing. Hello, Donny, this is Jasper. I know I'm not supposed to call you on your personal phone, but this is an emergency. I need a cooler, and just so I can stop bothering you, I'm going put my gardening instructor Mr. Gordon on the phone to explain."

Taking the phone, "Hello, Mr. Don, my name is Mr. Gordon, and first let me say what a marvelous job Jasper is doing… You want me to send you a purchase order? …Yes, sir, I'll do that. No problem, does Jasper know your address? …Oh, yes, of course, he would. Thank you, Mr. Don." Returning the phone to his pocket, "That was easy. He didn't want a quote, only a purchase order. This is good news because it means we can afford a cooler with a computerized temperature component that I can program from my phone."

"You see, Gordon, what Jasper wants; Jasper gets."

"Okay, Jasper, you have the money for the cooler. Congratulations! You've figured out how to use your parents' deep pockets, but you can't go on through life believing that family money will always come to your rescue. You'll need to find an occupation."

"That's a very good idea, Gordon, and I'll work on that one. See, Roy ol' buddy, Gordon is full of wisdom."

"There's another thing, Jasper. The cooler needs to be kept in a completely dark room so we can control the light, and we need a thirty amp circuit to run the cooler. I'm not sure if Mapledale will allow us to operate your piece of equipment."

"I'll work on it," Jasper said, as if he had the power to solve all the world's problems. "Say, Gordon, thanks for telling Big Donny that I'm doing a marvelous job!"

"It's true, Jasper. I've worked with many residents here at Mapledale, and you're a natural gardener."

Roy chimed in, "I was just thinking how much your prized rutabagas are gonna cost. I can tell you as a guy who grew up on a farm, you'll have the most expensive rutabagas ever brought to market."

"Well, ol' buddy, I gotta have the most something. If I can't win a ribbon at the State Fair, maybe I can be in the *Guinness Book of World Records* for the most expensive rutabagas."

Gordon clapped his hands. "Okay, men, let's get to work."

Roy and Jasper followed Gordon to another greenhouse that was packed with various sprouting plants. "This is where it all starts from seeds, and not just vegetables. We have many flowers around this property that must be started here."

Jasper took a deep breath. "Just smell the freshness of the plants. I just love gardening."

They walked over to the row of one-inch rutabaga seedlings. "Timing is everything," Gordon said. "The problem is we don't have the foreknowledge of which week will be the best time to plant so that it matures by the end of July. It's going to take lots of planting and strategy."

Jasper lightly touched the young sprouts. "It's just as I told you, Roy, this vegetable gig is exciting. Aren't they beautiful?"

"Well, it's obvious that a winning rutabaga is very important for you."

"It's everything, Roy. I love the plants, and they love me back. Do your parents love you?"

"Yes."

"Then tell me what that's like. Did they read to you at night, or tuck you in bed? Take you to school? Did your dad ever play catch with you, take you fishing, or teach you to swim? Because my parents never did."

"But Jasper, that doesn't make sense to me," Roy said. "A plant won't play catch with you, either."

"My parents think I'm a worthless loser. What's the point of getting a high school diploma if you know your parents won't attend your graduation? In the Army, I was labeled a loser, too, and now thanks to Gordon and my vegetables, I have a chance to prove them all wrong."

Jasper's eyes welled up and tattled on this painful past. Roy knew instantly that his friend had been deeply wounded over the years.

"I see you as a winner, Jasper." Roy instinctively sought to comfort Jasper, who responded to his ol' buddy with a simple smile.

"I just want to be exceptional at something besides making beds. I want to be an exceptional farmer. Is that asking too much? That's a hope that burns deep inside my gut."

"And I'd like for you to win that grand prize." Roy placed his hand on Jasper's shoulder. "I'm totally with you there."

"Over here fellas." Gordon said. "We have two greenhouses packed with vegetables and herbs that need to be planted today. Let's get started on this bed or we won't finish today."

Roy looked at the sizable field and estimated it to be nearly an acre. "This entire field?"

"Yes, my friend," Gordon replied, "the entire field. I'll show you where I want things planted. It seems like quite a bit of food, but the kitchen will use all these greens, and will probably need much more. There are ten bedrooms here, and the resident population is between eighteen and twenty every week. That's quite a bit of food the kitchen will need."

The long greenhouses were packed with lettuce, spinach, broccoli, basil, sage, parsley, and cilantro. Jasper and Roy loaded up the first two flatbed carts and pushed them over to the freshly prepared field. While on his knees, Gordon placed his hands over the plants—one hand over each cart.

Jasper gave Roy a gentle nudge. "Watch this. Gordon is gonna ask a blessing on the plants." He gave Roy a second nudge, "Uh, we bow our heads for this."

Out of respect for their customs and beliefs, Roy complied.

"Dear Heavenly Father," Gordon began his prayer. "As we plant your creations into the earth, the earth which you also made, we ask that you bless them and give them life. Allow them to grow strong and produce a bounty that will feed your children. Amen."

"Amen," Jasper said, and then turned to Roy. "It's kinda Gordon's secret sauce to make things grow."

Gordon looked up at Jasper with stern eyes. "It's not a secret! Believers are commanded to teach others that faith is not a religion but a relationship with our Creator. Prayer is how we talk with God, how we thank Him, how we praise Him, and how we ask of Him. The Bible says, we have not, because we ask not, so use your prayers wisely. I'm merely asking God to help these plants grow because we have many mouths to feed."

Jasper looked Roy squarely in the eyes. "Do you believe in God?"

"I've gone to church, and I was baptized."

"That's not enough," Gordon said. "You must have a true relationship with Jesus. He must be first in your life."

"Gordon's right," Jasper said. "All of us drunks here at Mapledale suffered because we worshiped liquor and not God. But Gordon straightened me out. Didn't you?"

"Well, so far so good, Jasper. Now, let's get started, but first watch how I plant."

Later, while working side by side in the garden, Roy confided in Jasper. "I got to thinking about what you said about your parents, and I think we have something in common."

"Are you saying that you don't get along with your parents?"

"No, it's not that. It's just that I've always wanted to be a farmer. My older brother Cole will eventually inherit the Dorman Farm, but because it can't support two sons, there's no room for me. I'm just the odd son out. That's why my parents sent me to college."

"And how did that work out?" Jasper asked.

"Not well. Not well at all. I was miserable in college and more miserable after I flunked out. Sure, my parents spent a good bit of money sending me to college and buying Angela and me a house, but to what end? All my life I just wanted to be a farmer."

"Well, I tell you what, ol' buddy. You just keep that farming dream in mind, and who knows? Maybe we'll be farming together someday."

"You know, Jasper, you're all right!"

CHAPTER ELEVEN

St. Louis, Missouri

Timothy David Higgins' Loss

All the guests had gone home, including Timothy's two grown daughters, their spouses, and children. Tim removed his tie and looked into his living room mirror above the fireplace. His black suit reminded him of his father's funeral, Tim Senior, who died five years earlier, and his mother Monica who died two years ago, and now on this day his wife Louise, who was laid to rest. *Enough of these painful funerals. I hope this is the last time I need to wear this black suit.*

"Do you see any more dishes?" the caterer asked as she popped her head into the room.

Tim saw her reflection in the mirror. "No, I believe you got them all, thank you."

"Would you like more coffee, Mr. Higgins? There's almost half a pot of fresh."

"No, thank you. How much longer do you think you'll need to clean up?"

"Not long. We're almost finished."

Louise was buried in the family plot next to Tim's parents. At the internment ceremony, Timothy looked down at the three gravesites, and as his wife's casket was lowered into the ground, Tim thought, *I don't have my wife or parents to enjoy, to humor, or to hug. I no longer have them to reminisce over the trials and joys of our past, or to consult with about major decisions. Yet, I have a duty to remain strong for my daughters. That's what my dad would say.* As he recalled his father's words, it suddenly seemed as if he could hear his father's voice giving him advice.

Tim's emotional pain was all-consuming. The difficult years of caring for his wife Louise culminated on this day, a final goodbye that ended all the trips to chemo, feeding and bathing her while watching her slowly wither away. It was a long and tiring road that he had traveled with his wife. Death's door had finally closed, but worse was the overwhelming loneliness.

Tim had sold his grandfather's practice on the other side of the St. Louis, just after he had taken over his father's dental practice. Over the years with the help of his two daughters—also dentists—they modernized and enlarged the office, purchased new equipment with the latest technology, and reconfigured the waiting room to accommodate more patients. Louise and Tim were so proud of their daughters for becoming dentists and for helping to upgrade the family practice. During the remodel, there was only one thing Tim kept: the dentist's chair where he was born, which now rested in the corner of his master bedroom.

Although Tim loved his daughters, they had their own hectic lives running the dental practice and tending to their husbands' and children's needs. This left little time for their father. The only time he saw his daughters was when they worked together as dentists, but when Louise became ill, it became imperative to turn his practice over to his daughters, who ran the business so well he was able to care for his wife.

During the funeral reception, Tim's daughters recognized their father's fear of being all alone, so they suggested that they start a family tradition. Every Christmas the family would vacation together in either Florida or at a ski resort. They could rent a large house so that his two daughters, their spouses, and the grandkids could all be together with Tim.

What a great idea. Tim smiled in the mirror. *Our first Christmas without their mother will be tough, but keeping the family together is important.*

What the daughters didn't know was that Tim had already begun to think about his future and how to start afresh. It was his way of staying positive in the middle of his emotional torture. He decided to sell his large suburban home, which had become a white elephant to maintain, and purchase a new car, perhaps an electric hybrid to travel long distances. Most of all, he wanted to fulfill his mother's request. After his father had passed, his mother recommended that Tim meet his biological father. Find out if David Johnson is still living, she said to him. Her encouragement made Tim believe that it would be a worthwhile visit for him and for Dave Johnson.

"I'm leaving now, Mr. Higgins," the caterer said. "My helpers have left, but if you need anything more, I'll be happy to get it for you."

"No, thank you. You've done a wonderful job. I know I can manage from here on."

CHAPTER TWELVE

Margaret

After a heavy breakfast, Cole sat with Dave on the front porch gently rocking with a second cup of coffee. The fresh air helped them think about their family, the farms, and the next planting season.

Dave rubbed his chin. "I wonder if Chip will ever marry and have any sons."

Cole leaned forward in his rocker. "Of course—someday."

"I'm not so sure." Dave sipped a little more coffee. "I'll never stop worrying about Chip until he gets married and has a least one son."

"Are you worried about Chip or your Johnson legacy?"

"Both, I suppose. Audrey always knew with great sadness that the name of her Evans Farm would change because it will eventually become Jenna's inheritance, but we had always hoped that the Johnson Farm legacy would continue."

"The Evans name is still on the cannery that Great-Grandpa started."

"That's because when your Great-Grandpa Evans sold the cannery, the new owner had no intention of changing a well-established brand name, but farm names are different. The name is always the same as the current owner. Right now, it looks like Hudson and Jake will be my only male heirs in their generation, and if that's the case, the Johnson Farm will also become a Dorman Farm. It also means your boys will also need to know how to run both farms. Hudson has a good work ethic, but Jake—I'm not so sure, but he's still young."

Jo Lynn stepped out onto the porch. "If you see Jake tell him he's to help Darcy in the garden this morning. I asked Darcy if he'd show Jake the difference between plants and weeds."

"Will do," Cole said. "See Grandpa, Jo Lynn and I have already started training our sons to be farmers."

Jo Lynn pinned up a wisp of hair that hung over her eyes. "I'm planning a big lunch with Mom and Aunt Marylou that will give us some nice leftovers for dinner and maybe a little extra to freeze, so it's important that someone keeps an eye on Jake. Boys at his age need supervision." She disappeared into the house.

"It pleases me that you found a good wife in Jo Lynn."

"She's more than that, Grandpa. Her loving presence in my life makes me feel complete."

"And that's a good thing. It also pleases me that you and Chip work so well together. You two cousins work in harmony like Jenna and your Uncle Robert. Your mama is a good farm manager and probably the best with the hired help. I can see those very qualities in you. Rob has always made sure the farm chores were all done properly and on time."

"Mom taught Darcy how to drive the Johnson tractor, and at the same time she made me teach Walter on Great-Grandpa Evans' tractor. Walter was a little skeptical because I was only eleven at the time. And yet, looking back at the situation, I should have been the skeptic since Darcy and Walter had just been released from prison."

"Your father Eddie and your Uncle Rob are good farmers and good mechanics on the older models, but only so-so mechanics on the new stuff. They complain that there's too much new technology to learn. That's why we rely on Chip, who loves to keep up with all that stuff. We all have important roles to keep this farm going. Take for instance your father and your Uncle Rob. They're terrific at getting the best market prices for seed and fertilizer, especially Rob. He's a great wheeler-dealer, just like his Grandpa Evans."

"I can see your point. It's important to pass on our skills to the next generation if we want to keep these farms going in the future."

The screen door opened, and Jake dashed out of the house and jumped off the porch before the screen door slammed shut. "Hey slow down," Cole said as he stood up. "Your mother wants you to work in the garden today with Mr. Darcy."

Dave stood up and tossed the very last of his coffee on the grass. "Come on son, let's walk the grounds and inspect the buildings. Jake, you run and catch up with us. We'll start by walking you over to the garden. I see that Mr. Darcy is there now, and you're going help him pull weeds."

As they stepped off the porch, Hudson popped out from the house, "Mom wants me to get your coffee mugs."

"They're on the porch, Hudson," Dave said. "Have you collected the eggs this morning?

"Not yet."

"I believe a few hens have been bragging about what they've laid."

"Then I'm on my way." Hudson said.

Hudson's daily chore was to collect and wash the eggs. The Dorman farm housed just enough hens to provide the Johnsons, the Dormans, and their workmen with a daily supply of fresh eggs. The henhouse elevation was low—not a problem for a ten-year-old, but adult heads would touch the ceiling when standing erect. It had an adjacent yard, fenced with chicken wire, where Hudson would fill a feeding trough with grain to attract the hens out of the house.

Hudson had been taught to always make a visual inspection for snakes before entering the henhouse. Every now and then a snake would make its way inside. If Hudson ever saw one, he was to call out for help to Cole, Dave, Eddie or one of the workmen, who would then use the pitchfork that hung just outside the door to stab and remove it. On this morning, Hudson inspected the henhouse and determined it was safe to enter, and so he did with egg basket in hand.

"Out! All of you, out!" Hudson waved his small arms at all the hens. "Your food is in the pen." The hens were eager to leave, except one, Margaret, Hudson's favorite. He lifted Margaret and saw that her nest was bare. "Margaret, I'm going to give you another chance." He returned the hen to her spot and said, "Come on

Margaret. You can do it. Just squeeze one out. You don't want to become chicken dinner, do you?" Margaret gave a muted reply.

Hudson collected all the eggs and then grabbed the pitchfork to put a new layer of straw on the floor. "Let's go, Margaret. If you're not up to laying an egg, you can watch me wash all of these. Margaret followed closely behind as Hudson walked over to the house and up the back porch steps.

Jo Lynn called from the kitchen, "The porch basins are ready for an initial wash and final rinse. Just be careful not to break any eggs."

"Yes, Mommy."

"You're being such a big help today, and that gives me time this morning to get the pie crusts ready for the strawberry filling."

Hudson opened the screen door and picked up his pet hen Margaret who was waiting patiently on the steps of the back porch. "Margaret, if you're quiet, you can sit here in the corner on this cabinet while I wash eggs." Margaret obliged while Hudson placed a foot stool in front of the double sink.

"Collecting and washing eggs is my job, Margaret, and if you're gonna live here on the farm, you gotta work, too. For you, it means laying eggs." Margaret clucked a bit. "Shhh…"

"Hudson," Jo Lynn called out from the kitchen. "Mommy's hands are full of dough, and I dropped a spoon on the floor. Would you please come here and pick it up for me and wipe up any mess you see with a paper towel? Your grandma and Aunt Marylou will be here shortly, and I don't want them to step on this mess."

He dashed into the kitchen, picked up the spoon and wiped the floor, but before he could return to the screen porch, Margaret let out a loud and proud cackle. Jo Lynn stepped out onto the back porch with Hudson on her heels.

"Hudson, did you let this hen in our house?"

"Not any hen, that's Margaret, and I think she is the most beautiful Rhode Island Red I've ever seen. Mommy, look! She laid an egg!" Hudson picked up the egg. "Great work, Margaret! I thought I heard your egg-song."

"Hudson, that bird needs to go back in the pen with the other layers, and let's keep the barnyard animals in the barnyard."

"Sorry, Margaret, you heard Mommy. You can't hang out with me today, but at least you're not going to be eaten."

"That's exactly why we don't like you naming the farm animals."

"But Margaret's my pet."

"Hudson, it's not okay that it's a pet. Now please go find your brother. He should be in the garden helping Mr. Darcy. You've been a big help this morning, and now I'd like you and Jake to go to the den and work on your home school assignments. I'll be there shortly to review your work and start on today's lessons."

Preparing the daily meals for the family and the workers was Jenna, Marylou, and Jo Lynn's daily job. It wasn't just the two families and two workmen they had to feed but sometimes a dozen more seasonal workers.

"We're here, Jo Lynn," Marylou said as she and Jenna entered the kitchen from the back porch. "Where would you like us to start?"

Jenna eyed all the strawberry pies Jo Lynn was preparing. "Would you get a load of all those pies? You certainly have a talent for sweet things."

"I wanted to use up all the frozen strawberries before we start putting up this year's crop. How many pies would you like Aunt Marylou?

"One is plenty."

Jo Lynn's eyes aslant, "Are you sure? I know how Uncle Rob loves my strawberry pies."

"Oh, yes, he absolutely loves them, but I don't want him wearing pies on his waistline. Rob can eat a whole pie for dessert, and I'm afraid if a second pie were available, he'd eat that one, too. I think one will be enough, thank you. Jo Lynn, you have such a way with your jams and pie fillings, will you be entering something in the Delaware State Fair?"

"I thought about it, but that's all I've ever done—think about it. I've never entered anything before, and I'm not sure how it's done."

"Well, I'm no help," Jenna said. "I've never entered anything either, but perhaps the three of us can help you figure it out. Do you have a favorite recipe you'd like to enter?"

"I've been toying with the idea of doing a medley of peach recipes—two different chutneys and a traditional peach jam."

"That sounds interesting," Marylou said. "Tell us about it."

"Well, I'd prepare three jars of different peach condiments, and then enter them as one in a custom wooden crate to add interest."

"Is there a category for this?" Marylou asked.

"I don't know, but I thought by having a unique idea might help my chances."

"It sounds interesting and fun." Marylou said.

"Now all I need to do is come up with the recipes, and I need to do it soon. The deadline for entry is June first."

"Well, I know you, and you'll do a spectacular job," Marylou said. "Jenna, have you heard anything from Mapledale?"

"Not from Mapledale but from Angela. She said Roy's blood test showed that his kidney function is not in the normal range, and that his test results were being sent to a specialist at Johns Hopkins. We should know more soon."

"Sounds like his lifestyle has caught up with him," Jo Lynn said. "I hope it's not serious."

"Angela said the Mapledale physician wasn't too worried at this point."

"Then it sounds like it's a manageable situation," Jo Lynn said.

"After a few weeks, he'll get another blood test, and if his condition improves or stays the same, there will be no radical treatments, just a healthy diet and lots of water, but I'm also very concerned, for Angela. She has carried so much weight on her shoulders."

"Have you said anything to Dad?"

"When he comes in for lunch, I'll have that talk about Roy's condition. I only got the call from Angela about an hour ago, and I don't want to alarm anyone unnecessarily. I think we should all stay calm until we know more." A knock on the back door prompted Jenna to investigate. "Excuse me for a moment."

“Morning, Mrs. Dorman,” the delivery man from Corinth Cleaners beamed. “You have anything for me?”

“Oh, yes! Thanks for asking.” She grabbed a fully stuffed laundry bag that hung on a nearby heavy peg. “Here you are.”

“Mrs. Dorman, I’ve left all the men’s work clothes in the bunkhouse, along with their towels and bed linens, but my boss told me to tell you that you need to invest in some additional work clothes for the men. The ones that they’re using now are plumb wore out, and they may not survive another wash cycle.”

“We certainly don’t want that. Tell your boss that I’ll have Angela give him a call to place an order.”

“Yes, ma’am. You have a nice day, now, hear?”

CHAPTER THIRTEEN

Rooting for the Rutabagas

After dinner and while heading back to their room, Jasper spotted Dr. Weir at the far end of the hall. "Come on Roy, I need you for support. I gotta talk with the Dr. Weir." The two jogged down the hall to catch up with her, and when in earshot Jasper said, "Dr. Weir, I have a very important matter I'd like to discuss with you."

"Can it wait until tomorrow?"

"I don't believe so. There are a couple of decisions that need to be made today."

"Then come with me to my office."

"Roy, too. He needs to come."

"Well, okay." Dr. Weir made herself comfortable in her chair behind her desk, while Jasper and Roy sat across from her. Jasper sat on the edge of his seat, bouncing his heels with nervous energy.

"Now, Jasper, what's this decision about?"

"You know Gordon…"

"That's Mr. Gordon."

"Yes, ma'am, Mr. Gordon. Well, you know about my rutabaga project."

"Yes, and Mr. Gordon has told me that you are working hard at this. You've set a lofty goal for yourself and are very enthusiastic about your rutabagas, which is a very good thing, I might add."

"Well, for me to have a rutabaga entry in the Delaware State Fair, I need to set up a florist cooler to fool the rutabagas into believing it's fall when it's really summer.

"You really believe a fall crop can be fooled by a florist cooler?"

"Gordon thinks Jasper has a chance," Roy said. "That is, if he can use a cooler."

"It's Mr. Gordon, if you please."

"Yes, of course. I know in theory it can work. I grew up on a farm and it's entirely possible with a controlled environment that Jasper's rutabagas will be ready for entry at the Fair."

Jasper stood up and leaned over the desk, begging. "Dr. Weir, I need a florist's cooler and a dark room with power. That's what's going to make it possible."

"And where are you going to get this cooler?"

"Oh, it's being delivered tomorrow. So, now the first decision that needs to be made is where to put it. I only need the space until the end of July."

"Did you have a particular place in mind?" Dr. Weir asked.

"Oh, yes!" Jasper reacted as if he knew the answer to the final Jeopardy question. "Dr. Weir, the small storage room next to the men's public restroom. It's ideal. There are no windows, which is critical, so we can control the amount of light my rutabagas get. The other important need is a thirty-amp power outlet. I checked, and there's one in there."

"And if I agree to let you use that storage room, where do you propose we keep the janitorial supplies that are currently filling that space? As I recall, every square inch is being used."

Eager to help his friend, Roy chimed in, "Here's the good news. We spoke with Mr. Begley, the kitchen manager, and he said Jasper could store those supplies in his outdoor shed behind the kitchen, but he wants his space back by August first."

"Well, Jasper, you and Roy seem to have made the decisions all on your own…and without asking me first."

"Thank you, Dr. Weir," Jasper smiled. "I'm not sure how Roy decides things, but I'm a natural. I was born this way."

"Now, Jasper, do you want to share the second decision we must make, or have you independently taken care of that one, too?"

"The second decision is all yours, Doctor. Please, Dr. Weir, I can't go home in June like I'm scheduled, because I need to stay here until the end of July. That's when the Delaware Fair starts. I need to be here so I can grow my rutabagas until they're harvested, or else I can't enter them in the Fair as my rutabagas."

"Jasper, you've come a long way since your family's chauffeur dropped you off at our doorstep. Residents normally come here with the full force of their family. You, Jasper, have had at best, minimal family support with maximum monetary provisions. That means if I were to say that you cannot stay here until your rutabagas are harvested, you will look at your stay here as another failure in a long line of failures."

"But I'm not a failure. Mapledale and Mr. Gordon have given me a new outlook on life."

"And I can see that you never want to go back to your old ways, so here's what I'll recommend. You can stay here until your rutabagas are harvested, but if for some reason the florist's cooler doesn't work, you'll have to leave Mapledale. My primary concern is your future behavior once you leave here. Will you be a contributor to society, or will you be a drain and a drunk? Jasper, I want you to raise your rutabagas, and I want you to win that prize at the Delaware State Fair, because I want you to feel successful even if you don't win the grand prize."

"Yes, ma'am, that's exactly what I want. I feel that I now have a God given purpose in life—organic gardening. Does this mean I can start moving the supplies out of the storage room?"

"Yes, Jasper, that's what it means."

"Oh, doctor, you're the best!" He dashed around the desk shouting, "thank you, thank you," hugging the doctor with such enthusiasm it caused her glasses to fall off her face.

"Jasper! A simple *thank you* would have been sufficient. Just give me a chance to say, you're welcome."

Jasper and Roy left Dr. Weir's office with smiles that stretched across their faces. "Yippee!" Jasper shouted as he ran down the hallways to the storage room, periodically jumping up to touch the ceiling. "Hurry up, Roy!"

"I'm coming, but I don't know why I need to hurry."

Jasper opened the storage room door. "Okay all you guys; you can all come out now! Start emptying out this place!"

While Jasper's voice echoed through the halls of Mapledale, several fellow residents came out from the storage room with buckets, mops and cleaning supplies, all eager to help Jasper make it ready for his florist cooler.

"Follow Roy. He'll show you where we're putting this stuff. You guys are great!" Jasper whooped as his friends shuffled past him with hands loaded. "You don't need to be sneaky. We have permission! Just head towards the kitchen with Roy, and Mr. Begley will show you where all the stuff goes."

Jasper placed his hand on his friend's shoulder. "Roy, ol' buddy, thanks for your support in Dr. Weir's office. You're the best."

CHAPTER FOURTEEN

The First Kiss – May

Dave and Cole sat on the front porch, sipping their morning coffee while admiring their wheat fields that had started to turn a golden color. The crop was now tall enough to catch a soft breeze and gently sway in unison.

Dave leaned back in his rocker and gazed up at the sky. "It's a beautiful day right now, but there's a wicked storm brewing—a fast mover. The radar shows its heading our way sometime late this afternoon. I hope it doesn't ruin our crops."

"There won't be much precipitation, so our wheat should be fine."

"Good, because we'll be harvesting soon," Dave said. "Knowing when it's peak time to harvest is what separates the good farmers from the great ones. We want the lowest moisture content in the crop, but if you wait too long, heavy rain can flatten a field, making it impossible to bring in the wheat. That's a financial loss we would look to avoid."

Cole knew all about harvesting. He also knew there were times when it was better to harvest early rather than risk a loss due to bad weather. But Cole was always glad to spend time with his grandfather, no matter how repetitive his farm advice and stories were.

"Now that wheat prices are high, I'm gonna empty the silos and make room for this year's crop. That's my priority this week."

"And a good one, too." Dave said, "You'll need that space, because it looks like we'll have a very high yield this year."

"I was thinking the same thing. Say, I've been meaning to ask. How are you and Pop making out on that dump truck?"

"Well, Eddie's still in the diagnostic stage with Old Red. I gave him a checklist, so he'll figure it out with the grandkids. He's not as good a mechanic as Chip, who in my opinion, is the best in the county; but Eddie has plenty experience to get that old dump truck running again. The work on a farm never ends."

"I'll say. I've gotta take out another section of old peach trees this fall and ready the soil for planting new—maybe sooner if I have time after the peach harvest. Grandpa, did you ever have any bad years, I mean really bad?"

"Oh, yes. The worst two years we had were when Jenna and Rob were about Jake's age. They were lean—very lean years. There was a long drought that lasted a few years. My pop died in the middle of that drought. During that last year, we failed to break even on our crops. The chickens did okay, but the drought increased the price of feed and ate up most of our profits. Thankfully, our peaches had a fair year—no untimely frosts or strong winds when they were in bloom, but they needed water, too. We had to take out a second mortgage on the Johnson Farm just to make the payments on our equipment, taxes, and other bills."

"But in the end, you made it work."

"Your Grandma Audrey and I were very blessed because when her parents sold their cannery, the proceeds of the sale paid off all the mortgages on both farms and all the loans on the equipment. Being debt free was one of the legacies your great-grandfather Evans left our family."

"And I will always be grateful for his generosity."

"Son, not every family has generous grandparents. A wise farmer doesn't gamble, but he'll use the best farm practices; and then after a good year, he'll squirrel away enough to hopefully carry him through bad times. Unfortunately, we didn't anticipate the drought lasting for so many years, which put us deep in debt."

"That's why Mom, Dad, and I appreciate Angela so much. She has the skills to manage cash flow and investments."

"And it's important that my great grandkids learn good farming practices, too, so it's up to you to make sure Hudson and

Jake are good farmers. The same goes for Chip's children—if he ever gets married."

Cole stood up. "Oh, Grandpa! Stop worrying about Chip. He'll get married and he'll have sons. If he doesn't, it's not the end of the world. I'm a Dorman, but I'm also a Johnson and an Evans."

"You're right, Son, but I'm proud of the Johnson name and the Johnson Farm. It would hurt me to see that name change."

"Grandpa, I think I'd rather focus on our successes. It's going to be a good year, and I know Chip has his eye set on winning the *highest yield* prize money."

"It's a tough mountain for Chip to climb, Cole. There are many great and talented farmers in our county who are using best practices and modern technology. What Chip needs at this stage are more pointers from Sandy, that new extension agent. Perhaps a little more technology and science from a pretty farm girl can give him an edge, or at least keep him on par with the other farmers."

"Sounds like you're playing matchmaker, Grandpa."

Dave shifted in his rocker and raised an eyebrow. "Just playing it smart. Cole, you found a wonderful partner. Jo Lynn is pretty and a good mother."

"And a wonderful wife."

"I'm glad to hear you say that, Cole. What will you be doing today?"

"I'm going over the finances with Dad, Uncle Rob, and Angela. She'll give us a new budget for the rest of this year, but I know Dad will have some ideas of his own."

"And your Uncle Rob?"

"He'll just sit there as he always does, listen to Angela, and nod in agreement. He trusts her."

"I trust Angela, too. She's very good with taxes, numbers, and forecasting, and most of all investing our profits wisely."

"Angela will be here soon. Do you have any questions you'd like us to ask her?"

"Not a one. I'm mostly retired and not in charge of the business side of things these days, so I don't need to worry about it."

"Well, in case you think of something, Angela will be around. Mom has invited her for lunch."

Dave stopped rocking and leaned forward. "Son, more than Jenna's fine cooking, Angela needs a big hug from all the Johnsons and the Dormans. This is not an easy time for her, and none of us want her and Roy to divorce. Right now we need to support Angela no matter Roy's health outcome or their marriage situation. For now, I'm pleased we're keeping her close inside the family circle because it will show how much we love her."

"I sure hope Roy comes home a changed man so he can hang onto Angela."

"We all hope for that. By the way, where's Chip? Is he joining us for lunch?"

"Nah, he says too much to do today."

"Too much to do!" Dave slapped his hands on the arms on his rocker. "Nonsense. What in the world is keeping Chip occupied over there?"

"He wants to work on the tractors today, and I left my truck over there."

Dave shook his head. "I better have a talk with that grandson of mine. No single man has too much to do when there's a pretty farm girl like Sandy on the loose who could be snatched up by any number of beaus. Ring him up, and then hand me your phone. Chip needs to contact that pretty gal even if it's only to help him win that prize money."

"Ah ha, Grandpa! You are playing cupid again?"

"Well, maybe. Our wheat doesn't mean as much to me as that girl."

Putting Cole's cellphone to his ear, "It's ringing."

"Hello, Chip. This is your grandfather. I was wondering how your fields are looking and thinking you might want to give that extension agent a call to help you cross the finish line for the prize money. ...Oh, you already called her. Great! ...Well, that shows me you're serious about your crops. Maybe serious about Sandy, too? ...Well, let me know her recommendations. ...I can guarantee the other farms are using every trick in the book, and you should use them, too. ...I'm sorry you can't make lunch, but Sandy's advice at this stage could be just what you need. ...Okay, bye Son."

"Well, well, Grandpa. Sounds like Sandy will be paying Chip a visit today."

"Very likely. Now let's hope she can make some time today to check out the Johnson Farm and Chip, too." Dave spotted an approaching car, "Is that Angela coming this way?"

"Sure is, Grandpa. I think I'll go inside and let you welcome her before we tackle all the paperwork."

After Angela parked her car, Dave stepped down from the front porch. "Angela, come on over here. I want to give my granddaughter a hug."

Angela melted into his fatherly embrace which felt like a balm to her troubled soul.

"Will you visit with me before going inside?"

"Of course."

As Angela took a seat, Dave noticed her forced smile and the anguish on her face. "Would you like a cup of coffee?"

"No, thank you. I've had my share this morning."

Dave took Angela's hand and looked at her with compassion in his eyes. "I hope you know that all the Dormans and the Johnsons believe you did the right thing by asking Roy to leave, and we are all here to help you. I can only imagine how difficult your decision was, but know we are grateful. You see, it was the tipping point that got him into rehab—something he desperately needed."

"Thank you for saying that, Grandpa." Angela held back her tears. "It's been a long struggle."

"And we are so sorry that you suffered alone. How do you see your future with Roy?" Dave's voice was soft and sincere.

She looked him in the eye. "That's something I can't answer now. I can't promise him a future with me when I don't know if he'll leave Mapledale as the man I once loved, or will he go back to the bottle, or will he be someone entirely different."

"That's a fair answer."

"Roy cannot move back with me when he gets out of rehab. He'll have to stay here on the Dorman Farm. Then in time, and if he remains sober, perhaps he can call me for a date. I want to take it one step at a time. Right now, I'm so worried about his kidneys."

"What's the latest you've heard?"

"Let me first say that Mapledale has been good for Roy, and their onsite doctor keeps me abreast of his condition. Johns Hopkins believes there is a chance that he needs dialysis."

Dave leaned back his rocker. "Oh, my! Have you told Jenna and Eddie?"

"I will soon. Of course, I'm praying that his kidneys will be good enough to avoid such treatment."

Jenna opened the screen door and slapped a tea towel in the air as she stepped out onto the porch. "These flies are all over! Guess we're gonna have a big rainstorm. Angela, my dear, stand up and let me give you a big welcoming hug."

"Thank you, mom."

"Dad, you can't monopolize Angela's time. We all want to visit with her, and besides, the men need to work on the financials."

"Sorry, Grandpa, duty calls. We'll visit more over lunch."

~ ~ ~

Chip paced around the barnyard in nervous anticipation as he practiced what he would say to Sandy. He kept a close eye on the farm's long lane for her white pickup and breathed in deeply a couple of times once he saw her turning off the county road and nearing the barn.

"Hi, Sandy, park anywhere you like."

"Chip, I have some very good news for you. If you give me a moment, I'll show you on my laptop."

For Chip, simply being in Sandy's presence was good news, and her great news about his fields made it better.

Sandy wore a green baseball cap with the Extension Service logo across the front panel, and her long soft ponytail poked through the back. As Chip stood behind her, peering over her shoulder to see the screen, he could smell the sweetness of her hair.

"Here are the aerials of your farm. Chip, your wheat looks better than your competition, except for your neighbor across the road. Mr. Stevenson's field is going to be tough to beat. I can show you the other farms later but look at this one section of your farm. You've got a low spot that could affect your overall yield."

"Oh, yeah, that's always been a trouble spot for me. It's the farthest away from the house and is difficult to reach after crops are in the field."

"But overall, it looks like the Johnson Farm has some extremely healthy fields. Chip, we should at least try to ride out there and have a look at it. Maybe the next time you get ready to plant you can take some corrective measures. I don't see a farm road to that section, so how can we get there from here?"

"It's a half-mile drive down the main road to our east farm road. When the farm road ends, we'll have to walk about a quarter mile to the back of the field. It's a big 'U' turn from here. Would you like me to drive?"

"That would be best."

"He opened the passenger side of his pickup. "Okay, hop in."

Chip turned off the county road and observed all the trees along the Johnson hedge row that needed to be felled after the leaves and poison oak died back. To Chip, it was just another winter job to add to his list.

When the road narrowed to a couple of feet in width, Chip parked his pickup. "This is it, the end of the road. You don't mind getting your cowgirl boots a little muddy, do you?"

Sandy laughed. "These are work boots, and they've seen plenty of mud, but you've seen my fancy pair that have only touched a dance floor."

"Of course, and I promise to notice them the next time we dance, and believe me, it won't be at Rodney's Roadhouse."

They both noticed ominous dark clouds in the distance.

"I'd love another dance, but right now we need to solve the problem in your field before it starts to rain."

"Just follow the foot path," Chip said. "It won't take us long to look at this section of the field, but we need to hurry before the rain starts."

The two moved several hanging branches away from their faces as they walked toward the rear of the property. "Sandy, I think after I bring in the wheat, I'll widen this path and extend our farm road."

"Sounds like a good idea."

When they reached the end of the field, Sandy leaned over the edge of the property and looked down into a ditch. "This is quite deep."

"Grandpa believes that it could be an old stream bed because water often flows freely here."

"Isn't that property on the other side of this ditch owned by Todd Bennett, my creepy dance partner?"

"Yep, it was. Anyone can see why his farm went up for auction. See that barn and all the outbuildings in the distance? They've been neglected for decades and are now only fit for a skunk or a coon, but the house could be saved with significant work."

"How did you know about the house's condition?"

"Easy—Dad and my Aunt Jenna won the bid at the auction. It has a common boundary to both the Johnson and Dorman farms, so it was a logical purchase for them. They haven't decided what its best use will be—more chicken houses, peaches, grain, maybe a combination of those ideas. They discussed possibilities for this farm with Angela. She's our accountant and my cousin's wife."

"It looks like a good acquisition for commercial purposes. The house is on a busy road, but one hundred acres is hardly enough tillable land for a family to make a living."

"Another poor farming decision by the Bennett family that forced them to sell. Not everyone is cut out to be a farmer, especially if you're not living on the premises. Buying this small farm as an investment was the Bennett's first mistake."

"Chip, that barn looks like it's ready to fall over with all its holes and the dead vines covering it."

"Cole and I will salvage any decent barn wood, and when that's done, the fire company will do a controlled burn to take care of what's left. After that, we'll regrade."

"Well, Chip, let's look at your field; that's why we're here." Sandy walked over to the worst area. "It's obvious that water is ponding in this hard-to-reach corner of the field, and with this deep ditch so close, you should be able to correct it after you harvest."

Chip recognized the problem without any of Sandy's suggestions. He even believed he had corrected it before planting, but the only thing that mattered now was to have Sandy by his side.

"It could have been more serious," Sandy said. "Fortunately, it's an easy fix. I just hope it doesn't adversely affect your overall yield for the contest because other area farms are also looking very good."

"You mean Mr. Stevenson? Sandy, his equipment is old and so is he. I can't see him doing as well as the Johnson Farm."

"Well, that old farmer may have a few tricks up his sleeve, because his fields look spectacular."

Suddenly, a strong wind began whistling though the tall pines in the hedgerow and whipping up the leaves of the trees.

"Chip, that storm is blowing in fast, and look at those clouds!" As the sky grew dark, chunks of debris began to swirl in the air. "Chip! Your field, it's being littered with old wood shingles." Sandy stopped, turned around, and discovered the source. "Those shingles are coming from the old Bennett farm."

Pea sized hail began to pummel the ground, and the sounds of thunder and cracking branches gave them cause to get to seek immediate shelter. Chip removed his heavy canvas jacket, and the two huddled beneath to shield themselves from the sting of the ice as they started to run for the truck.

"If I were back in Texas, I'd say this is leading edge of a tornado."

"We've had a few *F-1s,* but never this close to our farm."

"Believe me, Chip, this is close. I hope for your sake it stays on the other side of the Bennett Farm."

The clouds released a sudden downpour, drenching their clothes, and making the foot path slick with mud, while a loud clap of thunder indicated the closeness of the storm. "Come on, Sandy. We need shelter."

Chip held Sandy tightly to keep her under his jacket, but the muddy ground was too challenging and caused her to slip and fall onto the muddy path.

"Sandy! Tell me you're okay." Chip said as he helped her up. Her face, hair and the front of her shirt and jeans were coated with mud. "We're about half-way. Can you make it?"

She gave Chip an affirmative nod.

"Hold tight, and we'll get there." As they ran along the hedgerow another loud clap of thunder sounded nearby. "We need to get away from these trees. My pickup isn't much farther."

The two continued at a brisk pace until finally reaching Chip's truck.

"Don't worry about your mud, Sandy. Just get in!"

Soaked, dirty and winded, they sat and laughed for a few minutes while the rain pounded on the roof of the truck. A bright flash of light was followed by a loud crack of thunder that told them the storm was about to give up its last bit of energy.

Chip started his truck and hit the gas. "I'm moving to a safer place away from these tall trees."

"Good idea, but can you see well enough through this pouring rain?"

"I can drive blindfolded across our land." Chip moved his pickup and parked it along a cleared section of farm road.

Sandy looked at Chip and smiled. "We made it!"

He removed a small twig from Sandy's hair and handed her a small stack of napkins from his console, keeping one to gently wipe the mud from around her mouth. "There, that's better," he said before leaning over to kiss her soft lips. "I had to do that, Sandy, because, well, I just had to."

There were a few moments of silence as the two felt the beauty and tenderness of the moment.

"For what it's worth, Chip, I'm glad you did."

"Sandy, I think you're just about the prettiest woman I've met, but it's your sweet spirit that I admire the most."

Chip's phone rang. "It's Mom. I'll put it on speaker. Hi, Mom."

"Chip, your father and I are worried. We were under a tornado warning, but it looks like it's almost passed. I'd say by looking at the radar, we'll see clear skies in about five minutes. I hope you're safe."

"We are, Mrs. Johnson," Sandy said, "but we're soaked and muddy and in need of a shower."

"The showers I can help you with, but if you're using our east farm road, then you'll have to wait. We got a call from Clyde

Stevenson. There's a massive tree down blocking the entrance of that road. If you're trapped on that side of the farm, your father will need to use a tractor to clear the road."

"Yeah, we're trapped, all right. Don't worry, Mom. We're sitting in my truck, and we're out of harm's way."

"Mr. Stevenson told your father not to waste his time with one of the smaller tractors and suggested that he fire up *Big Mo.*"

"If it's the one I'm thinking of, that tree is huge."

"Well, sit tight. These storms are fast movers, and your father will be on his way in a few minutes."

"Okay, Mom. Bye."

"Isn't Mr. Stevenson your neighbor across the road?" Sandy asked.

Chip nodded as he gazed into Sandy's eyes. "Well, it seems like we're stuck here for a while, but I'm glad I'm stuck here with you."

"Even in my muddy condition?"

"Yes, especially with all this mud because it can't cover up your heart. Sandy, you're a special sort of lady, kind and sensitive to the needs of others. That's why I want to spend more time with you."

"Thank you, Chip. That means a lot to me."

As soon as blue skies began to appear, Chip put his truck in four-wheel drive. "I'm going to back up and look for that downed tree blocking our exit. Dad will probably need help, and you better figure on staying for dinner. It will take some time to move that tree and get cleaned up."

Chip's truck bounced and slid as he backed up toward the massive tree that blocked any hope of getting onto the main road. "Well, there it is, and it's gonna be a job to move it, but while we're waiting for Dad, I have something I want to ask you. Will you go out with me? I just want to know if I can finally get a *yes.* Will you'll go out with me?"

"Yes. The answer is *yes.*" Sandy climbed up onto the center console, leaned over, and gave Chip an affectionate kiss.

Chip pulled her close to his body. *Can this be happening? Someone I truly like feels the same way as I do.* The lingering kiss transported Chip to calm and beautiful places just as the loud rumble of Big Mo was heard heading towards them.

CHAPTER FIFTEEN

The Florist Cooler

Jasper and Roy started their day as they usually did, cleaning their room and making their beds. After breakfast they hopped in the Gator and took off for the greenhouses at breakneck speed with Jasper's usual reckless abandon, and Roy with hopes that one day he could take over the driving duties. Each stiff bounce of the Gator took the wind out of Roy's lungs as the two rode to the rear of the Mapledale campus.

"Jasper, I think you have a good shot at having the prize-winning rutabagas. So far, they're looking great…even though they're not in season."

"Yeah, so far so good, but Gordon wants to talk to me about the florist cooler before it arrives. He's not convinced it will work."

"That's not good. Did he say why?" Roy's head hit the roll bar. "Ow! Hey, Jasper, watch those bumps!"

"I always watch for bumps, and I find nearly all of them. Roy, ol' buddy, the Fair is the last week of July, which means, I need a good crop of rutabagas by then, because if the cooler doesn't work, it's curtains for me."

"Well, if so, then what?"

Jasper thought for a moment, as it wasn't something he had ever considered. "I just don't know, Roy. I just don't know."

"Well, lean on me. I'm your friend, and together we'll figure something out."

"Thanks, ol' buddy."

As they neared the greenhouse where Gordon was standing, Jasper yelled out, "Good morning, Gordon!" All his sadness about the coolers faded when he saw Gordon's smiling face. "You gotta love this guy." He placed one arm around Gordon. "You're the best!"

"Good morning, guys!"

"Gordon, ol' buddy, you wanted to talk to me about my cooler. What's the issue?"

"I'll just come out and say it. The cooler isn't going to work, but I have another solution before you lose faith in your rutabagas. I have a friend who has his own refrigerator truck. With diesel prices so high, he's not sure he can make money hauling loads. So, I think we can make him an offer to let us rent it for the rest of May, June and July."

"That sounds promising," Roy said. "But how would you control the light?'

Gordon was hesitant at first, and then said, "Pot growers have all the technology to control the light, and the refrigerator trucks provide the right temperature controls. For all that, we'll need a few thousand dollars more—maybe less if it's possible to rent the equipment."

"Rent? Why do that when I can buy?"

"The computer system we need is very expensive. It must adjust the light and temperature daily according to average daily norms. And, of course, we'll need an alarm system to alert you if something goes wrong."

"What could go wrong?" Jasper asked.

"Well, just about everything. The lights or temperature could fail, and then someone will need to restart the system immediately. It's not just the lighting, computers, and alarm system, we also need to rent the truck."

"How much for his truck?" Jasper asked.

"The owner makes about five thousand dollars a month on the road," Gordon said, "but that's not his net. He has fuel, tolls, insurance, and truck maintenance to cover when he's hauling loads."

"Do you want me to call my family's accountant so we can offer Hank five thousand a month?"

The numbers were spinning in Roy's head. "Wait a second, Jasper. You're giving Hank an opportunity to be at home with his family. If you pay him to stay home, there would also be less wear on his truck and fuel savings. Why not offer him no more than a thousand dollars per week, but start your bid at eight hundred?"

"Brilliant!" Jasper was grateful for Roy's excellent suggestion. "We only need it for one week in May, four weeks in June, and three weeks in July. That's only eight weeks!"

Roy was flabbergasted. "All this, so you can grow a twenty-thousand-dollar rutabaga? Am I missing some farm economics with your scheme? Are you really prepared to pay that much?"

"Me? I'm not prepared to pay anything."

"But I see another problem," Gordon said. "Where do we park the tractor trailer? Dr. Weir will never allow us to park it at Mapledale. My nursery has several acres, and we can park it there, but that creates another problem. Jasper wouldn't be a qualified entrant at the Fair."

"Yeah, I need to be a hands-on grower, and if I'm stuck at Mapledale, and my rutabagas are at Gordon's nursery, I wouldn't be hands on." He pondered for a moment. "I could always break out of this place."

"You can't do that!" Roy didn't want to see his friend get in trouble or fail when he seemed so close to solving his problem.

Gordon wanted to help Jasper, especially after all his hard work and commitment. "If Dr. Weir releases you, I have a travel-trailer at my nursery. You can stay there until the State Fair. It's located near where I'd park the truck."

"Perfect!" Roy said, "And you'll be right there in case alarms go off."

"My IT guy can make sure the alarm system is tied to your phone," Gordon said.

Roy was quick to bring everyone back to the financial reality of the situation. "Of course, this all depends on Jasper's family coming up with the twenty grand for his rutabagas."

"Gordon, what happened to the money for the coolers?" Jasper asked.

"I cancelled the order, so your family has it."

"So, I won't need to ask for much more money. I'll tell Donny Boy to think of it as money my parents would have spent on college tuition. After all, look what I'm learning."

Gordon said, "I think you need to speak with Dr. Weir first to see if you can check out of Mapledale."

Roy nodded in agreement. "Hey, Jasper, before you talk to Dr. Weir, maybe you should return all the janitor supplies to the storage room. I'm sure Mr. Begley would love to have his space back early, and I think it would strengthen your request to leave."

"Roy, Roy, ol' buddy, what would I do without you? I believe I can settle all this by the end of lunch! Gordon, Roy, will you go with me when I sit down with Dr. Weir? I'll need you to explain your offer of temporary lodging at your nursery."

"I would be happy to," Roy said.

"Me, too," Gordon agreed, "But for now, we have some serious work to do, so grab a shovel, and a hoe."

"I'm on it." Jasper said over his shoulder as he started to sprint away. "I'll be right back!"

Roy looked at Gordon. "This is all crazy talk to me. My farming family would never spend this kind of money on a crop that has no promise of a return, and yet, you keep encouraging Jasper."

"Roy, the prize isn't found in a State Fair ribbon, but through Jasper's willingness to take responsibility for himself. Through his gardening, he found God, and in finding God, Jasper found his self-worth. No one can put a price on that. If he wins a ribbon, that will be a bonus, and I will do my best to help him accomplish that. But if he doesn't win anything for his rutabagas, he now has a cherished relationship with the Lord. Jasper has learned the importance of working hard and setting goals. That, Roy, is a true accomplishment for a boy who was raised as an expensive accessory rather than a person of value."

"I never looked at it that way."

"Have a seat," Gordon offered Roy a nearby bench. "I've been watching you and Jasper these past few weeks, and I've noticed how your friendship has grown. You've been good for each other—supportive and kind. Roy, I don't know what caused you to think that alcohol would comfort you, because a person's true comfort comes from positive relationships, and I think that's how Jasper has helped you."

A few minutes before lunch, Jasper, Roy and Gordon met with Dr. Weir in her office, where Gordon explained that he could use Jasper as an employee to oversee his nursery while he was working at Mapledale.

"You see, Doctor," Gordon said. "I like teaching young people about the greatness of gardening. I know it helps them through their difficult battles of addiction, so I want to continue my work here at Mapledale as an instructor."

"I'm pleased to hear you say that."

"Thank you, but to do that, I would like to hire Jasper to oversee my nursery while I'm here, and I believe he is ready for the challenge."

"And where would you stay, Jasper? It's important for me to know that you'll be in a situation where you won't have a relapse."

"I can answer that, Doctor," Gordon said. "I have a travel trailer that Jasper is welcome to use. It's a one-bedroom RV with a full bath and kitchen."

"Would you be happy with that arrangement, Jasper?'

"You bet he would!" Roy's exuberance seemed a little out of line, but he knew how much this prize meant to his friend.

"Thanks, ol' buddy, for sticking up for me. Doctor Weir, for the first time in my life, I feel like I have a family. Gordon and Roy have been true friends, and I really want to work for Gordon. I want to give back to him for all that he has given me. Please help me, Doc. I really want this."

"Well, Jasper, you talk about giving back to Gordon, but how about Roy? I'll agree that you can leave anytime, but since you're paid up through May 31, I'd like for you to think about staying. You and Roy have worked so well together."

"What about your baptism?" Gordon said. "It's scheduled for the Friday of Memorial Day weekend here at Mapledale."

"At least stay here for that." Roy said. "I'd like to be present for your baptism."

Jasper put his hand on Roy's shoulder. "Gee, Roy, that's mighty nice of you to say that. When we love God, a baptism is our contract with the Lord, and getting dunked is like a signing ceremony where everyone witnesses you putting your signature on the dotted line."

"Jasper, I'm quite proud of you," Dr. Weir said. "Of all the patients we've seen here at Mapledale, you've been one of my favorite challenges."

"Since you put it that way, Doctor, I guess I'm staying until I'm baptized, and just so you know, Mr. Begley has all his storage back, and every mop, bucket and plunger has been returned."

"For Mr. Begley's sake, that's a good thing," the doctor replied.

As Jasper, Roy and Gordon left the office and headed down the hall, Gordon stopped Jasper. "Now all we need is several thousand dollars more for the truck and the equipment, and I'll have everything set up by the time you leave here and move into my travel trailer."

"Piece of cake, Gordon, but Donny Boy may have a heart attack when I tell him I have a job."

CHAPTER SIXTEEN

The Good Samaritan

On this sunny morning, Hudson rose from his bed, put on his clothes, and rode the banister downstairs to help his grandmother. He filled the percolator with ground coffee and asked if he could look for eggs.

"Don't you want to eat breakfast first?" Jenna asked.

"I don't know, Grandma. The hens were very noisy this morning. You can still hear them clucking. I bet there must be a dozen eggs ready for the collecting."

"Well, all right. You go ahead."

Hudson grabbed his egg basket from the back porch and ran across the yard and peered in the henhouse, only this time there was a black, middle-aged man inspecting the nests. Hudson thought he might be one of the seasonal workers that his dad occasionally hired, but Cole never hired someone to collect eggs. Hudson grabbed the pitchfork, prongs forward, marched into the henhouse and said, "You're not supposed to be in here."

"I'm not bothering anyone."

Hudson lunged forward and thrust the pitchfork into the ground as hard as he could, landing a few inches from the man's foot.

"Hey watch it there, buddy."

"Mister, you're not supposed to be in the henhouse without first inspecting for snakes."

The man looked down at his feet and saw a snake struggling to get free from three of the four prongs that had pinned it to the ground. Holding his chest, the man wobbled out the door and fainted in the yard.

"Daddy! Daddy!" Hudson yelled at the top of his lungs. "There's a snake in the henhouse!"

"I'll be right there, son," Cole hollered from the kitchen window, and then he noticed the man lying in the yard.

"Hudson, who's that man lying on the ground?"

"I dunno." Hudson shrugged his shoulders.

Cole dashed outside to see why a stranger had passed out in his backyard.

"He was in the henhouse, Daddy, collecting eggs, and he didn't see the snake by his feet, but I did, and I stabbed it with the pitchfork. I think it's still alive."

"Good job with the snake, Hudson, now get me a glass of water, quickly, and ask Grandma to call over to the bunkhouse. I need Darcy and Walter to help me, immediately."

Hudson returned with the water, escorted by Jenna.

Jenna leaned over and looked at the man lying on the ground. His clothes were tattered and filthy, and the holes in his soles revealed that he had no socks. "Who is this man?"

Cole attempted to give the man a drink by lifting his head. "Whoever he is, he looks very dehydrated and could use a shower and a good meal. Mom, his worn-out boots are military, which means he's probably a homeless vet."

"We can't allow anyone to suffer like this, especially one of our veterans," Jenna said.

The man blinked as he struggled to open his eyes. He looked up at Cole.

"Hey pal," Cole said. "Don't worry, you're in good company. Can you sit up and drink some water? I can help you."

As the man sat up, raw egg oozed from his back pocket. He gulped the water.

"Do you have a name?"

"Joe Colton."

"Joe, would you like a hot shower and some breakfast?"

"Well, if it's not too much trouble, I surely would appreciate it."

Darcy and Walter came quickly. They, too, wondered who the man was.

"Thanks for your help, guys. This is Joe. But first, Hudson says he stabbed a snake in the henhouse, and it may still be alive. Can one of you see about the snake, and I'll need some help getting Joe over to the bunkhouse. He needs lots of water to drink and maybe some coffee, too. Then, he'd like a hot shower. I believe there are some clean work clothes back from the laundry that will fit him."

"And I'll bring over a plate of breakfast," Jenna said.

"Walter, if you take care of the snake," Darcy said, "I'll take care of Joe."

Cole looked at Joe, "This is Darcy. He's going to help you walk over to the bunkhouse and show you where you can shower, and my mom will make sure you get a good breakfast."

"Thank you most kindly, sir," Joe said, as Darcy helped him to his feet.

"My name's Cole Dorman, but you can call me Cole."

Joe leaned on Darcy for support, as the two walked toward the bunkhouse. He looked over his shoulder and said, "Thank you, Mr. Cole."

"Daddy, do you know that man?"

"No, Hudson, I don't. But he needed our assistance, and God wants us to provide that help. Anytime you can help a stranger in need, especially one who faints in your backyard, then do it. Remember the Bible story of the Good Samaritan? God wants us to help strangers in need. That's what this is all about. Now, let's wash up and eat some of your grandma's creamed chip beef and home fries."

After breakfast, Cole sat down with Joe in the bunkhouse. "Joe, you're homeless, aren't you?"

"Yes, sir, and I've been for a couple of years."

"How old are you, if I may ask."

"Forty-seven."

"Are you a drinker?"

"No, sir. My mamma raised me right."

"Would you like a job here on our farm?"

"Yes, sir. I surely would."

"So, Joe, tell me about yourself and your family."

"I served in the military for twenty-six years—mostly Iraq and Afghanistan. I was honorably discharged. I'm proud of that. When I was thirty years old, I was engaged to be married as soon as I came back from a tour, but my time overseas was extended, and I guess it was too long of a wait for my fiancé. When I finally came home, I discovered that she had taken up with another man."

"I'm sorry to hear that. What did you do in the military?"

"I drove heavy equipment, mostly tanks, but there's no call for a tank drivers in civilian life."

"Joe, if you'd like to work with us, I'll need your social security number and your military discharge papers. Do you have a driver's license?"

"I used to have a Maryland license, but I misplaced it. I do know my social security number, though, and I could probably send for a copy of my discharge papers."

"Good enough. Joe, we supply work clothes, and linens for our workers, and your job comes with a bed, a small salary, and two meals—lunch and dinner. The men like to make their own breakfast. There's a small kitchen in the bunkhouse."

"I would like that very much, sir."

"We'll also need to get you a new pair of boots. The ones on your feet have more than served honorably. I tell you what, Joe. There's a Red Wing store in Dover, so let's plan on making a trip over there in the morning for a new pair of boots. And in the meantime, write down your social security number, so we can put you to work as soon as possible. I'll have our accountant Angela see if she can get your military records. Does that sound good to you?"

"Yes, sir. That would be very nice, sir."

"There's no pressure, Joe. If you don't want to work here, let me know by tomorrow if you decide you'd rather move on. At least you can leave here with clean clothes and a new pair of boots."

"Thank you, sir, but I believe I'd like to work here."

"Good." Cole shook Joe's hand.

"Is there anything you'd like me to do for you today, Mr. Cole?"

Cole was struck by Joe's willingness. "I tell you what, Joe. Darcy and Walter will be working the chicken house over at the Johnson Farm later today. That would be a good thing to learn around here, especially if we acquire more houses."

"Today, I'd like for you to just watch Walter and Darcy. They can explain the process, but for now, rest up, and after lunch, I can take you over there."

"That's very well, sir. Thank you, sir."

After lunch, Joe stepped into Cole's truck wearing clean work clothes and his barely soled boots that had a fresh piece of cardboard in the bottom to keep his socks clean. Cole drove Joe to the chicken houses and then showed him where they kept the disposable personal protection outfits worn while working around the chickens.

"Here, before you go any farther, put this outfit on over your clothes, and these booties over your shoes. There's an avian flu outbreak in the area, so we must take extra precautions because it's highly contagious. It's mostly spread by wild birds, but if anyone has contact with any bird, even pets, we won't let them past the yellow posts in the driveway.

Joe and Cole donned protective gear and entered the first chicken house at the west end of the row. "Everything is automated, the water, the temperature, and the feed. What Darcy and Walter are doing now is checking to make sure there are no clogs in the lines. I'll have them show you how they do it in the next house." Cole lifted the lid on a galvanized can. "They've already culled all the dead birds in this house."

"All those chickens died today?"

"Five is a little high for one day, because we don't like to see any dead birds. Come with me and I'll show you how we compost them. When we leave here, you'll remove your protective outfit, and put on a new suit before you go into chicken house number two."

"It seems wasteful to go through so many suits, Mr. Cole."

"The avian flu could devastate our entire poultry operation. You'll notice that Darcy and Walter are wearing rubber work boots. They disinfect their footwear by stepping into those shallow tubs before entering the chicken houses. That action will prevent cross-contamination."

The following morning Angela gave Cole the results of Joe's background check, and it came back clean. It saddened Cole that a retired military man with an honorable service record of twenty-five years could be homeless, alone, and so desperate. He couldn't imagine what could cause Joe's difficulty integrating into society, but he also knew that many returning vets had the same problem.

"Joe, I have some good news for you. I asked a sheriff friend to check to see if your driver's license was still current, and it is. This means all you need to do is apply for a duplicate. I'll take you to the Motor Vehicle Office later today."

"That is good news, sir."

"It sure is! But our first stop will be the Red Wing store for some heavy work boots and several pairs of new socks, as well."

CHAPTER SEVENTEEN

Timothy David Higgins

Dr. Timothy David Higgins had decided to retire long before his daughters suggested the idea to him. By May he finally mapped out all the places he secretly wanted to visit. The first step of his plan: sell his lavish six-bedroom home and downsize to a condo. This would allow him to leave on an extended vacation without worrying about house security and maintenance.

Selling his house was emotionally hard for Tim and his daughters—so many memories of holidays and birthdays spent with Mom. In the end, a fresh start seemed like the right thing to do for all concerned. Each daughter currently spent Thanksgivings with their in-laws, so the daughters and Tim made a family decision to spend every Christmas vacationing together somewhere exciting. It was to become an annual tradition for Tim, his daughters, and their families.

Tim looked over all the household treasures, and finally decided that he only wanted his personal belongings, the family Bible, the framed photos of his wife and family, and his father's old dentist chair—the one he knew at his birth. His daughters could have anything they desired if they removed those items from the house before the end of the month. All remaining furniture and furnishings would be sold at auction or donated to charity.

The handymen and painters were scheduled for the first week of June, so his huge suburban house could be listed with his realtor soon after. Tim just wanted to get on with his life and was anxious to see a *for sale* sign on the lawn of his expansive front yard.

In the meantime, the first days of May were occupied with his realtor, house-hunting for his perfect condo.

"Ah ha! This is it!" Tim told his realtor. "A high-rise with a beautiful view of St. Louis from my living and dining rooms, and from my terrace, too. Look! I can even see the Gateway Arch from the balcony!" But it was the proximity to both of his daughters, and the underground parking for his new car that clinched the deal. "I don't want to move in right away. The place is in desperate need of a decorator."

"I can tell you have good taste, Dr. Higgins; you must admit it's a great floor plan."

"It certainly is. How soon can I own this place if I pay cash?"

"Let me make a few calls, and I believe you can take possession before Memorial Day. That way all the fuss of decorating will be over by the end of June."

"That's all I needed to hear. I'm anxious to pack up and start my new life right here in the downtown area."

"It's a marvelous condo, Dr. Higgins, and you can't beat the location." Opening her laptop, she assured him, "I'm so pleased we were able to find you something that suits you perfectly. Give me a moment, and I'll have a contract ready for you to sign."

CHAPTER EIGHTEEN

First Day of Class

Eddie dusted off two old wooden bar stools that he kept in the corner of his barn and placed them next to Old Red. This was how Eddie looked after his grandkids when they needed an adult eye to keep close tabs on them—watch Grandpa work. "Hudson, Jake can you get up on these stools or do you need a little help?"

Hudson had no problem, but Eddie was a little concerned for Jake.

"I can do it, Grandpa," Jake said, as he clambered up on the stool with ease.

"Today will be your first lesson on how to fix a farm truck." Eddie gave Hudson as stern look. "Why is that hen waddling around in here?"

"That's Margaret. She likes to follow me."

"You know, we don't name our farm animals. It makes it too hard to eat them when their time comes."

Hudson jumped off his stool, picked up Margaret, and held her in his arms. "Can she stay just for today?"

"All right, just for today, but you're responsible for anything Margaret leaves behind. Your daddy goes to great lengths to keep this cement floor clean."

"Okay, Grandpa, I will."

"Good! Now, where were we before, ahem....Margaret showed up?" Eddie picked up a colored marker. "Right...repairs. You boys should know that your great grandpa, your father, and I are all counting on you boys becoming great farmers. It means you must know how to fix vehicles and equipment. Great-Grandpa had a class for both your father and cousin Chip when they were the same ages as you two boys."

"Did they sit on stools like we're doing?" Hudson asked.

"They sure did, in fact, on these very stools."

"Look, Jake," Hudson rubbed his fingers over the carved letters. "Your stool has daddy's name on it. C-O-L-E, and mine says Chip."

"The reason why your father and Chip sat where you're sitting is because they realized that to maintain the two farms, they had to learn about being a farmer, and one place where it begins is the maintenance of all our vehicles and equipment."

"Where's Uncle Roy's stool?' Hudson asked.

"Well, Roy's life took a different turn. He knew the farms would eventually go to your daddy and his cousin Chip, so Roy lost interest in mechanics. Right now, your great grandpa owns both farms. Your grandmother will inherit the Dorman Farm and your Uncle Rob will get the Johnson Farm."

"Then what?" Hudson asked.

"Well, it looks like your daddy eventually will get the Dorman Farm and your cousin Chip will get the Johnson Farm. After that, we don't know. The important thing for you two boys is to learn all you can about farming just in case you're next in line. Now, let's not worry about that and get back to work."

Margaret reacted with her contented murmurs.

"Boys, see this big white board? There's another one in your Uncle Rob's barn. We use the boards to write down all the items we need to check and any spare parts we need to buy. Today I've written the first few items on your great-grandpa's checklist. They're potential problems the dump truck might have which is keeping her from running."

"Gee, Grandpa, is all of that broken?"

"Well, we don't know. This is just a partial list of things your great grandpa says we should check, and hopefully after we do, Old Red will start. But if the dump truck doesn't start, then we'll write a few more things on this whiteboard from his list, and we'll check those things, too."

"Maybe then it'll run like new," Hudson said.

"We hope so. Hudson, can you read the list on the board for me?"

Hudson, the ever-eager grandson said, "Check Battery cable ends—loose or corroded. Check ground wire to see if it's well attached to engine and chassis. Check cables on starter, and the last one, test start relay."

"Very good, Hudson, and after we finish checking these items, and if Old Red doesn't start, I'll write down four or five more things to check. We'll keep doing this until everything on Great-Grandpa's list is checked. Now, do you boys know the names of all the tools?"

"Daddy taught us the names of all the tools," Jake said.

"And if you forget the name of a tool, Jake, we can always learn the names again."

"Mom says we can get credit in homeschool if we learn about machines, how they work, and how to fix them," Hudson said.

"And I say you should, too. Now, let's get started. Are you ready, Hudson? How about you Jake? And don't worry, I won't forget Margaret."

Hudson gave Margaret a gentle nudge, and she replied with a *cluck.*

CHAPTER NINETEEN

Chip's Date with Sandy

Chip bounded down the stairs and into the kitchen. His mother tilted her head with disbelief. "It's two-thirty and you're showered and dressed to go out?"

There was no doubt in anyone's mind that Chip Johnson was a hard-working farmer who spent most of the daylight hours in the fields or in the shop. That's why Marylou was surprised to see her son showered and dressed so early in the day.

"It looks like you might have a date with Sandy Moore. I know your grandpa will be pleased to hear this. When your family approves of the person you're dating, that's a good start for any relationship."

Chip headed for the back door. "You got that right, Mom. I spent the morning cleaning and polishing my pickup."

He walked out to his truck where Dave was standing nearby. "Chip, your dad said you have a date with Sandy."

"It sure didn't take long for the word to spread."

"I'm glad Sandy changed her mind." He shook Chip's hand and slipped him a one-hundred-dollar bill. "I want you two to have a great time."

"Thanks, Grandpa."

"You're welcome, and where are you taking this lovely gal?"

"Rehoboth Beach."

"Have you told Sandy you're taking her to the beach?"

"Of course. I'm thinking we'll walk on the beach and the boards, and then head over to Lewes for dinner. I made a reservation at a great restaurant."

"I'm surprised you could even get in. Memorial Day weekend means it will be packed with tourists especially the restaurants."

"You're right about that, but I know the chef. Our reservation is for eight o'clock, which means I'll get Sandy home before midnight. Say, I'm running late, Grandpa. I gotta go, and thanks again for the money!"

When Chip arrived at Sandy's door, he was again awe-struck by her simple elegance and natural beauty. She had on a stunning pink and coral blouse with a coordinated lightweight sweater, white capris, and strappy sandals.

"Sandy, I thought you looked pretty when we were soaked and covered with mud, but tonight you are downright beautiful."

"That's a lovely of you to say, and I think we should go before my head gets any bigger."

Chip took her hand as the two walked out to Chip's truck where he opened her door. "Sandy, no one can go to the beach without at least one round of miniature golf. Are you up for it?"

"Absolutely! I love putt-putt golf."

"Great, because Rehoboth has some great courses."

Chip and Sandy had a romantic afternoon, holding hands as they strolled along the beach, stopping a few times to kiss. They walked the boards and window shopped along the way, topping the evening with a candlelight dinner. Chip made sure a long-stemmed red rose was waiting for Sandy as they were seated. He was mesmerized by her beautiful broad smile and how her eyes sparkled after she smelled the sweet aroma of the flower.

"Chip, you're so thoughtful. The rose is perfect, and today has been magical."

"I feel the same way. That's why I asked for two glasses of champagne before we order."

Sandy reached for Chip's hand. "Can it get any better? You've shown me such a wonderful time. I can't thank you enough."

"Sandy, you know all about my family, tell me about Texas and your family."

"Well, I have four older brothers, two are living on the ranch and helping Dad. That's Brad and Mark. They're both married. Brad has two children, and Mark and his wife are expecting their first. The main house is quite large and it's where all cooking is done. We have both indoor and outdoor kitchens. Near the house is a casita where Mark and his wife live. It has a bedroom, living room with a kitchenette, and a full bath. It's considered a guest house. The ranch has about nine thousand acres, which by Delmarva standards is huge, but our herds of cattle depend on lots of grazing land."

"What crops do you grow?"

"Quite a bit of wheat and hay, but most of all, we grow strong family ties like the Johnsons and Dormans. It takes a strong, close-knit family to work our ranch, and it is hard work as you well know. Outsiders may think we're crazy to live with parents and in-laws, but not us."

"And your other bothers?"

"My oldest brother Jeff lives in Austin with his wife and three children. He's an architect and a Naval Academy graduate. I first discovered Maryland when our family attended his graduation in Annapolis. My other brother Don is a salesman. He also lives in the Austin area with his wife and one daughter. Neither one of those brothers liked ranching, but whenever they're home, they'd saddle up and help with chores."

"And do you love farming?"

"I majored in it, and you know what job I chose."

"How stupid of me! It's remarkable how just being here with you in the candlelight made me forget the work boots, the mud, the flannel shirts, and everything else that our jobs require. All I see tonight is a woman who is lovely inside and out."

"Your champagne," the head waiter said as he poured.

CHAPTER TWENTY

Jasper's Baptism

Roy walked down the hall to his room. It was time for Jasper to be baptized. "Come on Jasper. What's the hold up?"

Jasper came out from the bathroom. His long blue hair had been shaved bald and his nose ring removed. "It's a new beginning for me. Since being here at Mapledale, I've changed on the inside, so I wanted look different on the outside, too. It's quite a statement. Don't you think?

"I can say this much, you do look different. And I see you're wearing your formal Hawaiian shirt."

"Only the very best for the Lord."

"Come on, Jasper, the preacher is waiting for you in the lobby, and most of the residents are sitting around the pool. Too bad your parents won't be here."

"Donny Boy said Mom and Dad are in England for the Queen's Jubilee. They're celebrating a silly overseas ceremony and skipping my baptism, but it's nice that Mapledale put my baptism on the schedule."

"Yes, it was nice, so don't keep your guests waiting."

"Roy, according to Dr. Weir, I'm checking out today for good. Our family chauffer is coming today to take me home, and you're leaving Mapledale on the thirty-first. Ol' buddy, this could be it for us, so will you pray with me now?"

"Of course."

Jasper bowed his head and placed his hand on Roy's shoulder. "Dear Heavenly Father, Roy and me, we know we're sinners, in fact, we've been real stinkers, or we wouldn't be here at

Mapledale. We're asking for forgiveness of our sins—all of them—because we've racked up plenty. Isn't that so, Roy?"

"Yeah, especially me."

"So, Lord, please give us guidance and help us to be not so naughty. You know, like lead us not into temptation, and please deliver us from evil. Basically, guys like me and Roy, we know how much we need you—I mean, like really need you—and we appreciate you saving us and always being there for us. In Jesus name, Amen."

"Amen," Roy concurred.

"Did you really mean that prayer, Roy, especially about us being stinkers?"

"Well, yeah, I was that, and I never want to go back."

"And were you sincere when you asked God to forgive you?"

"Yeah, I was sincere, and I now know what it means to be under the grace of God."

"Good, because after today, what if I never see you again? Roy, you and Gordon are like the best friends I've ever had. That's why I had to know that you had repented and really love Jesus."

"Oh Jasper, I always said I was a Christian, but I never felt it until I met you and Gordon."

Jasper hugged his friend. "Come on, let's go."

Mapledale set up a lectern and a microphone by the pool. First up was Pastor Miller who explained that Jasper's baptism was both a solemn and joyous occasion. "I have asked Jasper to prepare his testimony, explaining why he wants to be baptized. We ask this of all the adults whom we baptize. Jasper, please, come forward."

Jasper walked up to the lectern and adjusted the mic. He spread his arms wide and said in a loud, thunderous voice, "Welcome alcoholics!" Then, in a lowered tone, "Me included. Yep, I'm one of you, an alcoholic. I don't know about all of you, but I never want to touch a drop of alcohol again. With the help of God, I won't."

The audience applauded and a few cheered.

"Here it is the Friday before Memorial Day and as we all know, it's a popular time to get drunk, but no longer for me. I'm a changed person. I'm being baptized today, because my folks never had me baptized, and God says that we must believe in Jesus, repent, and be baptized. But before this ritual of baptism that symbolizes the changes in my life, I want to thank all of you for coming. I also want to give a special thanks to Dr. Weir for making this event compulsory."

He looked out over the smiling audience. Among them were two older men dressed like they had just come from a round of golf, and there was a smattering of younger tattooed men and women who could have come from a carnival. The rest of the audience was made up of ordinary people, housewives and blue-collar folks that had no outward appearance of a past drinking problem.

Jasper continued, "I have other folks to thank; Pastor Miller for being here today, and Mr. and Mrs. Gordon who invited Pastor Miller. I didn't always believe there was a God. My parents don't believe in God, but then I met Mr. Gordon. He taught me about Jesus. Thank you, Mr. Gordon for that, and thank you for offering me a job at your nursery and a place to stay!"

The audience gave a polite applause.

"This means I'll be leaving Mapledale, and I want to thank all my fellow residents for the support and kindness you've shown me. But the most wonderful thing I learned here at Mapledale was how to pray. I give Gordon all the credit. Did you know that the Bible is a love letter to all of humanity? So why would anyone not want to read a love letter? Gordon also taught me the Lord's Prayer. Some of you might call it the *Our Father* prayer, but it's a sinner's prayer. Can we all agree that alcoholics have hurt others while drunk? That qualifies us as sinners, right?" Cupping his ear, "Can I get an *Amen*?"

A few in the audience, along with Pastor Miller and Mr. Gordon replied, "*Amen*."

Jasper continued, "There's a prayer, a fully complete prayer that you can say in the quiet of your room and it begins, Our Father, not *my* father. That's because all of us have a Father in heaven who loves us. Mr. Gordon taught me this prayer, but he also taught me that Jesus died for my sins. I believe in God because I've personally experienced His love and mercy. Then one day while working in the garden with Mr. Gordon, *shazam*! God opened my spiritual eyes and ears, and I could clearly see that I needed a Savior. Here's a news flash! ...We all need Jesus."

"Amen," a heavily tattooed lady stood up and screamed out. "Only Jesus has the power to wash away sin!"

"That's right, Lenora, and thank you for saying that," Jasper said. "Even with a bar of Lava soap, you can't wash your sin away because sin is inside of you."

Lenora chimed in again. "Hey, some of you high and mighty folks! You may think you're spotless, but you're not."

"Thanks again, Lenora." Jasper walked around the pool where she was seated and gave her a hug before returning to the lectern. "It's our bad behaviors and negative attitudes toward others that makes us sinful. Do we really love one another? Are we kind and forgiving to others, even when they're not kind to us? Do we always tell the truth? Aren't we all drunks? Hey, folks, none of us would be here at Mapledale if we weren't alcoholics. That pool isn't gonna wash away my bad past or my future sins. It's only a representation of what Jesus did for me at the cross. He washed away all my sins with his blood and gave me a new start on life. He is our Passover lamb, so today I'm publicly accepting his grace, and believe me, I sure need it!"

Pastor Miller stepped into the shallow side of the pool. "Jasper, will you join me, please?"

When both men were waist high in water, Pastor Miller said, "Jasper, I baptize you in the name of the Father, Son, and Holy Ghost. Hold your nose if you like."

"Not a bad idea," Jasper said just before he leaned backward so Pastor Miller could immerse him completely.

When he came out of the water, Pastor Miller said, "Let's give Jasper a round of applause!"

The audience complied, and some cheered joyously.

Roy gave him a standing ovation, but his applause was abruptly interrupted by dizziness and nausea. As he collapsed onto his chaise lounge, he realized he needed medical help. Jasper, while putting on his bathrobe, noticed Roy in distress and hurried to his side. "What's wrong, ol' buddy?"

"Jasper, can you walk with me to the clinic? Something's not right."

"Sure. Just lean against me, and we'll go the back way. It's closer."

Halfway to the clinic, Roy was winded. "Jasper, I need to sit down."

"Right now?"

"Yes, now."

"Okay, ol' buddy. No rush. Just sit right here on the lawn. When you're ready, I'll help you up. Take your time."

When the two reached the clinic, the staff doctor immediately put Roy in one of the clinic beds, asked him a series of questions, and then drew blood for testing.

"Roy, the bloodwork we're sending to the lab is to see if your symptoms are caused by your weakened kidneys or perhaps something else. Hopkins suspected that you might eventually need dialysis. This round of bloodwork could possibly confirm that. Regardless, you're staying in the clinic until I get your tests results back from the lab."

"Then what?"

"I'll share the results with the doctors at Johns Hopkins, and then we'll know what our next move will be."

"Doctor, how soon will you get the results back?"

"We'll it's a holiday weekend, so I'm sure the labs are running with a limited staff. I would say Tuesday at the latest, but I'll put a rush on it, so it could be as early as tomorrow morning. It depends on how well staffed the lab is. In the meantime, I'll call Hopkins and see what protocols they'd like me to follow."

"Doctor, do you think it's my kidneys?"

"It seems likely, but I can't say absolutely at this point. When your blood work comes back from the lab, you and I will have a talk. In the meantime, we're going to follow the advice from Hopkins while we wait. Be prepared to take an ambulance ride to Baltimore today if that's the order from Hopkins."

CHAPTER TWENTY-ONE

Time to Downsize – June

Tim's condo purchase was finalized the last week of May, and good weather during the first few days of June allowed the painters to finish their work on the outside of Tim's expansive suburban home. They estimated that the interior work would be finished in two weeks so the house could go on the market. In the meantime, Tim was living with his older daughter Robyn—not ideal because of the lack of closet and storage space—but it was only a temporary situation.

At his new condo the main bedroom closet was off-limits to the decorator, since it was the only area that the previous owners had modernized with any degree of taste. After moving all his clothes into the grand closet, which was as large as a bedroom, he admired all the built-in drawers and shoe racks. He opened a velvet-lined jewelry drawer and arranged his cuff links and his father and grandfather's watches along with a special ring box that his mother had given him. Inside the box was a beautiful engagement ring and a note which reminded him of conversations that he had had with his mother about the man she almost married.

My Dear Timothy,
This is the ring that Dave Johnson gave me. Here is his address in Corinth, Maryland. If he is still living, I hope you can meet this fine man someday.

Tim placed the ring and case back in the drawer and thought about how much he had longed to meet his biological father. Now that his wife and parents were gone, perhaps this would be the time to finally meet Dave Johnson.

He looked around the massive half-full closet. It reminded him that his life was also only half-full without his precious Louise. While packing an overnight case to take with him to his daughter's house, he couldn't stop staring at the empty shelves and rods on the right side of the walk-in closet. He imagined seeing his wife's wardrobe filling more than half the shelves and rods. He remembered a certain blue gown that Louise always prominently displayed on a hanger. *How stunningly beautiful you looked in that dress when we went out on the town. And I must laugh, darling, how indecisive you always were about which pair of shoes to wear. You had shoes of various colors, styles, and heel heights, too numerous for the closet in our house. Ah, but here in this condo there would be ample space for you, Louise. I wish you could see this closet. You would love it!*

Tim's eyes welled up as he leaned against the wall, holding his chest as if his wife were pressed against him. It reminded him of how much family life and a sense of belonging meant to him. He breathed in a long deep breath and exhaled. *Oh, Louise, how I miss you. How long must this grief burden my heart?* He wiped his eyes, shut off the light, and walked out of the closet, closing the door behind him.

The following morning, Tim hired a mover to take his father's dentist chair from his daughter's garage to the condo, where he had a face-to-face meeting with his decorator. "Please use my dentist chair as part of your design." He positioned the chair directly in front of the wall of windows that overlooked the city. "There, that's exactly where I want it. I'll be able to see the cityscape from the most comfortable reading chair I've ever owned."

"As a dentist, I can see why you like this old chair, but it's quite unconventional to use such a strong industrial piece in high design."

"Sorry, but since I'll never part with it. You don't have a choice."

"Do you mind if I have it reupholstered?"

"The problem is you don't understand the sentiment behind this chair. This is exactly how it was when my father gave it to me, and you must admit that it's in excellent condition."

"Then, that's exactly how it shall remain," she said with authority. "It's a design challenge, but I know in the end you'll be pleased with my solution."

"Good. I've left all my family pictures on the kitchen counter. They're of my wife, children, and grandkids. You can have them reframed if you like, but I want them prominently displayed. My family is my life." He removed a key from his key ring and handed it to the decorator. "It's a spare. Will I have a brand-new place before the end of the month?"

"That's my plan, Dr. Higgins."

"Thank you, because one month is about all I can take living at my daughter's place. Don't misunderstand. My daughter and her family are a joy to be around, but I don't like the feeling of always being a guest. It's also important for me to be completely settled in this condo before taking off on vacation."

"Of course."

"Oh, and one other thing, nearly all my clothes are now here in my closet, so you'll be seeing me quite often should you have any questions."

CHAPTER TWENTY-TWO

The Emergency Call

Angela was home and working in her office when she received a call from Mapledale. It was Roy. His voice was weak, and his speech garbled, which troubled her.

"Angela, I just received some bad news about my health. Can you come here as soon as possible and talk to my doctor?"

"What sort of bad news?"

"It's about my kidneys, but you better hear it from the doctor and not just me. Will you come here soon?"

"Yes, Roy, I'll leave right away."

It was a hard decision for Angela. She wanted to do the right thing and support Roy's recovery, even though she struggled with her anger and disappointments. She grabbed her purse and keys and headed to Mapledale, feeling in her heart that it was only on behalf of her Dorman family whom she dearly loved.

When Angela arrived, the doctor met her in the hallway. "I'm glad you could come, Mrs. Dorman. Roy's kidneys have deteriorated further since we last spoke, and after Johns Hopkins received his last blood test results, they believe he should be transferred immediately to Baltimore for a more comprehensive evaluation and treatment."

"And that can't be done here?"

"You see, Mrs. Dorman, we are not set up to care for residents who are suffering from any ailment beyond alcohol withdrawals. That's when we must transfer seriously ill residents to other facilities."

"But Roy is scheduled to be discharged next week. Why must he go to Hopkins now? What's the urgency?"

"Mrs. Dorman, in his current condition and without immediate medical help, Roy could die."

Angela's legs weakened. She sat in a nearby chair. "May I have some water?"

"Sure. Let me get it for you. I would be negligent if I didn't put him in an ambulance and transfer him directly to Hopkins where they're expecting him this evening. We have an ambulance waiting now, except Roy isn't cooperating. I need you to give him a push."

As she sipped on some water, she realized how much Roy truly meant to her and that this was the time to be strong for him. She stood tall, entered the clinic, and walked over to Roy's bedside.

"Angela, thank you for coming. Tell them I don't want to go."

"Roy, don't be stubborn! Your life is in danger. You're going to Hopkins, and I'll let your family know."

The doctor stepped closer to Roy's bed. "I wanted your wife to be here, to help you with this critical decision. She can also update your family about your situation. I know they'll be worried, and she's the best one to explain why you must leave Mapledale."

Roy lifted his head slightly. "Doctor, I don't want to go."

Angela's firm voice was filled with anger "Roy, this is life threatening, and if you don't get into that waiting ambulance now, all I can tell your parents is call the funeral home. I'd rather tell them that we are doing everything in our power to help you."

Roy looked at the doctor and then at Angela with woeful eyes in search of sympathy.

"Doctor, I want to forgive Roy, but it's not easy when he's caused so much pain. I also want what's best for him, so wheel him out of here. He's going to Hopkins. Roy, I'll meet you there!"

While driving to Baltimore, which was on the other side of the Chesapeake Bay and over an hour away, Angela thought about the difficult days ahead. She realized she must keep her hurt feelings to herself if Roy were to have any chance of recovery. She loved the

Dormans so much that anything she could do to help Roy was a gift to his family.

At the hospital Roy was assigned a room, and Angela was there by his side when the doctors decided to put a port in Roy and begin kidney dialysis.

"Roy, I need to go."

"Angela, thank you for coming. It may seem pointless to apologize for my past behavior, but I hope you can forgive me."

Angela took a deep breath. "I need time, Roy, and you need to get better."

She remained doubtful about her future with Roy, but compassion led her to remain silent about the subject, while helping Roy recover. "I'll be back tomorrow to hear what the doctors have to say. Tonight, your parents deserve to hear from me, and I need to go home and pack a few things so I can stay longer in Baltimore. Now, try not to worry. You're in one of the finest hospitals in the country, and the angels of God are looking out for you."

It was almost midnight when Angela headed back to the Eastern Shore. She called the Dormans from her car to let them know that she would be stopping by with an update on Roy's condition.

That night she sat down with Eddie, Jenna, Cole, Jo Lynn and Grandpa Dave. "Roy is very sick and weak, and the doctors at Hopkins want to keep him for at least a week, maybe two, depending on how well he responds to treatment. Tomorrow the doctor will give Roy and me a full analysis of Roy's problem. They're limiting the number of Roy's visitors, but I'm assuming some of you would like to be present for that."

Eddie looked at Jenna and saw a tear on her cheek. "Dad, why don't you go with Jenna and Angela? I can go the following day."

If there was one quality that was plentiful in Dave's heart, it was his fatherly love. "I like that idea. Let's leave right after breakfast."

"Don't worry about a thing here, Mom," Jo Lynn said. "Aunt Marylou and I can take care of the meals for the workers."

The following day Roy's family met with the doctor in a conference room. "When I saw the second results of Roy's bloodwork and compared it to the first, I knew immediately that he should be hospitalized. Roy is weak and cannot walk on his own. He will need regular dialysis, and after a few treatments we'll understand how far gone his kidneys are. But for now, we need to keep him here."

"And then what?" Jenna asked.

"Angela has agreed to keep you informed. That way I only need to talk with one Dorman family member to update you on Roy's condition. It's one day at a time."

"Can I see him now?" Dave asked.

"Yes, of course. Angela knows where his room is."

Angela took Dave and Jenna's hands. "Be prepared. His appearance is poor."

As they walked the corridors Jenna paused. "Angela, I want you to know how grateful I am that you are still willing to help Roy. He has been less than a good husband, and you have been an angel." She kissed Angela's cheek, and Angela returned a tight smile.

"Mom, Grandpa, know that I'm here doing this just as much for you and family as for Roy."

The door was open to Roy's room, so they walked in and found him lying motionless.

"Hey, Roy, it's Grandpa. Your mom and Angela are here too."

Roy opened his eyes and looked at his family. "Mom, I feel so tired. Grandpa, I'm so sorry that I did this to myself, and I hurt all of you."

Jenna brushed back a wisp of hair that covered his eyes. "Roy, you don't have to feel alone. We are all here to help you recover."

"But I can't stop this awful feeling of guilt."

"You don't know what caused your kidneys to fail."

"Mom, please don't do that!" Roy cried hoarsely. "I know exactly what I did, and I'm sorry for all of it. If I could change my past I would. If I could undo all the pain that I caused all of you, especially Angela, I would. I'm so sorry. If Mapledale taught me anything it was to take responsibility for my actions."

Dave took Roy's hand. "Roy, you are my grandson, and I will always love you, and I have already forgiven you. Notice we're all here to show you our love and support. But as for your guilt, well, you'll have to give it to Jesus, and He promises to shoulder your burdens."

"We all can take that advice," Jenna said. "And thanks, Dad, for reminding us about the true source of forgiveness.

Dave looked at Roy with a serious eye. "Here's what my father taught me. That would be your great-grandpa Johnson, who learned it from a wise preacher. If you live in the past, you'll always feel regrets and sorrows. If your focus is always on the future, your life will be full of fear because we don't know what tomorrow brings. That's why God wants us to dwell on the present and live without regrets or fears."

"I like that, Grandpa."

"Now, here's something you can do right from that bed, and it will keep you positive on the present."

"What's that?"

"Your mom and your Uncle Rob bought the Bennett property that runs behind both farms. So, I want you to think about what we should do with that hundred acres of farmland to make it profitable. It has remarkable frontage on the highway, so factor that into your thoughts."

Roy's face lit up. "How are the soils?"

"We're having them tested," Jenna said, "and I'll share the results with you as soon as we get the report."

"And those worthless buildings?"

"In a few days, the fire company will do a controlled burn on all the outbuildings if the weather holds," Jenna said. "Cole and Chip are salvaging the barn wood, if there is any to salvage, and we haven't decided what to do with the old house."

Roy smiled. "I'd love to work on a plan."

"There, you see, Roy, something positive to think about." Dave patted him on the shoulder. "Perhaps it's about time we leave and let you get some rest."

Jenna was grateful that her father knew exactly how to leave Roy on a positive note. She took Roy's hand and kissed his forehead. "You can be a great help to your Uncle Rob and me if you can come up with an idea to best use that land."

"I will, Mama. Thank you for coming. I needed to see that you're not angry with me."

CHAPTER TWENTY-THREE

The Final Class

While Jenna and Grandpa Dave were at the hospital, Eddie looked at the large white board inside the barn and decided he would keep his grandsons busy by working on Old Red. He wrote out the final steps on the board and surmised: Old Red ought to start when these tasks are done. He put down his pen and headed back to the house where Marylou and Jo Lynn were washing windows. "Jo Lynn, I want to take those boys off your hands for a little while."

"Dad, you're always welcome to do that. Are you working on Old Red today?"

"That's the plan. This will be lesson number five, and it should be the last."

"Is that the end of Grandpa Dave's to-do list?"

"Yep, the very end, so after this, I'll be shocked if Old Red doesn't start. I saw Jake in the yard, so I'll go fetch him. Just let Hudson know to meet us in the barn."

Jo Lynn stepped out onto the back porch. "Hudson, are you almost finished washing your eggs?"

"Just two left."

"Good, because you're working on Old Red today with."

"Jake, too?"

"Yes, Jake too. They're waiting for you in the barn."

Hudson stepped into the kitchen. "Mommy, is Uncle Roy going to die?"

"Well, he's very sick, but we should be grateful that he is in the finest hospital. That's why we don't want you to worry. Just depend on God to take care of this matter. Now, you run along. Your grandpa is waiting, and I'll finish up here. You did most of the work and an excellent job washing the eggs."

"Are you coming, Hudson?" Eddie called from the yard.

"Here, Hudson, take this towel and dry your hands. I want you to learn a few mechanical things today."

"Oh, I will. Grandpa says that I'm going to be the next Dorman farmer."

"That's right, but only if you're properly prepared to take on the responsibility. That's why Grandpa wants to teach how to work on farm machines, so don't keep him waiting."

Hudson stepped off the back porch where Margaret was faithfully waiting for him. "Come on Margaret, follow me. I think Grandpa's finally convinced that you're part of the family."

As much as Jo Lynn objected to her son making pets of farm animals, she made an exception with Margaret. "Aunt Marylou, what can I say? I guess Margaret is now a family pet."

"I laugh whenever I see that hen following Hudson around, and the way he hugs her like she was a puppy. It's just as precious as it is comical."

The women finished preparing meals for the workers and loaded them into Jake's little red wagon by the back door and wheeled it off to the bunkhouse.

"Aunt Marylou, Joe has been here for over a month. Don't you think he deserves a bed that's better than a bunk bed, and how about some privacy?"

"Absolutely. He keeps his area so tidy, and he's such a hard worker. I think we can carve out some space in the bunkroom to give him a proper bedroom with a decent sized bed. What do you think?"

"It's doable," Jo Lynn said. "We never have more than eight seasonal workmen, so we only need four bunk beds. Let's talk it about it over at lunch with the men. Mom said she and Grandpa would be back by then."

"Good idea. In the meantime, let's walk over to the barn and look in on Eddie's class."

"I'd love to!" Jo Lynn said, as they started for the barn. "Both Hudson and Jake seem to be quite willing to help their grandfather work on his dump truck, but I think it's because he's very aware of their short attention span."

"That's why grandfathers are so good with kids. They understand those things."

Eddie saw Jo Lynn and Marylou enter the barn. "Well, hello, ladies. You're just in time. We're going to see if Old Red will start. We've checked out everything on the truck, and it all seems to be in working order. Right, right fellas?"

"Yep! We checked off every item on Great Grandpa's list!" Hudson said.

Jake showed off his wide and proud smile. "Yep, top to bottom, Mommy!"

Eddie hopped up onto the driver's seat, gave it a little gas, and turned the key. Nothing happened. He tried again. Nothing happened except the unfortunate quiet click of the key turning the switch.

"What do we do now, Grandpa?" Hudson asked.

"We talk with Great-Grandpa some more. That's what we do."

"Lunch will be ready soon," Marylou said. "We'll serve it when Grandma and Great-Grandpa get back from Baltimore."

"Come with me, boys, so you can get washed up," Jo Lynn said.

"Mom! Mom, they're here! They're here!" Hudson shouted as he saw Jenna and Dave drive up to the house. "Can I tell them lunch is ready?"

"That would be very nice," Jo Lynn said.

When Jenna and Dave entered the house, Eddie and Marylou didn't know what to think because Jenna and Dave looked so forlorn. "How is he?" Marylou asked.

"Not good, but can we talk about it when the boys are not around?" Jenna said.

"That's wise," Dave said. After Chip and Rob arrived, the entire family gathered around the dining table. "Today," Dave said with a crack in his voice, "we will dine and pray as a family for Roy who is foremost on our hearts and minds, and then we'll have our family discussion."

After their meal, Hudson and Jake were sent outdoors. It allowed the adults time to discuss Roy's situation out of earshot of the little ones.

Jenna looked at everyone seated around the table. "I wish Angela were here."

"I'd like that, too," Eddie said, "but I'm glad she's staying in Baltimore. That's either a real commitment of marriage, or an example of how kind and responsible she is."

"It's both," Dave said.

"Thank you for saying what we all believe," Jenna said. "As always, Angela has been wonderful, and if Roy's condition worsens, let us never forget her devotion to this family. I will love her with all my heart for the rest of my life."

"I know you're all worried about Roy's condition," Dave said. "When Jenna and entered his hospital room, it was difficult to be positive, even for a few minutes. His color was poor, and he looked so frail. Wouldn't you say that's true, Jenna?"

"Very true. Roy went downhill very quickly, and I so am grateful the doctor at Mapledale immediately contacted Johns Hopkins and arranged to transport him there. Roy is getting dialysis three times a week, and more if necessary."

"The doctor told us the first hurdle is to stabilize him. He needs to get his appetite back, and his tests need to improve dramatically," Dave said.

"We can't tell you much more," Jenna said, "but perhaps there will be more to say in a week. Roy's doctor will tell Angela if there are any changes in his condition, and she'll let us know right away."

"So, is that all we know?" Cole asked.

"There's not much else to say, except we need to stay in prayer and wait upon the Lord," Dave said. "There is one other thing. Visiting times and the number of visitors will be limited."

"Well, I want to see my son," Eddie said, "so I'll go up to Baltimore this evening."

"And I'll go with you," Jenna said.

Eddie took Jenna's hand. "Thank you, dear. I want to apologize to Roy. All these years he had a dream to be a farmer, and instead of sharing in his dream like a loving father, I wrongly tried to shape it. I almost feel like it was me who drove him to the bottle."

"I think I'm the culprit," Dave said, "and so is tradition for instilling in everyone's mind that only the oldest son can be the next farmer."

Jenna embraced her husband. "Eddie, Daddy, please don't do that to yourselves. I want us all to look to the future and leave our self-doubt and reproach behind."

Jo Lynn stopped rinsing the dishes and looked at everyone. "I know perhaps this isn't the right time to bring this up, but we still have a farm to manage. Good workers are hard to find, which means we need to keep our best help. Joe is not only a great farmhand, but Darcy and Walter really like him. The three of them pray together over meals, and Joe wants to start a Bible study with them. Joe deserves his own bedroom, and I think we can add another bedroom inside that bunkroom."

Eddie said, "It's true, there's plenty of room there, but don't you think Cole should first talk to Joe? We need to know if he'd like to become a long-term employee before we build him a bedroom."

Jake burst into the kitchen screaming as loud as he could. "Daddy, Daddy, Grandpa, Grandpa!" His over-the-top excitement sounded ominous. "Grandpa, Grandpa, Hudson needs help!"

Eddie, Cole, and Dave jumped to their feet. "What happened?" Eddie asked.

"Hudson got Old Red running, and he's real scared. He doesn't know how to turn it off!"

The men couldn't leave the room fast enough. They dashed outside and ran toward the barn to see what was going on with Hudson. The rumbling sound of truck grew louder as they neared Old Red.

Cole was first in and saw the driver's side door open with Hudson behind the wheel. He jumped up on the running board, leaned over his son, and turned off the engine. "Hudson, how did you manage to start Old Red?"

"Yes, I'd like to know, too," Eddie said. "Show us how you managed to fire up this old dump truck."

"You mean, you're not sore at me, and it's okay if I do it again? I won't get in trouble, will I?"

"Trouble? No, Hudson, you're a hero!" Cole laughed. "Show us how you did it."

"I couldn't reach the key, so I had to balance myself on this brake pedal in order to turn it." Hudson demonstrated. "Like this. See, it starts."

Everyone laughed and cheered while Dave tucked his head below the steering wheel and looked behind the brake pedal. "Eddie this model never came with a brake safety switch. That's why you and I never considered it. Audrey's dad must have added it. He was always safety conscious. He even installed these seat belts."

Eddie also looked behind the pedal. "Well, I'll be! Depressing the brake releases the safety switch, so you can start the engine. Hudson, you are hereby a graduate of my mechanics' class."

Dave ruffled his great-grandson's hair. "Hudson, and I also declare you an official farmer!"

CHAPTER TWENTY-FOUR

Teamwork

Darcy, Walter, and Joe were busy painting the outbuildings. They each had a spray gun and believed the bunkhouse could be finished before lunch.

Cole stopped by to see if they needed more paint, and he also wanted to have a conversation with Joe. "Joe, can you come down off your ladder for a moment? I like us to have a little chat." The two walked inside and sat down in the bunkroom.

"Joe, you've been doing great here, and that's not an exaggeration. You work hard, and everyone here likes working with you. That's why we'd like to ask you if you'd want to stay on with us. We'd like to give you your own bedroom and a more comfortable bed, but it depends on if you want to stay on."

Joe seemed surprised that he would be offered such a gift. "Are you serious?"

Cole walked over to one corner of the bunkroom and stood between two windows. "Joe, we can put up some walls here and bring in heat and air conditioning vents for you. But before any of this can happen, I need to know if you want to be a long-term employee, or do you think you might be moving on?"

Joe took out his handkerchief and wiped his face and nose.

"Joe, I want you to know that I'll never think less of you when you shed tears. I can't imagine what you went through on the battlefield or after that, but you persevered. I also know how much your self-confidence has improved in the short time you've been here."

"It has, and I feel much so better, too, thanks to all of you."

"In the past you may have been abandoned by friends, family, and even our country, but the Dormans and the Johnsons believe in you, and we want you to stay, that is, if you want. You don't need to give me an answer today, just think about it."

"Thank you, Mr. Cole. Can I really stay for as long as I want?"

"Yes, Joe, as long as you want."

"Then, please, Mr. Cole, I'd like that bedroom."

"I'm glad to hear you say that. You see, Joe, you've been a blessing to our family, and everyone will be happy to know that you want to stay."

"Thank you, Mr. Cole. Can I finish my painting now?"

"God bless you, Joe, but I have another job for you. I'll have Darcy and Walter make sure your paint sprayer is cleaned, so you can go with me over to the Johnson farm. Do you think you can drive a combine?"

"I know how to drive an Abrams tank at sixty miles an hour."

"Well, a combine won't go that fast, but if you can drive an Abrams, then you can probably handle a combine."

"I'd like to try it."

"Both farms own a combine, and they operate in a similar fashion. Uncle Rob and I want you to learn on his combine, because the Johnson farm will be where you're most needed."

"When will I start?"

"After supper, we'll work in shifts around the clock to ensure that all the wheat is harvested before a powerful rainstorm comes our way. When your shift is up, get some rest and something to eat. Chip goes between farms, inspecting the combines at the end of every shift to make sure there's no build-up of chaff and wheat that's trapped around the engine or exhaust lines. That debris could easily start a fire, so we keep a leaf blower in the cab. If you're driving into the wind, you could have some serious build-up of debris, so I'll show you where you should periodically check and blow off anything that could start a fire. There's no wind now, so you shouldn't have a problem.

"Can a combine really catch fire?"

“We know of farmers who have had combine fires. We’ve never had one, and I give Chip the credit for that. It’s his job to check the equipment and keep the combines safe for the drivers. But, Joe, if you should ever see smoke, grab the fire extinguisher, which is next to your seat, and get out of the cab as fast as you can. Make sure your phone is always strapped to your arm so you won’t have to return to the cab and retrieve it during an emergency.”

“I’ve seen Chip work; he’s a good mechanic.”

“He certainly is, and he’s proved it many times over. Between shifts he also checks the lines, hoses, and belts, and he always insists that the combines rest at least twenty minutes before the next driver takes over. This gives the combine a needed break and allows the equipment to cool down for refueling. Once we start harvesting, the shifts never stop until all the wheat is in.”

“Will I be working all night?”

“Not all night but into the night. These next few days are peak times for harvesting. We just need to make sure it all happens before the rain comes, or we’ll get hit with a lower return, maybe even a loss. It’s a race against time and nature. That’s what makes it an around the clock operation.”

“How many men will be running the combines?”

“My dad and I will be harvesting on the Dorman farm, and as you can see, we have about four hundred acres to bring in. My Uncle Rob will be doing likewise on the Johnson farm, which is three times as large. We also have Walter and Darcy to pitch in on both farms. They’re both very good on the combine. Chip usually pitches in, too. That’s why he doesn’t get much sleep when we’re bringing in crops.”

“I think Uncle Rob is ready to give you a test drive, so let’s take a ride over to the Johnson Farm.

~ ~ ~

The activity was brisk in the Dorman kitchen as Jenna, Marylou, and Jo Lynn prepared meals for the workers.

“I have a surprise for you.” Jo Lynn lined up three jars on the counter. “Aunt Marylou, Mom, I need you to sample my entries for the State Fair. These were all made with frozen peaches, but once our peaches come on, I'll make them with fresh ones which should improve the textures and flavors.

"Tell us about these three jars," Jenna said.

"The first jar is a peach chutney, made with peaches, Vidalia onions, raisins, balsamic and cider vinegars, and sweetened with a touch of maple syrup. The next jar is similar, but it has a spicy kick to it, and the last jar is a peach jam made with peaches, orange zest, and a hint of orange liqueur. All three recipes have been entered, so I can't change the ingredients at this point. The deadline for entry was June first."

Sampling the jars, "Oh, Jo Lynn, these are all delicious," Marylou said. "Each one is a winner. How will you enter them, separately or together?"

"I don't really know, but I need to decide before I get to Harrington."

"Then you are all of invited to our house tonight for dinner," Marylou chimed in. "Bring your appetite and chutney, Jo Lynn, because I happen to have lots of pork chops in our freezer. We can have a taste testing. I want to see how the men and your boys react to pork with peach chutney."

"I think they will all be pleasantly surprised," Jenna said, "and I'd also like to see their reaction to the preserves and the jam."

CHAPTER TWENTY-FIVE

Excelsior

The first week Tim's suburban house went on the market, he received several offers. He sat down with his realtor as she went over the papers. "This one is the best. No inspection, it's over list price, no contingencies, and a thirty-day settlement date."

"Then that's the offer I'll accept. I'm leaving on vacation after Independence Day, so I'll have my attorney draw up papers to allow my oldest daughter to sign any necessary documents."

"You're leaving that soon?"

"I'd leave sooner, except every Fourth of July both my daughters plan a family barbeque. I wouldn't want to miss that. The kids hang out by the pool, and we play games and eat, and eat and eat. It's so much fun."

"Sounds like you have a close family."

"I do, and the Fourth is a big family day that only lasts a few hours. My daughters and their children are precious to me and so are the times we spend together."

"How is the construction coming along on your condo?"

"I'd move in now except the kitchen and two bathrooms are completely torn apart. The decorator says that it will be all put back together by next week. It really doesn't matter whether it's finished before I leave on vacation, because it won't delay my trip back east."

"Sounds like you're eager to get started."

"I'd like to visit historic cities like Philadelphia, Baltimore, Washington, D.C. if I have time, but most of all I want to look up some old friends. It will be a laid-back car trip that I've been looking forward to for many years."

"Well, let me just say, congratulations, you have just sold your house, and I'll be in touch to arrange the closing."

Tim was relieved that his big house sold so quickly, and now it was onward and upward to his next bucket list item—to meet his biological father. Tim wondered. *Should I phone or write first? Maybe I should get an intermediary to break the news. No, I should just show up and have a private conversation with Mr. Johnson—if he's still alive. I'll have to make Dave Johnson as comfortable as possible before I introduce myself as his son.*

As Tim contemplated Dave's reaction after sixty years without so much as a hint from Monica, he worried how he would be received. *Will Dave find me credible or chase me off his property as a fraudster? Mother's ring ought to help him realize that my story is true, but only if recognizes the ring and remembers her. What if he has dementia? How will his wife and family react to me? It would be wonderful to discover more family members to know and love, provided they are willing to accept me. And what a great pleasure it would be if Dave were to call me son, but I must not get my hopes up. Oh, I'd love to have some siblings, but would these new brothers and sisters accept me? Will they consider me an intruder or a spoiler? I need to trust God and give everyone a chance to see me as family.*

CHAPTER TWENTY-SIX

Love Thy Neighbor as Thyself

Acres of ornamental trees and shrubs could be seen from the busy highway along with countless potted flowers prominently displayed to attract the attention of passing drivers. The sign in front of the well-stocked garden center proudly announced *Gordon's Great Landscapes and Gardens.*

Jasper had settled into his new home, a one-bedroom travel trailer parked in the rear of the nursery. It had a full awning in the front and an outdoor kitchen in the back, and although Jasper always had access to the very best in life, to him, nothing could be better than his simple life in a trailer. He sat on a camp chair under the awning and looked at the large amount of money in his checkbook, twenty-five thousand dollars. It was all the money Donny Boy had sent him for his rutabaga project.

As Jasper continued to look at the large number, he questioned why his parents never thought twenty-five thousand dollars was too much to pay for a basket of rutabagas, but the answer was simple. They used money to keep Jasper out of their lives rather than to draw him closer. Thanks to Gordon and Roy, he was introduced to a different philosophy of teamwork and friendship. They had become the family that his soul longed for and never had. So, with his checkbook in hand, he marched over to Gordon's office.

Jasper loved Gordon like a father, and he had much respect for the man who taught him that life is so much more than naughty thrills and getting drunk. He learned the joy of looking outward and finding ways to help others.

"Gordon, I've been thinking about that rutabaga project of mine and have decided not to do it. Now don't get me wrong," Jasper chuckled. "Who in their right mind would pay twenty-five thousand for a rutabaga? Nobody! Well, my parents paid it, but that's how they do things. Roy was right, and you knew it all along."

"Jasper, your eyes have been opened, and I was honored to be a part of the process. I knew the thousands of dollars your parents doled out meant nothing to them, but to you, it meant finding a dream, working the dream, and seeing it through to the end. That's a lesson I want you to take with you throughout your life."

"Thanks, Gordon, I will, but now I want to help you. Will you allow me to be a part owner, a very small owner, for twenty-five thousand dollars?"

"Ah, Jasper, that's very generous and thoughtful, but I cannot accept your offer. So, my recommendation to you is keep your money, and some day you will know where and how to spend it. Focus on the well-being of others, and God will take care of you."

"But how will I know how to spend it?"

"Jasper, God has entrusted you with this money for a reason. Now you must trust Him with all your heart, and don't lean on your own understanding. But rather, in all things acknowledge God, and He will show you how this money is to be spent. In the meantime, you need to be a good steward of what God has given you."

"Gordon, you are the wisest guy I've ever met."

"That's because you don't know many people. Why don't we take the rest of the day and drive to Johns Hopkins to see Roy? I heard from the doctor at Mapledale today. Roy probably would like our company because he is gravely ill."

"Gravely ill! Oh, man, that's bad."

"I'm sorry for him, too, my friend, and I know he'll appreciate a visit from us."

"How soon can we leave?"

"Right now, Jasper."

"Let me change my shirt, and I'll meet you by your car."

When they arrived at Hopkins, Roy was sleeping. Angela met Gordon and Jasper in the hall. "I know Roy wants to see you because he spoke so highly of you. When we enter, I'll wake him and announce you, and then don't stay too long. He's very sick. Are we ready?"

Jasper and Gordon followed Angela into the room. She gently touched Roy's hand. "Roy, you have some guests. Gordon and Jasper are here to see you."

Roy stirred and opened his eyes and spoke with a weak voice, "Jasper, your formal Hawaiian shirt."

"Nothing but the best for you, ol' buddy."

With a soft voice Roy said, "Gordon, I never got to thank you for teaching me about organic gardening. If I ever get a kidney, could you help me start an organic fruit and vegetable farm? My family has some spare land."

"Of course, I'll help you; I promise," Gordon said.

"Me, too, ol' buddy. And don't lie there worrying about gettin' a kidney. Baltimore is one of the murder capitals of the world. Surely some stiff will be found soon to donate one for you."

"I wouldn't have said it quite like that," Gordon said. "But I do believe God will provide you with a kidney, and, Jasper, this would be a good time to pray for Roy. Shall we all lay our hands on Roy as we pray?"

When Gordon and Jasper returned to the car, Jasper wailed. "We're going to lose our good ol' buddy, Gordon. I never saw anybody look that bad. Roy always appreciated me, and after five other roommates who begged Dr. Weir to let them transfer out of my room, Roy stayed. He really liked my company. Oh Gordon, I'm about to lose my best friend."

"Jasper, please, keep your faith, and look in my glove compartment for some tissues. You must accept that if we should lose Roy, remember it's God's will."

"Then God needs to draw up another will, because seeing Roy in that awful condition has punched me in my gut, and I don't like it one bit, Gordon." Jasper blew his nose and wiped his eyes. "Roy is my good ol' buddy, and I don't want to lose him."

CHAPTER TWENTY-SEVEN

The Harvest

Cole sat down with Joe, Darcy, and Walter in the bunkhouse while eating lunch. "The timing couldn't be better for harvesting. The wheat is at its peak, and the weather looks like it will hold, but we have only a two or three-day window to bring it all in on both farms."

"We can do it," Walter reassured. "We're using both combines, right? And if we break it up into shifts, and if the bad weather doesn't come in sooner, it'll get done."

Cole asked, "Do you want six or eight-hour shifts?"

"Eight," the men concurred.

"Then that's the pace we should set," Cole said. "As long as we allow time for Chip to do the maintenance between shifts and refuel, we'll be fine. The downside is that we must start harvesting immediately after dinner."

"I'm in," Darcy said as he lifted his water glass. The other men concurred with raised glasses.

"I'll talk with Chip and Uncle Rob and let you know the shift schedule. The good news is Old Red is running, so we now have three trucks to haul the Johnson grain to market. Remember Chip has entered the Highest Yield contest, so the Dorman wheat is to be kept separate and siloed."

"What about the two chicken houses?" Walter said.

"I'll ask Mom, Jo Lynn, and Aunt Marylou if they'll take chicken duty while we're harvesting," Cole said.

During the last hours of daylight, Joe took his first shift on the Johnson farm. Chip wanted him to be accustomed to harvesting while the sun was still shining and before he had to tackle the job using headlights. Rob was second up on the Johnson rotation, and after an hour in the field, he called Chip's cellphone. "From what I can see, son, Joe did a great job."

Over at the Dorman Farm, Eddie was first up. He started a two-hour run to make sure both farms were not on the same rotation schedule, allowing Chip to alternate his inspections between farms.

The first evening harvest went smoothly, and as the sun peeked over the horizon, the first full day was about to begin. Jo Lynn, Marylou, and Jenna worked tirelessly to assure there would be plenty of food and coffee to help the men make it through the day and into the night. Later in the day they would have to work in the chicken houses, so the women decided it was time to start teaching Hudson and Jake this new chore.

That morning, Eddie stopped in to get a kiss from his wife and rest his weary bones.

"Eddie," Jenna said. "You need to sleep between shifts. If the men get too tired on the combine, I don't mind taking a turn."

"Now that's the spirit! But honestly, with Joe out there harvesting, we'll finish on time—but I'll keep you in mind." Breathing in the kitchen aromas, "Smells good, ladies. I think there's gonna be some fine meals today."

"Eddie, please let everyone know that we'll keep plenty of snacks in bunkhouse." Marylou said. "And we'll make sure there will be cold drinks and lots of coffee there, too."

"I made two pies for dessert," Jo Lynn said.

"I'll be sure to tell them." Eddie went upstairs to shower before starting the new day.

The following day, while the sun was high in the sky, Sandy made the rounds to see how the county's harvest was progressing. The Extension Service and farmers across the county knew that they had a narrow window to reap before heavy rains were expected.

Just before noon Sandy arrived at the Johnson farm. She heard in the distance the sounds of a cow in distress and realized the cries were from the birthing byre. She parked her truck nearby and walked over to the distraught cow.

"Easy Mama. I see you're having a hard time with your baby." Knowing from experience that cows love music, Sandy began to sing in a soft tone to the cow. "*Jesus loves you, this I know, for the Bible tells me so…*" She fastened the lead that was around the mother's neck to the railing, as she continued to sing. "*Little ones to Him belong, we are weak, but He is strong.* You like lullaby music, Mama? I see your baby's legs, Mama, and I'm going to give them a tug. *Yes, Jesus loves you. Yes, Jesus loves you…*" She pulled on the front legs of the calf until it was fully outside of its mother. Along with the calf came enough water to soak her work boots and the legs of her jeans. "Oh, look, you have a beautiful little bull calf with great markings. Good job, Mama." She untied the lead and stepped back from behind the rail. "That's good, Mama."

After all that excitement, Sandy decided to walk up to the Johnson house rather than step into her truck with slimy boots. When she knocked on the back door, Marylou appeared and looked at Sandy's unkempt clothes. "Sandy, how nice to see you again, and what have you been up to?"

"Just helping one of your Belties calve a little one. I hope you don't mind if I use your hose and rinse off my boots."

"Go right ahead, and thank you for your help. With everyone focused on the harvest, we hadn't checked on that cow lately, though we did manage to get her into a birthing stall."

"I heard a familiar distress call and decided to help. May I leave my boots outside on your steps and clean up a bit on your back porch?"

"Of course. Go right ahead. There's soap and a clean hand towel on that shelf."

"Thank you, Mrs. Johnson."

"And, please, join me for a cup of coffee."

"Thank you, and may I be the first to announce the latest addition to your herd—a beautiful bull calf. That's why I'm a mess."

"Oh, I'm sorry."

"It's part of the job. I grew up on a cattle ranch. The poor thing was worn out trying to calve, but don't worry. Everything's fine, and I stayed until the calf took to its mother's teat."

"What brings you to our farm today? Please tell me it's to see Chip."

"My boss had asked me to visit as many farms as I could and report back how the harvests are looking. If I see Chip, I'd be surprised on this busy day, but it would be a welcomed surprise."

"Cream, sugar?" Marylou said as she poured two cups of coffee. "I'm just sitting here watching my biscuits to make sure they're not overbaked."

Marylou was eager to get to know Sandy a little better as the two sat down at the kitchen table.

"Mrs. Johnson, all the area wheat farmers know that they are in a race against time. I've already reported that so far it looks as if the men can beat this big storm heading our way. I've been keeping an eye on the radar maps, and I suspect most farmers will be working throughout the night."

"They did last night," Marylou said, "and they will tonight. They're not tired now, but this time tomorrow will be rough. They want to stay ahead of schedule in case the storm decides to come early."

Sandy's cellphone rang. She answered and realized she was running late. "It's my boss, and I've got to go. Mrs. Johnson, thanks for the coffee. I'm sorry for rushing off like this, but I've got to go." She left in a hurry, put on her wet boots, and headed down the driveway.

After dinner, the men began their second full day. Their stomachs were full and their trucks were empty and ready to accept the grain from the combines. Chip was certain the equipment was in good working order and decided to take a much-needed nap.

He met his mother in the kitchen. She was washing the pots and pans from dinner. "Mom, I'm going to lie down, and I'll need you to wake me in about two hours."

"When this is all over, you men need to have a real good sleep rather than all these cat naps. Oh, and just so you know, Sandy came by today."

"Was she looking for me?" Chip asked.

"No, but she smiled when she said it would be great if she ran into you. Sandy wanted us to know that we have another Belted Galloway—a bull. She heard the cow's distress call and assisted in the delivery. She's quite a gal, Chip."

"I know."

"Now, please go upstairs and get some rest. You look so tired. I'll let you know when it's time to get up."

The day turned to night, and as the hours wore on the men kept on schedule while Rob kept a close eye on the weather radar from his shop in the barn. Eddie showed up with a thermos to keep him company.

"It's way after midnight, Rob, so I brought you some coffee. How are you and the men holding up?" Eddie asked.

"It's hard for me to take my eyes off this radar. If we can beat this storm, we'll have a great harvest, but if we don't, it will hurt us in the pocketbook, but not too badly. Chip's been doing a great job keeping the combines running, though he always worries about overheating, especially the Dorman combine."

"I saw Chip a couple of hours ago heading home for some shut eye, and he looked beat."

"Don't worry about him. He's tough, he even insists on relieving the men for an hour so they can stretch their legs."

"We have some fine boys, don't we?"

"Excuse me, Eddie, but my cell phone is vibrating. Who would call me at this hour? Hmm, it's our neighbor, Clyde Stevenson. Hello, Clyde, how's it going over there?"

"Rob, my combine broke down in the middle of my field, and I can't get it going. Do you think Chip could lend me a hand?"

Rob knew Clyde would be in great financial trouble if he didn't get his combine working soon. With a heavy rainstorm heading toward Corinth every hour was critical. "I'll make sure you get help, Clyde. Which field are you in?"

"It's the one closest to you. I'll leave my headlights on so you can't miss me."

Rob didn't want to wake Chip, but this was an emergency for his neighbor, so he walked over to the house. During harvest, Chip always slept with his clothes on, so when his father came into his room, he only needed to slip on his work boots.

"Chip, I need you up."

Woozy and exhausted he answered, "What time is it, Dad?

"A little after two. Clyde Stevenson had a breakdown on his combine. He's been down two hours already."

"Does he know what the problem is?"

"He doesn't know, and it sounds like he needs a trouble shooter."

"Call him back. I'll be right there, and let Cole know where I am. I can only work on Stevenson's combine for about an hour before I'm needed back here, but I'll do the best I can."

Chip jumped in his truck and drove to the end of the lane. He grabbed his tool bag, jogged across the road, and over Clyde's already harvested land, where he saw Clyde's combine in the middle of his field.

Clyde had worked up a worried sweat trying to figure out the problem. "Thank you, Chip, for coming so fast. I didn't start harvesting as soon as I should have, so this breakdown is very serious to me."

"Hey, no one can afford to lose time. How long have you been down?"

"Almost three hours."

After checking several areas of the combine, Chip said, "I think I know what the problem is. Could you point your flashlight over here?"

"Sure."

"Mr. Stevenson, you're in luck, and I have the part you need in my shop. I'll be right back and get you going again. It will only take me a half hour, and don't worry about your lost time. We're ahead of schedule, so as soon as we have a free combine, I'll come back and help you catch up."

With the financial success of his farm resting on getting the crop in before the rains, Clyde didn't have the words to express his deep gratitude. As a lone farmer, a few lost hours with a big storm on its way meant Chip's help would be invaluable.

As Chip entered his shop, his cell phone began to ring. It was Cole asking if he had overslept. "Cole, if Uncle Eddie is awake have him start the cleaning process and check the hoses. Make sure you're cooled down before you refuel. I'll be there soon. How much more cutting do you have left to do?"

"Only a few more hours. Probably by breakfast time the Dorman Farm we'll be all done, so you can start using our combine."

"That's good, Cole, because I promised Mr. Stevenson I'd catch him up. He had a breakdown, but I think I can fix it pretty quick. He's running behind, and we're ahead of schedule."

"Do you want me to cut Clyde's field?" Cole asked.

"I think it would be better if after breakfast you help Dad get our grain to market so we can free up some trucks."

"Okay but let me know if you need anything else."

"Great! Thanks, Cole."

CHAPTER TWENTY-EIGHT

A Job Well Done

Before the storms came, all the Dorman wheat was safely siloed, the Johnson wheat had been taken to market, and even Clyde Stevenson's entire crop was harvested. The heavy drops falling on the roof were a pleasant sound for a long-deserved rest in bed.

Jenna and Marylou sat at Marylou's kitchen table and tallied the profits. As they tapped away on their calculator keys, it became apparent that this would be a record harvest that could carry them through a drought should one occur in late summer or in the following year. Ultimately, they would need Angela's advice on how much to set aside for taxes and for bad times, but for now, both women felt a great financial relief.

"The chickens are going to market this week, and if our peaches come in strong, this could be our best year ever," Marylou said.

"I hope so because after several years of good weather, we're overdue for some rough times."

"Jenna, there's something I want to say about Joe. I know Cole hired him before we discussed wages, but Rob and I believe Joe is a blessing to our operation, and whatever was promised will be fine. Cole is a wonderful manager. We trust him, and we couldn't be prouder of our nephew."

Jenna gently touched Marylou's hand. "I knew it would be fine but thank you for saying it."

The high profits were good news and couldn't have come at a better time, but there was a downside to Jenna's joy as the family waited to find out how much Roy's health insurance would cover his medical care and rehab.

"Any more word on Roy?"

"Nothing other than his condition is worsening. Each day I pray for a miracle."

Marylou looked into Jenna's eyes. "And we are praying, too. Every night when we lie in bed and say our prayers, Rob cries out to God for Roy's recovery."

"Rob has always been sensitive to my needs. I think it's because we're twins."

Just then, Chip came downstairs for a snack. He opened the refrigerator and poured himself a glass of milk.

"Wouldn't you like to have some breakfast, or in a couple of hours will have some lunch?" Marylou asked.

"I'm not that hungry, just plain worn out. I feel like I've been wrestling with a bear."

"Maybe this will cheer you up. Your mother thinks you're a contender for that highest yield prize, because this is the best harvest we've ever seen."

"I think all the farmers are probably feeling the same way," Chip said. "This was a good year for everyone, and while I was over at the Stevenson Farm, I noticed that his yield looks very good."

"When will they announce the winner?" Jenna asked.

"The first Saturday after Independence Day at the Farm Bureau dinner."

"We'll all be there to cheer for you, and I bet Sandy would like to go."

"You're right, Aunt Jenna, and I've already invited her to go with me. As an extension agent, she's required to go."

"I think we should start the planning for our family Independence Day barbecue." Jenna said. "We can have it at our place again, under all the nice tall oaks in our front yard."

"It's another opportunity to spend time with Sandy," Marylou said.

"Mom, I'm not sure who's more anxious about me and Sandy—you, Dad, or Grandpa."

"We all like her, and you must admit she's very nice and quite talented," Marylou said.

"Eddie and I like her, too, and we'll be pleased to see her again," Jenna said. "I think I'll ask Cole and Jo Lynn to oversee the games and entertainment. There will be lots of children when we invite all our friends and neighbors."

"I'm all for it, right now, I'm going back upstairs. My bed is calling me."

"And you deserve a good sleep."

"I'm only resting until this rain stops and the fields are dry enough to plant soybeans. Dad wants me to turn under a wide swath around the Bennett barn so the fire company can burn it without burning down the county."

"Chip, do you mind if I ask Roy to rename that farm? It's no longer the Bennett property, and it will keep his mind off his poor health while he's in the hospital," Jenna said.

"Aunt Jenna, I never liked the sound of the Bennett Farm, so please tell Roy to rename it soon."

CHAPTER TWENTY-NINE

Independence Day

While the Dormans were eating breakfast, they heard a disturbance in their front yard. Rob had rented a bouncy castle for the children, and the company was in the process of setting it up on the front lawn.

Eddie walked out onto the porch, "Okay, Uncle Rob, I see you're trying to have one up on me with the grandkids."

"I hope the location is okay because it's not too late to move it."

"It's fine where it is. Jake and Hudson will go nuts when they see it. Say, is that a new flag on our pole?"

"Yep," Rob expanded his chest with pride. "One flag, one land, one heart, one hand, one nation evermore—Oliver Wendell Holmes said that. I bought the flag yesterday to replace your faded one, along with a few boxes of sparklers for later tonight."

"Well, Uncle Rob, you've certainly outdone yourself. Since you're here, come on in and have a cup of coffee."

Rob followed Eddie inside and to the kitchen. "Hi Pop," Rob said, placing his hand on Dave's shoulder. "And hello to my lovely sister, and you, too, Cole and

Jo Lynn."

Eddie couldn't hold back and had to say, "Hudson, Jake, you'll never guess what your Uncle Rob got for you, just for today. Here's a bunch of sparklers, and some men in the front yard are blowing up your big surprise."

"A bouncy house!" Hudson got up from the table and ran to the front door. "Jake, come look. We have a bouncy house." Jake ran to the front door in his pajamas, hollering, "A bouncy house! A bouncy house!"

"That's a lot of excitement for two kids," Jenna said.

Rob waited for the children to leave the room. "I know we're all concerned for Roy. Has there been any luck in finding a kidney donor?"

"There's no problem finding a donor," Cole said. "Chip and I have both volunteered to give him one of ours, but Roy won't let us give up our kidneys because we're family. He insists that he won't accept a kidney from any family member and will only accept from a stranger."

"We're visiting Roy on Thursday," Jo Lynn said, "and we're taking the boys. They've made get well cards, and I hope it will give him some cheer."

Jenna offered, "You're welcome to come, Rob, because Dad isn't going."

"No, thanks. Too much to do around here, and besides, the hospital limits company, and I know you'll want as much time as possible with your son."

Eddie asked, "What time today do you want me to start the grill?"

"I think about three-thirty or four would be fine," Jenna said. "We'll feed the boys lunch before their friends arrive around two. The bouncy house will entertain them until it's time for hot dogs. I also bought a gallon of ice cream in case the boys want cones. They'll be in bed by eight or nine, but it will be dark enough for sparklers."

Hudson and Jake dashed into the kitchen. "Mom, the castle is all blown up. Can we play in it now?"

"Not in your pajamas. Go upstairs, change, and brush your teeth. Then you can play all you want."

"What games have you lined up, Cole?" Rob asked.

"Corn hole, croquet, horseshoes, and whiffle ball."

"That should entertain the crowd."

"Is Sandy coming?" Jo Lynn asked.

"I sure hope so," Dave said. "She's coming even if I have to invite her myself."

"Now, Dad," Jenna said. "Chip and Sandy are not exactly strangers to one another."

"Then, Rob, you need to encourage your son a little. He ought to pick her up at her apartment. A little nudge from his dad won't hurt."

"That's funny, Dad," Rob said, "when you've practically dragged him by his ear to get him to pay attention to her."

Jenna, always the voice of reason, said, "Let's just see how it goes this afternoon. In the meantime, tell your Uncle Rob about your State Fair entry."

"Cole has made this doll's cradle that perfectly holds my three small mason jars. That's my display. Then I'll have three large containers for sampling the product, and I bought lots of these tiny spoons for tasting."

Further boasting, Jenna chimed in, "The lids on her display are covered with cloth, embroidered the words *peach chutney, spicy peach chutney, traditional peach jam.* It's so creative. Jo Lynn ought to get an award for the most attractive display."

"Well, if you enter the chutney that you served me, then you're a winner." Rob stood up and pushed his chair under the table. "I guess I need to get home and get a few things done before our big day."

"And have Chip bring Sandy," Dave said. "Don't let her drive here by herself."

Typical for July, the day was warm and slightly humid. As he stood over the hot grill, beads of sweat started to appear on Eddie's forehead that his ball cap didn't capture. Stacks of hamburgers and hot dogs indicated that the crowd would be large and there would be plenty of food for everyone.

The barbecue was destined to be a success as carloads of neighbors joined the party, over sixty guests in total. Jake and Hudson took a break from jumping in the bouncy house to take turns with a dozen playmates. The women prepared many side dishes and salads. The cornhole boxes, the croquet course and the horseshoe stakes were all in place. Cole even cut boards for whiffle ball bases and Jo Lynn laid out burlap bags for sack races.

Chip took his father's advice and drove to Sandy's apartment. He knocked on her door, and when she answered, her beauty rendered Chip speechless.

"Well, are you going to just stand there, or are we going to a family barbecue?"

"Sandy, I haven't seen you in nearly a month, and, well, you just now took my breath away like the first time I saw you." He continued to stand in her doorway.

"That's a lovely compliment." She stretched up and gave him a sweet kiss. "And it's wonderful to hear, but you didn't answer my question?"

"Question?"

"Are you coming in, or are we leaving for your family barbecue?"

"I suppose we're leaving."

"Then, let me grab my guitar. We can't have a cookout without some singing."

Clyde Stevenson was the first to notice Chip's truck turning into the Dorman driveway. Wow, look at how attractive his girl is."

'Yep," Rob said. "Chip's a lucky guy. Sandy even knows all about cattle, which makes the Johnson Farm lucky, too."

"Is that a guitar case I see in Chip's hand?" Marylou said to Dave. "It looks like we are going to have some music today."

While Cole, Jenna, and Jo Lynn played corn hole, Joe, Walter, Darcy tossed horseshoes, and Eddie, who was grilling food, called out, "Hot dogs, Hot dogs! Come and get your hot dogs and sweet corn. The steamed crabs will be ready soon!"

"I believe that means we can start eating," Dave said. "But first, Reverend Hayworth, would you please give the blessing."

"Speaking of blessings," Clyde Stevenson spoke up. "I want to thank my neighbors, the Dormans and the Johnsons, for hosting this grand celebration, but more importantly, I want to ask a question of all of you. Raise your hand if the Johnsons and the Dormans have been a blessing to you."

"I see everyone has a raised a hand," Clyde said, "and I'm raising my hand, too. Okay, Reverend, we're ready for the blessing."

And after the Reverend gave a sincere and heartfelt prayer, everyone said, "Amen."

"And now, I better make sure all the side dishes are unwrapped," Marylou said.

Jake, Hudson, and a few of their playmates were first in line followed by the adults. Chip and Sandy filled their plates and sat under one of the shade trees.

Chip's engaging eyes caught Sandy's attention. "Our time at the beach stayed with me all during the month of June. I even pressed the rose you gave me."

"I'm sorry that I couldn't find time to see you—even for a few minutes."

"You don't need to apologize, Chip. I know how taxing farm work is. I was raised on a farm."

"Yeah, but this past month has been especially busy with the wheat, the shop work, and getting our beans in the ground, which we haven't finished planting, and you'll notice the Bennett barn is gone."

"Will you have some free time soon?"

"Of course, and I'd like to be the one to take you to the Farm Bureau Dinner this Saturday."

"I can't think of anyone I'd rather be with."

The sweet interplay between Chip and Sandy caught the eye of Dave who was glad to see them as a couple.

After mealtime, Cole yelled out, "Whiffle ball! That includes Hudson, Jake and all of their friends." As people started walking toward the impromptu diamond, Cole turned to the workers. "Joe, since you're our latest employee, you are going to be a captain."

Joe put on a blue ball cap that said *Captain*.

"Darcy, since you are the next to the last employee, you head up the other team. Here's your red Captain's hat. Okay, everyone, listen up. It's going to be the Joe's against the Darcy's."

Jenna reached into her pocket. "I'm flipping a coin to see which captain will choose first."

"Okay, listen up," Cole said. "The rules are as follows: It's only a called strike if you hit the ball into foul territory or if you swing and miss. You only get three strikes, and there are no walks. Everything else is like baseball—sorta."

They played until dusk, but it didn't stop players from eating between plays. That's when Jenna declared, "Game over, and the Joe's are the winners! And now, it's time for ice cream!"

Jo Lynn asked, "Would you kids like ice cream cones, or would you like to make your own sundaes?"

There was a unanimous answer, "Sundaes!"

"I thought so," Jo Lynn said. "There are sprinkles, gum drops, chocolate sauce, whipped cream, and maraschino cherries."

While the young ones were preoccupied with sundaes, Sandy brought out her guitar, started singing *God Bless America*, and the adults were glad to sing along.

After the first song was finished, Dave said, "This may sound old-fashioned to some, but there is a nice thing about July Fourth celebrations. Both young and old are all entertained, and it's also a wonderful time for friends and family to come together."

As the sun set over the horizon, Rob opened the boxes of sparklers and demonstrated how to hold them safely. "This is our nation's Independence Day, so we must be joyful but very careful when we celebrate freedom."

Sandy turned to Chip, and the two decided it was time to leave. She packed up her guitar, thanked the Dormans and the Johnsons, she then said her goodbyes to her whiffle ball teammates and the opposing team, and the couple headed down the road.

Chip parked his truck in front of Sandy's apartment and retrieved her guitar from behind his seat.

"Do you want to come in?"

"Yes, I'll come in."

"Sandy unlocked her door, and they stepped inside. "Chip, today was such fun, and I want to thank you for inviting me. Back home barbecues and backyard family gatherings are quite normal, but so are generational farms."

"I guess we're lucky to have a close family."

"Today reminded me of home and how much fun families and neighbors can have. It made me a little homesick."

Chip didn't answer; he put his arms around Sandy and kissed her, and then he kissed her again with more passion. "I think I should leave while I still can, but don't forget we still have a date on Saturday."

"Yes, a Farm Bureau Dinner date."

"I'll pick you up about five-thirty."

CHAPTER THIRTY

The Visitor

Dave walked outside and onto the front porch with Jenna, Eddie, Cole, Jo Lynn, and the two boys. He watched as they piled into Eddie's SUV for an early start to Johns Hopkins to see Roy. Their early breakfast allowed them to beat the city traffic as they headed to Baltimore.

"Now, remember," Dave said, as he closed Jenna's car door. "Roy wants to use the Bennett farm to grow organic vegetables, so encourage those thoughts. It will help him remain positive."

Jenna smiled. "Rob and I have already agreed to help Roy in that regard. He can have the front half of the farm rent free, and if he can make a go of it, we'll deed the entire farm to him. After all, he's a farmer at heart and from great farming stock. If he needs to hang onto that organic farming dream to get well, his uncle and I will be there for him."

Dave waved goodbye and prayed for his grandson. It wasn't that long ago when his wife Audrey had died. Facing another family loss so soon after his wife's passing stirred up unbearable emotions. *Lord, please heal my grandson. He's too young to leave us.*

Later that morning, a strange car drove up the Johnson driveway while Chip and his father were working inside the barn. The well-dressed gentleman was seated in a Toyota hybrid with Missouri plates. He spotted Chip and Rob curiously poking their heads out from the barn.

The driver got out, and said, "Your sign out front says that this is the Johnson Farm, but it doesn't say if it's the David Johnson Farm. I'm looking for Mr. David Johnson."

"Well, you've come to the right place. This is Dave Johnson's farm, but he doesn't live here anymore," Rob said.

"Oh. I'm sorry. I didn't realize he had passed."

"Oh, no!" Chip said. "He's alive and well. He's been living over at the Dorman Farm since his wife passed. You probably drove by it on your way here."

"Well, then I'm in luck. Please excuse my poor manners, my name Timothy Higgins, and I thought I'd look up an old family friend since I was in the neighborhood. Both my parents are deceased, but they would have been thrilled to know that I could meet Mr. Johnson. And yes, I did see the Dorman Farm sign, and I know exactly where it is. I didn't mean to bother you, and I'm sorry for interrupting your work. I guess I'll get on down the road. Thanks for your help."

"I hope you have a nice visit, Mr. Higgins." Rob said.

As the two watched Tim drive away, Chip turned to his father and said, "I wonder how Grandpa knows someone from Missouri."

Rob shrugged. "Probably through the Farm Bureau."

"Dad, this may sound weird, but that Higgins guy reminds me of you. His face and build—he even has some of your mannerisms—you know, like the way you talk with your hands."

"Me? Nah!"

~ ~ ~

Through the living room window, Dave noticed a car approaching the house. He walked outside to greet the unknown guest, wondering who it could be. A handsome man about sixty years of age stepped out of his vehicle.

"Mr. Johnson? I'm assuming Mr. David Johnson?"

"Yes, what can I do for you?"

Tim's smile showed great relief. "My name is Timothy Higgins, and you don't have the faintest idea who I am, but if you give me a little time, I think you'd like to hear my story."

"Well, okay, I like a good story. Here, pull up that rocker and have a seat."

Tim made himself comfortable next to Dave but was nervous about how to start his story.

"Many years ago, you met my mother Monica Dawson at the Delaware State Fair. Do you remember her?"

"Why yes! How could I ever forget? She was a real beauty. Is she still alive?"

"No, I'm sorry to say that she and my father are both gone now. They died some years ago and within three years of each other. But after my father died, my mother encouraged me to pay you a visit someday."

"Well, my relationship with your mother was a long time ago."

"She told me that the two of you wanted to be married, but Mom realized she could never be a farmer's wife, so she broke off the engagement."

"She did, and that was the smartest thing she could have done for both of us. It was unfair of me to think that a sophisticated city gal could be happy tied to a farm. I must tell you; your mother sang like bird—swept me off my feet with her voice, she did. I stayed a whole week at the Delaware State Fair just to hear her sing, and I almost bought one of the microphones that she was peddling."

"Mr. Johnson, are your other family members within earshot? You may not want them to hear us talk about your old sweetheart."

"Oh, I don't think it would matter, now. Anyway, they can't hear us because none of them are here. They've all gone to Baltimore to visit my grandson, Roy Dorman. The poor fellow is in Johns Hopkins, and he's probably going to die."

"I'm so sorry, Mr. Johnson. Did I come at a bad time?"

"No, there's nothing I can do here while Roy is in Baltimore, so tell me what's on your mind."

"Mr. Johnson, because we're alone, I'd like to tell you something important." Tim squirmed in his rocker. "This may not be the right time or place to tell you, but I've come a long way just to meet you, and to let you know that I happen to be your biological son."

Dave gasped and looked wide-eyed at Tim, whose appearance was much like his son Rob. Processing this news was not easy, and it made him uncomfortable. He wondered. *Could this man be a shyster who's looking for a way to swindle me? Or is he telling me the truth?* "Mr. Higgins, I'm somewhat in shock. This is a lot to take in."

"Yes, sir, it is. I remember how I felt when I first learned that my father, whom I adored, adopted me. Mr. Johnson, I'm not here to cause trouble, and I'm certainly not interested in your money or property. I have my own wealth. I just wanted to meet you."

"This is so puzzling. Why didn't Monica tell me? She had sixty years to say something."

"Late in my mother's pregnancy she wanted to tell you. Instead, she found out you had recently married. How could Mom tell a newlywed man that she was carrying his child? She believed it would have been a big mistake to say anything to you. She cared about your happiness and worried that news of a child would be upsetting to your new wife and marriage. But, Mr. Johnson, my life had a happy ending because she married my wonderful father."

With a lowered voice and a sunken heart, Dave said, "I'm glad to hear your father was a good man, but I'm still in shock by your news which I cannot confirm or deny."

Tim reached into his pocket and pulled out a small box. "My mother said that when you proposed to her, you gave her this diamond ring. She told me that it's rightfully yours, so please take it."

Dave opened the small ring box. "Well, what do you know?" He held it between his fingers and examined it closely. "Yes, sir, this is the very ring." He looked up at Tim. "This may seem odd, but you look like a Johnson."

"It's not odd because I believe I am part Johnson."

Examining the ring more closely, "It's a little more than a carat, and I can still hear the pawn broker bragging about its quality."

"Mom always felt guilty that she didn't give it back to you immediately, and now I feel good that it's back in your hands."

"I must tell you; I'm absolutely stunned by this revelation. Can this story be true? Yes, this is the ring I gave Monica, but it's so unbelievable. Tim, tell me more about yourself. What do you do?"

"I'm a dentist, like my father and grandfather, although I'm now retired. I have two wonderful daughters, Robyn and Julie, who are both dentists in St. Louis, and I have three grandchildren. How big is your family?"

"I have a sister Millicent in Denver. She's a widow. Her husband was an executive with a big oil company in Colorado, and my wife blessed me with twins, a girl Jenna and a boy Rob."

"Jenna and Rob, they'd be my brother and sister. But again…I don't want to cause any family disturbances. I just wanted to meet you, sir, and how great it is to meet you in this peaceful setting."

"Jenna and Robert are all grown and have their own children. Jenna will inherit this farm and eventually pass it on to her older son Cole."

"Sounds familiar. I recently passed my dental practice on to my daughters."

"My son Rob will inherit the Johnson farm."

"I believe I met Rob before coming here, but I didn't tell him about my reason for being in Corinth other than to see an old family friend."

"His son Chip will eventually inherit the Johnson Farm, if I can get him married off to a nice farm girl. I want Chip to have a wife and at least one son so the Johnson Farm can remain the Johnson Farm. I'm fussy about that father-son tradition."

"Tradition is a powerful thing."

"Tim, would you like to go inside and have coffee, and I bet there's a slice of pie available, too?

"Sure, I'd love to."

"Good." Dave stood up and opened the screen door. "Follow me."

Before Tim sat down at the kitchen table, he noticed the family pictures on the wall. "Your family, no doubt."

"Yep, everyone of 'em." Dave poured two cups of coffee. "There's cream and sugar on the table."

Dave proudly pointed out all his children, and when he came to Roy's photo, he lowered his head and said, "This is Roy, Jenna's younger son. He's in bad shape. We might lose him at any time. His suffering wears on me every minute of the day, especially after losing my wife not long ago." Dave pulled out a handkerchief from his pants pocket to dry his eyes and blow his nose.

"I'm very sorry, Mr. Johnson."

"Please, drink your coffee, and don't worry about that now. Roy's wife has been by his side nearly the entire time. He's at Johns Hopkins waiting for a kidney. We pray constantly that he can hold on long enough to get one."

"Oh, Mr. Johnson, you and your family must be feeling quite low. I may not know this young man, but I know the pain of losing a loved one. I lost my wife to cancer this year, and I would have done anything in the world to save her. It was a desperate time for my two daughters and me, and I still feel a horrible loneliness when I think of her."

"Roy's brother and cousin both tried to donate a kidney, but my stubborn grandson wouldn't accept a kidney from either one. He said he couldn't live with himself if he took a kidney from a relative."

"Then Roy may not have a chance, if he's that bad off."

Dave rested his forehead in his hand while his elbow was planted on the table. "That horrible notion has devastated me."

Tim finished his coffee and wanted to embrace his father as if he were the son coming home from the war, but deep inside he felt it was not the right time. "Mr. Johnson, can we talk again sometime?" He looked at his watch. "I'd love to stay a bit longer, but I really must be going. Can I see you again?"

"Yes, please, come back."

"Here's my card. My dad's name was also Timothy, but when we practiced together, I used my middle name David. There's my cell phone number, and you can always write to me at the dental office. One of my daughters will make sure to pass on any mail from you."

"I must say, Tim, meeting you…well, I'm still in shock, but I'm glad that you came."

"Mr. Johnson, I've spent many years wondering all about you, and I'm very pleased to know that you are the honorable family man exactly as my mother described. It's been a great pleasure to meet you."

Tim felt an overwhelming urgency to leave, so he said his goodbyes and left feeling satisfied that he finally got to fulfill his mother's wish to meet his biological father, the man she almost married.

Dave didn't know what to make of the visit. He could understand why Tim wanted to meet his biological father. That was clear, and his story seemed plausible, but if he were truly his son, wouldn't he want to stay and visit a bit longer? Dave felt there was something odd about his story. If his mother Monica died some time ago as he said, why take so long to meet me? He looked at the business card with the name, *Timothy David Higgins, DDS*, and decided to keep his past a secret for the time being.

When the Dorman family returned home, Jenna lingered on the front porch with her father. Dave could tell that she wanted to speak with him.

"Jenna, why don't we have a seat on the bench under the old redbud tree? We can talk more freely without being bothered by anyone running in and out of the front door."

"I like that idea," Jenna said as they strolled across the front yard.

"Your mother bought this bench for serious times like this." Dave dusted off the seat with his hand. "Come, sit. That's it. Now tell me all about it."

Jenna buried her face in her father's chest. "Oh, Daddy, it was awful!"

"There now, let's not give up hope." Dave put his arms around his daughter.

"I know, but I hurt so much. My baby is dying, and I can't do anything about it. What's more, I don't want Hudson and Jake to see how I'm suffering."

"Oh, but my dear Jenna, you need to let the grandkids know that it hurts, because it hurts them, too. Maybe not as much as a mother, but pain and suffering are a part of life."

"I know."

"Show them that you still have faith because God absolutely knows that you're hurting. Remember when Lazareth died? Jesus wept. He wasn't crying over the death of Lazareth—no siree! Why would Jesus shed a tear for the guy that He was about to bring back to life? Jesus cried because he could feel the great torment Mary and Martha were suffering over the loss of their brother. That story tells me that Jesus hasn't abandoned you, but rather He's crying right now for you. Oh, Jenna, let's not give up hope, so dry your eyes and go talk things over with Cole and Jo Lynn on how all of you will handle this situation with the boys."

"Thank you. Oh, how I love you, Daddy."

~ ~ ~

Tim parked his car in the Hopkins parking lot and found his way to Roy's floor as if guided by angels. After explaining his visit to one of the nurses at the desk, Roy's doctor was summoned to the telephone.

"There's a gentleman here, a Mr. Higgins, who wants to donate a kidney to Roy Dorman, and he's willing to go through any tests needed to see if it could be possible." When the nurse hung up the phone, she instructed Tim to have a seat. "The doctor is faxing us a directive that will list all of the tests we will need, and we have some papers we'll need you to sign."

For the next two days, Tim went through all the necessary examinations and met with several technicians and a couple of doctors. Because of Roy's declining condition, test results were given the highest priority.

While lying in bed a doctor approached Tim's bedside. "Mr. Higgins, no one wanted to get Roy's hopes up before we know that you are, in fact, a good candidate," the doctor explained. "It appears that you are, but right now, we must make sure your health won't be impaired by having only one kidney. We should know by tomorrow."

That evening Tim wondered and prayed that somehow, he could save Roy's life. Giving his nephew a chance to live would be a great joy and blessing. He understood Dave's suffering, because he had felt the same helplessness when there wasn't anything he could do to save the life of his beloved wife Louise.

CHAPTER THIRTY-ONE

Award Night

For months Chip had hoped this evening would be his big night. The award was sponsored by banks, seed and fertilizer companies, machinery stores, farm insurance companies, and several small businesses that supported the farming community. In addition to the twenty-five-thousand-dollar prize money, the winning farmer earned coveted bragging rights for such a farming achievement. There was one problem. Even though Chip's yield was the best recorded on the Johnson farm, every farmer's field had a bountiful season.

Chip drove to Sandy's apartment, knocked on her door, and when she appeared Chip said, "My, oh, my! Sandy, when we walk into that hall tonight, you're gonna to be turning heads. Really, you look stunningly beautiful, and all my single friends will turn John Deere green with envy."

"Aw." She gave him a sweet peck on the cheek. "Thank you. Shall we go?"

Chip was not exaggerating about Sandy's appearance. She wore a simple sleeveless, form-fitting, white dress embellished by a print silk scarf of white, turquoise, and black. That, along with her high heels, up-do hair, and pearl earrings gave her a look of sophistication not normally seen at Farm Bureau dinners. As she entered the room, many wondered who was with Chip, until they got a closer look. Then whispers murmured around the room.

The long fire hall was decorated with lots of red, white and blue bunting and photo displays of previous farm queens and highest yield winners. Chip pointed to a table in the rear of the room. "Over there, Sandy. Mom and Dad saved seats for us."

Dave stood up until Sandy was seated. "Good evening, Sandy, it's always a pleasure to see you, and tonight you are truly radiant."

"I must tell you what a great time I had at your Fourth of July party. There is no doubt that it took lots of effort to organize all that fun, and I thank you for including me."

Chip and Jo Lynn sat across the table, but Eddie and Jenna didn't show. Jenna was too distraught after her visit with Roy and decided to stay home with the grandkids.

Cole asked Chip, "Are you getting nervous about the *Highest Yield* announcement?"

"My stomach is in knots. Every farmer had a good year, so the winner could be almost anyone here tonight."

After the prayer and the Pledge, dinner was fried chicken, mashed potatoes with gravy, green beans, coleslaw, and for dessert, an apple dumpling with a dollop of vanilla ice cream.

Mr. Simms, a local banker and the president of the local Bureau was the emcee for the evening. His first bit of business was to announce the guests. As the names of county and state elected officials were called, they stood up and waved as if they were a famous movie star. It didn't matter that no one recognized them, the audience gave them a respectful applause.

Then with great surprise, Mr. Simms called out, "Sandy Moore, will you come up to the stage. All you farmers here tonight have probably met our newest County Extension Agent, Sandy Moore, but some of our other guests may not know her." She walked onto the stage, smiled and waved before returning to her seat. "My, oh my, if our county agents start looking like this, I'll have to buy a tractor!"

He continued, "Tonight we are going to crown our county's Farm Bureau Queen, who will go on to the State competition across the Bay and represent our County to compete for the title of Maryland Farm Bureau Queen. Ladies, whoever wins tonight, please come back and tell us where in the devil those fairgrounds are located. I don't believe anyone here has seen them."

The audience roared with laughter, because nearly all in attendance go to the Delaware State Fair. Mr. Simms continued. "Excuse me, my mistake. Our last year's winner Connie Burks went to the Maryland State Fair last year, and I understand represented our county very well. Are you ready to pass your crown to the next county queen?"

Connie Burks smiled and waved to the audience. "Yes, Mr. Simms."

"So, let's meet this year's contestants. I know I want to hear from all these lovely ladies."

The audience applauded vigorously, led by the mothers of all the contestants.

Mr. Simms continued, "Every year we enjoy seeing these talented farm ladies compete for the title of Farm Bureau Queen. This annual event draws the biggest crowds to our meetings. Too bad we have only one annual Farm Bureau Queen contest a year. Five contenders will be called to the stage to give a short presentation about life on a farm before the judges announce the final winner."

After the Farm Queen was announced and the tiara placed on her head, Mr. Simms returned to the lectern. "And now I'd like to announce the winner of this year's *Highest Yield* contest. When we looked at all the yields per acre, our committee discovered that this was the best year ever for our county. Yes, we had a great growing season this year, so, every farmer in this room is a winner, and we can all thank the Good Lord for that."

Everyone applauded in agreement, and Chip held his breath as Mr. Simms unfolded a piece of paper.

Mr. Simms continued, "This year's winner is Clyde Stevenson. Congratulations, Clyde, please come up here and collect your check."

Clyde stepped up onto the stage and went directly to the microphone. "Thank you, Mr. Simms, but I cannot accept this check."

Gasps were audible in the crowd.

"I cannot accept this check because I'd like the bank to reissue it in the form of two checks. Half for me for the highest yield, an honor I'm quite proud of and will not give up." He took a bow, and the audience laughed. "But the second check must go to Chip Johnson for being the farmer of the year."

A noticeable silence followed as the audience wondered why.

"Now, let me explain," Clyde continued. "It was after midnight when my combine broke down in the middle of my field. I worked on it until I realized I needed help. It was after two in the morning when I called my neighbor. Now, raise your hand if you're not tired at two in the morning."

No hands went up.

"I thought so. We were all tired at that hour, but Chip Johnson came immediately. Mind you, there was a powerful storm brewing, and everyone knew it had disastrous potential if we didn't get our wheat in on time. It was a race against nature, but Chip took time away from his critical work on the Johnson Farm and came to my rescue. He saw what part my combine needed and without hesitation or asking for money, he went back to his shop, got the spare part, and fixed my combine. But the story doesn't end there. Knowing that I was hours behind on my harvesting and a monster storm was headed our way, Chip came back just after daybreak with a combine and helped me bring in my crop before the storm hit. I can tell you that if I hadn't had his neighborly help, I wouldn't be this year's highest yield winner. My wheat would have been flattened by that rain, the fields a muddy mess, and this good year we are all having would have been a bust for me. Chip, would you come up to the stage, please."

Chip, stunned by Clyde's announcement, walked onto the stage.

Clyde continued, "Chip Johnson represents the best qualities of a farmer and a human being. This is what family farming is all about. We have a heart. We love our neighbors, and we help our neighbors. Let us never forget that *America is great because America is good.* My highest yield award is only because Chip acted with utmost kindness and speed to help save his neighbor's wheat, and with that said, can I hear a thunderous applause for Chip Johnson, farmer of the year."

After the applause, Mr. Stevenson concluded, "Okay all you newspaper folks, and I believe we have a radio station here tonight, too. I want you to report that, due to unanimous acclaim, Chip Johnson is the *Farmer of the Year*! Over the decades, city folks have forgotten the importance of the farmer, the importance of hard labor and honorable behavior. Reporters, you have a responsibility never to let America forget. Mr. Simms, does the committee have a problem with reissuing the check in this manner, half for me and half for Chip?"

Simms answered, "Chip, Clyde, your checks are in the mail."

Chip gave Clyde a bear hug and returned to the table, where his family stood in honor of their son.

"Wow, I'm floored. I sure didn't expect this," Chip said.

Sandy hugged Chip and said, "I'm so proud of you. Tonight, you are the one who is causing other farmers to turn green."

Nothing could please Dave more than to see the joy between Chip and Sandy. There was now no doubt in his mind that they were meant for each other.

CHAPTER THIRTY-TWO

No Greater Love

While Tim was seated by the nurse's station, an assistant came by to escort him to a conference room where the surgeon, via teleconferencing, was waiting to speak with him.

"Mr. Higgins, I think your kidney is a great match for Roy, and after consulting with other physicians on staff, we believe that despite your age, you are in remarkable health and fit to be a donor. Are you a relative? I ask because most people don't just walk into a hospital and donate a kidney to a specific person unless it's a relative."

"Doctor, I've never met Roy Dorman, and he doesn't know me. Yes, I am a relative. I'm Roy's uncle, but because I was born out of wedlock, I'm asking that you keep my relationship with Roy confidential. Doctor, from the first moment I learned of Roy's need, I had an overwhelming sense, perhaps a divine sense, that I can help this young man. Can we leave it at that?"

"Of course, and I'm glad you told me this. Your secret will not be disclosed."

"However, I would like to meet Roy before the surgery. When will it be scheduled?"

"Tomorrow morning, so please don't have anything to eat between now and the surgery."

"Duly noted. Now, where can I find Roy? I want to be the one to tell him that he's getting a kidney tomorrow."

"I'll have a nurse show you to his room."

Tim and the nurse walked the halls and took an elevator to Roy's room. The nurse peeked inside, "Angela, Roy, you have a visitor, and I'll leave you to get acquainted."

Tim pulled up a chair and sat beside Roy. "Mrs. Dorman, Roy, my name is Timothy Higgins, and I have great news for you. Tomorrow morning Roy will get a kidney."

Angela gasped and noted Tim's fancy street clothes, "Are you a doctor?"

"No, I'm the kidney donor. I passed all the tests, and we are a great match." Tim gently laid his hand on Roy's shoulder. "Get ready, Roy, because the surgery is scheduled for tomorrow morning."

Roy turned his head, looked at Tim. His shaky hand reached out.

Angela dug in her purse for her phone. "This is an answer to prayer. I must call Mom and Dad!"

"Please, don't!" Tim implored. "Please wait until we're out of surgery, and the surgeon has declared the operation a success. That's my only request. If you say anything to your family, ask them for fervent prayer. I don't want to add to your folk's anxiety; besides, what harm would it do to wait?"

"We can wait," Roy said.

Angela put her phone back in her purse and looked bewildered. "As you wish, Mr. Higgins, but please tell us how you found us, and what made you do such a selfless act?"

"I recently lost my wife to cancer, so I know how you and other family members are suffering when it seems there is no hope."

"This is so incredible," Angela said, her face flush with disbelief. "There's a verse in the Bible that says: *Be kind to strangers because you never know when you're entertaining angels.* And you, sir, are certainly an angel." Angela grabbed the box of tissues by Roy's bedside. She had difficulty stopping her tears.

Roy looked at his wife. He wanted to hold her, but his lack of strength only allowed him to reach for her hand.

"Roy, Angela, there's a verse in the Book of Zephaniah that says the Lord will create calm in our lives with His love. Tonight, we need that calm, so let's stay in prayer and think about God's great love for us." Tim looked at his watch. "I'm going to check into my room now and get lots of rest because tomorrow is our big day."

As soon as Tim left, Angela placed Roy's hand on her heart. "God has given you a second chance, darling, and perhaps a second chance for our marriage. I realize the good that Mapledale has done for you and for me. If this transplant is successful, and if you can stay sober, then I would like to renew our marriage vows if that's what you want, too."

Roy cried tears of joy, nodded his head, and wept in weakened silence.

CHAPTER THIRTY-THREE

A New Kidney and a New Bedroom

Walking alongside Roy's gurney, Angela softly kissed Roy one more time. "I'm going to give you the biggest kiss when you come out of surgery."

Over the past few weeks, Angela saw that her husband was a changed man. Mapledale had helped him to recover, and most of all, helped him to understand how alcohol had nearly cost him his marriage and possibly his life.

Just before Tim was wheeled into surgery, Angela squeezed his hand and said, "Thank you, Mr. Higgins. You have given me great hope."

In pre-op Tim looked up at the surgical assistant just before he was asked to count backwards. "Can you place me near Roy when we go into the recovery room? It's very important to me."

"Of course, and that's the positive attitude we like to hear, that *both* of you will be in recovery."

~ ~ ~

At the bunkhouse, Chip and Cole unloaded a new headboard, frame, mattress, and nightstand off Chip's pickup. The construction of Joe's bedroom was complete, and all that was needed were the bed linens. Joe was already using the closet, but the new furnishings would be a surprise.

"We have to get this done before Joe comes here for lunch," Cole said. "That means putting on the sheets and blankets, too. Mom has a lamp she's bringing over, and she wants this bed made before she comes."

"I hope they're fitted sheets, because I'm lousy at making beds," Chip said. He opened the package and was relieved. "They're fitted!"

After setting lunch on the bunkhouse table, Jenna peeked inside Joe's new bedroom. "Great job, fellas! It's now a comfortable room. Excuse me. I believe I hear the men coming." Jenna returned to the lunchroom where she met the men. "Joe, we have a surprise for you in the bunkroom. Come take a look."

Joe walked back to his room. "A bed! My very own bed. This is beautiful! Thank you, Miss Jenna, Cole, and Chip!"

"You can also thank Jo Lynn who instigated this project," Chip said. "Joe, you are doing a great job here and deserve your own space. You also served our nation honorably, and the Dormans and the Johnsons will never forget that."

"However," Cole chimed in, "You, Darcy and Walter will be getting some temporary company in the bunkroom," Cole said. "Dad told me that the seasonal workers will be here on the twentieth of the month to pick peaches, so we wanted to make sure you had your own secure room apart from the others."

"Man, this is wonderful." He sat on his new bed. "And I gotta thank Mr. Eddie and Mr. Rob, too. I didn't know why God led me to this farm, but I want to thank the Good Lord for looking out for me."

Jenna smiled at Joe. "Welcome home, Joe, and please make the Dorman Farm home for as long as you like."

~ ~ ~

After a four-hour agonizing wait, Angela was called to the surgery desk, where a nurse receptionist asked her to join the surgeon in a private conference room. She held her breath wondering about the outcome as she entered the room.

"Have a seat, Mrs. Dorman," the surgeon said. "The surgery went well. Mr. Higgins is slowly waking up, and we're still waiting for your husband to come out of his anesthetic."

“Will Roy be all right? I just want to know if I still have a husband.”

“I believe so, but it depends on many things. Rejection of an organ is always a primary concern. His aftercare is critical, but we’ll have a nurse go over all the things you’ll need to know. Average recovery time for kidney recipients is about eight weeks. It can be longer, but right now, we have a success story on our hands.”

“Thank you, doctor.”

As soon as the doctor left the conference room, Angela wasted no time and called the Dorman house. Dave was standing next to Eddie when he answered his cell phone. “Dad!” Angela cried. “I have great news. Put me on speaker. I want everyone to hear it at the same time.”

“That won’t be hard because we’re all here eating lunch.”

“Grandpa, too?

“He’s standing right here,” Eddie said. “You’re on speaker now, Angela.”

“Thursday, after you and Mom left the hospital, a gentleman out of nowhere volunteered to donate a kidney, and both the donor and Roy are out of surgery. Roy isn’t awake, but the doctor feels it won’t be much longer before he is.”

“Do does the donor have a name?” Dave asked.

“Yes, Timothy Higgins.”

Dave’s heart sank. Overcome by disbelief, he sat down on a chair.

“Jenna! Did you hear that?” Eddie hugged his wife. “Our boy got a kidney!”

Jenna buried her head in Eddie’s chest. “Oh, Eddie, tomorrow after breakfast, let’s leave for Baltimore.”

Angela continued, “Oh, Mom, it was a miracle! The nice man walked into the hospital and donated one of his kidneys. The surgery was this morning, and the doctor believes that Roy will recover.”

The sigh of relief was unanimous as were the shouts and tears of joy.

In the recovery room Tim's bed was close to Roy's, close enough to see his face. He could also tell that he was breathing. With a soft voice he said, "Roy, you need to wake up and open your eyes. You have a new kidney. Roy, you'll make me a happy man if you would just open your eyes."

"Don't worry, Mr. Higgins," the nurse said. "The kidney patient doesn't wake up as fast as the donor."

Tim wouldn't take his eyes off Roy until he knew he was awake. Ten, then twenty minutes passed before Roy finally opened his eyes.

"Roy, your surgery is over and it's time to wake up," the nurse's compassionate voice declared.

Roy reacted with a smile.

Tim knew Roy would live as soon as he felt God's words filling his soul: *Well done, my good and faithful servant.*

~ ~ ~

Later, just after supper, Dave went to his room and closed the door. He opened the top drawer of his bureau, retrieved Tim's business card, and called him.

"Hello, Tim, this is Dave Johnson. The first thing I want to say is thank you for saving Roy's life. My family is overjoyed by your noble generosity. Are you okay? There are always two patients with a transplant."

"Yes, I'm fine, thank you; just a little drowsy and somewhat sore."

"I'm glad, Tim, but I'm also conflicted by your sacrifice."

"Mr. Johnson, hang onto the overjoyed part. Roy is my nephew, and if you saw his condition before surgery, you would also understand my deep pleasure, as well."

"How long will your recovery be?"

"They're telling me four weeks after I'm released from the hospital."

"Then I want you to convalesce right here on my farm in Corinth. We have a spare room on the first floor over at the Johnson farm, and I'm sure that my son Rob and his wife Marylou would be thrilled to take care of you."

"I'd like that."

"I want you to call me the minute the hospital releases you, and I'll ask Chip and Cole to drive to Baltimore and get you and your car. Most of all, Tim, I'll need you to help me explain your lineage, and why I didn't know about you before now. Have you told Angela and Roy that you're related?"

"No, not yet"

"Well, I give you permission to tell them, and let them know that we will be nursing you back to health right here in Corinth. Believe me, after your sacrifice, it will be our pleasure to care for you."

"I'm scheduled to be released sometime this week."

"Then, that's when you're coming home."

Home. The sound of the word warmed Tim's heart. He never expected Dave to accept him as family, but just hearing him say that he wanted to welcome Tim home to the Johnson Farm filled his soul with joy.

CHAPTER THIRTY-FOUR

Tim is a Johnson

That afternoon Jo Lynn picked up a couple of peach baskets and walked out to the orchard with Hudson and Jake. She asked her father-in-law if he could spare one of his workers long enough to pick two bushels of the ripest fruit. The Delaware State Fair was fast approaching, and she couldn't wait for the seasonal workers to harvest the orchard.

"How about Darcy?" Eddie said. "He's the best at that sort of thing."

"That would be wonderful. Can you call him and let him know where we are?"

While waiting for Darcy, Jo Lynn demonstrated to Hudson and Jake how to discern a very ripe peach. "Look at Mommy's hand. It's big enough to cradle a peach. I place the peach in my palm, then use my entire hand to feel whether the peach is soft without squeezing it with my fingers and causing it to bruise."

She picked up two peaches from the ground and handed one to each son. "Your hands are smaller than Mommy's, so you need to use two hands to cradle the peach. Now, see if you can tell if the peach is ripe by putting gentle pressure on all sides."

"My peach is ripe!" Hudson blurted out.

"Very good, Hudson." There was no doubt in Jo Lynn's mind that it was possibly overripe because it was on the ground, but it would be usable in her peach jam, so she placed it in the basket."

Jo Lynn was happy to see Darcy come so soon. "I so appreciate your help. You know how dizzy I get on a ladder."

“Not a problem, ma’am. Just please remember that me and the boys like a warm peach cobbler.”

“One peach cobbler coming up! I only need two baskets, but I’d like to have a third basket to give to the women’s shelter.”

“Not a problem, Ma’am.”

“Thank you, Darcy. Come along children, Mommy needs to get back to work in the house. We’re going to have lots of peaches to wash and skin.”

“Mommy,” Hudson asked, “When is Uncle Roy coming home from the hospital?”

“He needs to stay in Baltimore a little longer, but the nice man who donated one of his kidneys for your Uncle Roy will be staying with your Aunt Marylou and Uncle Rob. We’re expecting him sometime today.”

At the Johnson house, Marylou and Rob were readying the downstairs bedroom for their new guest. Both the Johnson and Dorman houses had upstairs and downstairs main bedrooms with private full baths. The downstairs main bedrooms were reserved for grandparents. It made for a much better situation when the two or more generations were living under one roof, and it was well understood that farmers, no matter how old, had to live on the farm.

Dave waited at the Johnson house for Tim’s arrival, in order to assuage any awkwardness. “Thank you, Rob, and of course, you, Marylou, for taking care of Tim Higgins.”

“Oh, but Dad,” Marylou said, “Rob and I are honored to do it. It feels like a great pleasure.”

Dave made a second request, “Marylou, would you please invite the rest of the family tonight for dinner. I want everyone to meet our family’s hero.”

When Cole and Chip arrived with Tim, the two carefully escorted Tim up the back steps, through the kitchen, and to a comfortable chair in the living room.

“Hello, Tim. How are you feeling?” Dave clasped Tim’s hand as he greeted him.

"Quite woozy. I took some pain killers for the car ride, and it was a good thing. My back could feel every bump and pothole along the way."

Dave pulled up a chair and sat next to Tim. "I know we spoke on the phone, but it's only the second time we've met. Tim, from the bottom of my heart, thank you for saving my grandson's life. What you did was totally unexpected. Roy's family will be here for dinner, so you'll get a chance to meet them."

"I'd like that very much."

Dave tapped Cole's shoulder. "Can you and Jo Lynn arrange for a sitter, because I'd like for you both to be here this evening for dinner?"

"That's not a problem."

Chip entered from the back door. "Mr. Higgins, I'll put your bags in the guest room."

"Thank you, Chip. Dave, you have the nicest grandsons. I have two daughters, two granddaughters, and a grandson, and they are the joy of my life. Rob, Marylou, I know I just sat down, but do you mind if I lie down until dinner? I'm a bit tired after that car ride, and I would like to be lying down when my medication wears off."

"Sure, it's no problem," Rob said. "Let me help you out of that chair, and I'll show you to your room. Our downstairs guest room gets afternoon sun, so I'll close the shades if you like."

As Tim lay in bed in the quiet of his darkened room, he thought about the recent loss of his wife Louise. His pain had not faded, and it seemed as if there was no relief for the loneliness. And then, there was Angela and Roy, who were a joy to be nearby. After he disclosed his identity to them, their immediate reaction was to hug their new uncle, which soothed his soul.

I must respect Dave's feelings. After all, he just learned about me. Oh, how I want to feel some familial acceptance, and yet, to push the matter might alienate the very family I long to embrace. It would be so wonderful if Dave would one day call me "son." He drifted off to sleep, knowing that Rob would later return to wake him for dinner.

That evening when Jenna and Eddie arrived through the back door, Jenna immediately spotted Tim sitting in the living room. Without so much as a pause, she put her casserole on the kitchen counter, went to Tim's side, grabbed his hand, and kissed it multiple times.

Noticing the stream of tears on her cheeks, Tim said, "Jenna, if I were standing, I'd hug you. It was my pleasure to help Roy, and seeing how happy you are makes me doubly glad to be here."

Rob went to his twin sister's side. "Come here, Jenna." He handed her a few tissues and took Jenna in his arms. "It's always going to be this way. When you hurt, I hurt. When you're happy, so am I."

At dinner, Dave gave the blessing, and then he asked everyone to listen to his story from sixty years ago.

"Before I married Audrey, I met a wonderful woman named Monica at the Delaware State Fair. We fell instantly in love. I wanted to marry her, so I proposed, and she said yes, but before the fair was over, she changed her mind, and rightfully so."

"That fast, Grandpa, you knew you wanted to marry a girl after one week?" Chip said.

"Yes, it was that fast, except there was a problem. You see, Monica was a city girl who wanted a city life. As soon as I realized that she was not cut out to be a farmer's wife—two days after I gave her a ring—she broke off our engagement. I was heartbroken, but more than that, I was remorseful for having had an intimate relationship with her. I got on my knees and asked God to forgive me, and my eyes were opened. I could see clearly that Audrey, the girl next door, was the woman I should marry."

"Allow me to take it from here," Tim said. He didn't want Dave to be put in a position to declare him as him as a *son* until he was ready. "You see, Monica was my mother. She died a few years ago, but one of her requests was that I meet David Johnson because he is my biological father."

Jenna's back straightened. "Rob! Tim here is our brother!"

"It's true," Tim said. "But I'm here not to cause family upset or make claims to your inheritance. I'm here to feel whole. Children who are adopted have an insatiable curiosity about their birth parents, and I hope you'll understand why I had to meet Dave."

"We do understand," Jenna said, "and we are glad to meet you, as well."

"Thank you, Jenna. My mother spoke highly of your father, and I believe she was truly in love, but a farmer's wife she could never be. Heck, Mom couldn't cook or clean, but boy could she entertain. She had a great singing voice and could tell funny stories better than anyone."

"I'll attest to that," Dave said. "More importantly, I want you all to know this. My years have been filled with both peaks and valleys, but after my affair with Tim's mother, I opened my soul to the Lord and asked for mercy. That's when God took control of my steering wheel, and from then on, I found that I could navigate through life's ups and downs with comfort knowing that God would never leave me nor forsake me."

"When my mother found out she was pregnant, she, too, had asked God to forgive her and to help her raise her child. Well, the day I was born, she met my father. Oh, boy, do I wish she were here to tell the story of my birth! You would be rolling on the floor with laughter. The happy ending was that God was there for my mother, and I was adopted by a wonderful man who became my father. He made me feel as if I were his own blood."

Dave interrupted, "I was alone at the house when Tim first came here to meet me. That's when he discovered that Roy was gravely ill and needed a kidney. I even told him that Roy didn't want a kidney from a relative, but I never imagined that Tim would be the one to give life to my grandson."

Tim continued, "When I learned of Roy's dire condition, I headed straight for Johns Hopkins. I recently lost my wife and would have done anything to save Louise, but cancer got the best of her. Eddie, Jenna, I have also felt the despair of not being able to help a loved one. The pain of losing my best friend pains me daily, but this time I could do something to spare others the same torment. That's why I donated a kidney."

"I was completely dumbfounded when Tim left so quickly," Dave said. "It even made me doubt his birth story."

"Ah, but, Daddy," Jenna spoke up. "Look at Rob and then Tim. Look at their profiles, their hair color, and eyes. They look like brothers!"

Rob leaned over to Marylou and smiled. "We have an entire month to get to know our brother, and he's staying in our guest bedroom!"

"But I'll only be in your way until the middle of August."

"Now, that's nonsense," Rob snapped back "You're welcome here at any time."

"I thank you for that, but mid-August is when my doctor said it would be safe for me to drive back to St. Louis, and that's when I need to get back on the road. My two daughters deserve to know why I'm missing a kidney. But right now, why don't we eat, and we'll talk more later."

CHAPTER THIRTY-FIVE

Jasper's Good News

"Here comes Jasper," a strong voice in the hospital hall proclaimed. Jasper popped into Roy's room holding a birthday cake with a single lit candle on top and a cardboard tube under one arm. Roy was able to sit up in bed and was beginning to gain strength. It was a great milestone for him, and a welcomed sight for Jasper, who instantly noticed how good he appeared since his last visit.

"Jasper! Hey, good to see you. Is that a new shirt? It certainly is the brightest orange shirt I've ever seen."

"All my Hawaiian shirts are new. Hey, ol' buddy, we have some celebrating to do." He began to sing: *Happy birthday to me. Happy birthday to me. Happy birthday, happy birthday, happy birthday to me.* I just turned twenty-one. Do you know what that means?"

"Please don't tell me you're going to buy alcohol."

"Nope, never again. Not that I ever bought it in the first place when it was plentiful at all my folks' places. My twenty-first birthday means the trust fund my grandparents set up for me is now mine! I'm a rich man. Of course, super rich people will only claim it's only pocket change, but it's more than ten million."

"That's a nice windfall. What do you plan on doing with it?"

I'll tell you in a minute, but first let me set this cake down. Unfortunately, the nurses said you can't have cake. Personally, I think it's because they want to eat it, so I'll leave it for them. Now, for the good part. You and I, ol' buddy, are going to have the greatest organic fruit and vegetable farm on all of Delmarva and maybe even the world!"

Roy perked up. "What did you say?"

"I knew that would excite you. We are going to put our organic gardening expertise to work. You told me that all you really wanted to be a farmer, right?"

"Well, yes."

"So, when you described your family farm, I had to see it. As I pulled up to your mom and dad's house, I knew right away you and I had possibilities. I also met with your Uncle Rob and your mom over a cup of coffee. I told them about this idea of mine and about our time at Mapledale. Then they drove me over to the Bennett Farm. What great road frontage that place has for a business!"

"Yeah, but that Bennett name has to change."

"And it sure will. Roy, ol' buddy, you have the land, I have the capital, and together we have the expertise. Here's the vision." Jasper pulled out a plan from the cardboard tube and rolled it out over Roy's bed. "I had a professional land planner sketch out the possibilities. Take a look. The house will get a major makeover, keeping its historical details in the front, and it will become our produce market. Over here is where our greenhouses will go and look at the available parking."

"Of course, Mom and Uncle Rob are only letting me use half the property."

"Roy, ol' buddy, they've allowed us to use the front fifty acres, which is more than enough to get us started. Besides, it takes three years to certify the land as organic, but in the meantime, we can grow organic vegetables in the greenhouses as starters for backyard gardeners."

"Am I dreaming?"

"Nope, not at all. Gordon also promised to help us get started, and he said he'll even provide us with plants and shrubs to sell on consignment."

Roy's smile stretched across his face. "You're really serious!"

"Of course, I'm serious! Ah, Roy, ol' buddy, it's good to see a smile on your face. You and me are gonna be organic farmers, and your family can't be happier!"

"Jasper, when I first met you, I wasn't sure why God chose us to be roommates. Now I'm beginning to believe it's because He knew we were destined to become business partners."

"Now that you got that new kidney, we'll sit down real soon and plan out our joint venture. What did I tell you when we first met? Organic vegetables, that's our calling and where it's happening."

"Jasper, tell me again about our organic farm, or I'll think I'm dreaming."

"It's even better than I could imagine. Your family has a commercial chicken operation, and we'll need all that luscious chicken manure to grow the best organic vegetables around. But first, you have to get well. Will you promise me that?"

"It's a promise."

"Good, then it's settled."

"Jasper, if it takes three years to get certified, what will we do in the meantime?"

"Gotcha covered. I have six huge greenhouses with all the accessories waiting to be delivered as soon as we want to get started. If we need more greenhouses, I'll get more."

"Thank you, Jasper." Roy took Jasper's hand and held it tight against his chest. This gives me something to look forward to. In fact, I can't wait to get started."

"That's all I wanted to hear. Say, I gotta go. My chauffeur doesn't like hanging around this section of Baltimore. It creeps him out."

CHAPTER THIRTY-SIX

The Winners

While the Dormans were eating breakfast, and Cole was nowhere in sight, Jenna asked, "What time are we leaving for the Fair?"

"We should leave before noon," Jo Lynn said. "I don't want to miss any entry deadlines. I have all my food packed and my displays are ready whenever we are."

"The grandkids and I are going to have a great day at the fair," Eddie said. "Isn't that so, boys?"

Hudson gave and enthusiastic, "Yeah!"

"Then, tomorrow we can return to collect all of Jo Lynn's ribbons," Jenna said.

Cole popped into the kitchen while the others were finishing their meal. His excitement could be felt throughout the room. "Mom, Dad, Grandpa, come see what I have parked out front. Chip's out front. He came over to see it, too."

They gathered on the front porch to look at a huge motor coach.

Jo Lynn's face lit up. "Oh, Cole, Monty let you borrow it!"

"Yep." Cole opened its door. "Go ahead look inside. It belongs to a friend of mine. It sleeps four adults and two kids. Mom, Dad, how would you like to go with

Jo Lynn and the kids to the fair in style? I can have this beast for one night, and I know that kids will love it."

"Oh, go on, Jenna, say yes," Dave said. "You'll have lots of fun."

“I’m all for it,” Eddie said. “I always wanted to travel in one of these things, and now we won’t have to make two trips to Harrington.”

“Then we need to pack our overnight bags, and if we’re quick, we can still leave before noon,” Jenna said.

“That’s the spirit,” Eddie said. “What’s on your agenda for the day, Dad?”

“Well, let’s see. I think I’ll have a talk with Darcy to see how much longer he needs the seasonal workers. Those peach trees ought to be nearly picked clean. Then, I’ll check in over at the Johnson Farm and see what’s going on over there.”

After Dave and Chip waved goodbye to the Dormans, Dave asked Chip to sit with him on the porch for a while. “With all the excitement of fairs, Roy’s surgery, and new relatives coming to town, we haven’t talked in some time—you know a good old man-to-man talk.”

“You sound serious, Grandpa. What’s on your mind?”

“Sandy Moore. She’s on my mind. I think you should ask her to marry you.”

“What! We just met in April.”

“I’ve been watching the way you look at each other. It’s quite heated if you ask me, and as your grandfather, I want to help you avoid a possible misstep.”

“But marriage? She wouldn’t go out with me until Memorial Day, and now it’s only July. You think that’s enough time for me to ask a girl to get married when I don’t really know her?”

“I’m glad you don’t really *know* her because it’s important to save that for your wedding night. If you want to have a joyful life, then avoid this tempting sin. Oh, yes, God can always turn a repentant life around, but you must do your part by respecting the Lord’s commands. Son, if you and Sandy love one another, and the physical desires are strong, then you must do the God glorifying thing and ask her for her hand in marriage and do it now before your emotions overtake your morality. Let me ask—do you love her enough to spend the rest of your life together?”

“Well, yes, I think so.”

"Are you sure? Because I've heard more enthusiasm out of you after you've rebuilt a starter. I'm asking you if you love her enough to have a long-term committed relationship."

"Well…yes."

"And do you believe she would make a good farmer's wife?"

"Grandpa, she grew up on a farm."

"And that's my point, son. She's a smart, good-looking farm girl, who loves Jesus. Not only that, Sandy has a warm personality and a degree in agriculture. She has proven to our family that she's not some prissy gal. Look how she took it upon herself to help one of our cows calve. Chip, all those things together are why I think you should ask her to get married."

"So soon?"

"Yes, so soon. I once got engaged after three days. You heard what Tim said about his mother. She did love me, but cooler heads prevailed. We were young and foolish. Monica was no farmer's wife, but Sandy is the real deal in so many ways."

"I'm afraid if I ask Sandy to get married so soon, she'll feel I'm rushing her and think I'm nuts."

"No, she won't, not if she's the sort of woman I believe her to be, but you'll need a little enticement with your proposal to show that you're truly serious. Wait right here." Dave went into the house and returned. "Here's what you need to do. Chip, you want to marry this girl, don't you?"

"Well, yes."

"That's good because I don't want to go to all this trouble if you don't. Okay, so the first thing you need to do is find a quiet private spot where you can both sit down together. That will make your proposal much easier."

"I don't think this will be easy for me."

"That's why we're rehearsing, so pay attention. After you find a quiet place, get down on one knee and say, *Will you marry me.* What's hard about that? Now, here comes the part that will sweeten the offer. When you pop the question, show her this ring. You must do it at the same time." Dave opened the small box. "You can give her this ring. It's more than a carat, so surely Sandy will say, yes, when she sees it."

"And if she doesn't?"

Dave looked at Chip with a wry eye and snapped the box shut. "Then I want my ring back." Dave took a deep breath and exhaled his frustration. "Chip, you and Sandy belong together. I can see it, and I believe you both know it. The wedding ceremony can wait until winter when there's a lull in farming, but this engagement needs to happen now. If she says yes, then you've got yourself a great gal."

"I don't know, Grandpa. It seems so sudden."

"What do you have to lose? Nothing! Look, son, over the next several months, should either one of you discover that you're not compatible, call off the marriage. There's not a soul on earth who would blame you, because when you say *until death do us part,* you both must mean it. Are you going to see her today at the Fair?"

"This afternoon after she's done judging livestock."

"Okay, then that's when you spring the question. Look, Chip, the trouble with guys today is they'll go with a girl for a year or two and even longer before they pop the question. Many won't even do that. Cowards, heathen cowards, who would rather shack up, but that's not for a decent man like you."

"Did you have this talk with my dad?"

"You bet I did. I knew Marylou was perfect for Robert, and I didn't want her to get away. That's when I marched Robbie straight to the jewelers to pick out a ring."

Chip pondered for a moment. "Do you really think Sandy will say, yes?"

"You bet I do! Chip, there's one other thing. Before you go and get yourself a fiancé, you need to talk it over with your mom and dad."

"I don't need their permission."

"No, but you need their blessing. It may require Rob and Marylou to change their living situation over at the Johnson house, so they need to be kept in the loop."

"Sandy and I talked about that—not a whole lot, but she did say that more than two generations are now living under one roof in Texas."

"I had a feeling that was the case. The other option is to build a separate house over there, but a separate house means a big mortgage."

"Grandpa, that could be tough for me to handle, especially if we were to get a string of dry years."

"I went through the same thought process with your grandma Audrey before we were married."

"That's why you decided not to build."

"Not just me. It was a mutual decision because there was enough room in the Johnson house to accommodate two generations, and there still is. Audrey and I had the upstairs master bedroom, and your dad and Aunt Jenna had the other two upstairs bedrooms. It worked out fine, because having my parents living in the same house while Audrey was coping with two newborn babies was a blessing."

"I can see how that would be an advantage."

"Look at my situation here. I'm living with all these Dormans. We're a four-generation family all living under the same roof, and we manage. Of course, this huge five-bedroom house with an extra den helps us stay out of everyone's hair. Chip, all I'm saying is it would be best to first talk it over with your parents to see if you and Sandy can have the upstairs like Audrey and I had. Your grandma and I were glad to move downstairs when Robert married Marylou."

"Do you want me to talk with Mom and Dad right now?"

"That would be wise. Then if it's okay with Rob and Marylou, you need to have this housing conversation with Sandy in the coming days. She'll need to be happy with whatever plan you wind up with—move in with folks or take on additional debt and build new. Those are your two options because if you want to eventually own the Johnson farm, you must live on the Johnson land."

~ ~ ~

A welcomed interruption to Delmarva's long hot and humid summer is the highlight of the season—the Delaware State Fair, located in the town of Harrington. Every year the experience of walking the fairgrounds to the lights and the music becomes almost magical. Chances are Maryland residents will see their old friends, neighbors, and classmates. It's also a chance to experience new consumer products, foods, and games. The excitement of the concerts, rides, animals, and amusements are a refreshing elixir to forget the daily drudgery of life.

And there is nothing more exciting than seeing the eyes of children light up as they watch people enjoying the rides and hearing the music of the Fair. When the Dorman family arrived, the first thing Hudson and Jake wanted to do was to check out the thrilling amusements.

"Grandpa, Grandpa, can we go on the rides now?" Jake asked.

"It's fine with me if it's fine with your dad. I'll remind him that it's better to spin and flip before you youngsters eat." Eddie said.

"It's fine with me, Dad, and I'll catch up with you later," Cole said. "I need to help Jo Lynn and Mom with their display." He picked up two of the crocks and followed Jenna and Jo Lynn across the fairgrounds until they reached the food pavilion.

Jo Lynn found her assigned table and said, "Right here, Cole. Just set them down next to my name and go have fun with the boys."

"Jo Lynn, your chutney will surely win the grand prize rosette ribbon," Jenna said.

"If only you were a judge, Mom." Jo Lynn picked up an envelope setting next to her name and read the message inside: *Please stop by our desk to discuss your entry form.*

Jo Lynn's heart sank. "I'll be right back, Mom. There seems to be a problem with my entry."

"Oh, dear! Do you still want me to start setting up the table?"

"Sure, Mom," although Jo Lynn was anything but sure.

While Jenna arranged Jo Lynn's table, two middle aged ladies and an older gentleman stopped in front of Jo Lynn's table and noticed the three jars in a cradle that were handsomely arranged.

"I love this idea," one of the women said. "Your display is very eye-catching. I can even see it in one of our catalogs."

“Oh, but you’ll really like the peach delights in these jars,” Jenna said. “Here’s three spoons for each of you. Why don’t you sample them?” Jenna removed the lids of the sampling crocks, and they took a spoonful from each.

“What do you think?” the first woman asked.

“I think this is a winner,” the gentleman said.

“Are you judges?” Jenna asked.

“No, we’re from Dayton & Mauby Foods,” the gentleman said. “We operate a commercial kitchen in New Jersey. Here’s our card. We prepare various foods in mass quantities when small entrepreneurs don’t have the capacity.”

“And would you be interested in these peach products?”

The gentleman immediately chimed in. “We have customers across the country, and one of our clients makes specialty foods for holiday catalogs. I believe they probably would be very interested in these peach recipes. They’re unique and delicious.”

“What exactly does that mean?”

“It means that if we can come to some agreement on price, our client would like to have exclusive rights to your recipes.”

“You don’t say!” Jenna looked across the room and saw Jo Lynn heading back to the table, then waved vigorously to get her attention. “Jo Lynn, you need to hear this,” she called out. She turned toward the visitors, “Jo Lynn is my daughter-in-law and she’s the one who prepared these condiments.”

“Then we’d like to talk with her. I know our client will pay top dollar for these recipes. They are uniquely delicious, and if she wins a ribbon or two, we can use those awards in our marketing.”

~ ~ ~

With the diamond ring in his pocket, Chip arrived at the fair around one o’clock and began searching for Sandy. He looked in the various livestock pavilions, asking anyone with a Delaware State Fair badge if they had seen Sandy Moore. Finally, someone directed Chip to a food court where she was having lunch with her fellow judges.

“Hi Sandy, did I catch you at a bad time?”

She stood up and said, “No, not at all. I just finished my lunch, and my judging duties are over.”

“That means we can enjoy the fair.”

“It sure does.” She curled her arm around Chip’s and turned back to the lunch table to say goodbye to the other judges. “See you next year.”

“Sandy, before we go too far, can we sit down for a moment?”

“Hey, are you backing out on our date already?”

“No, but how about we sit over there at the Quillen Arena? The horse shows and rodeos aren’t using it right now.”

“Well, okay.”

They walked to the covered arena that was filled with bleachers and sat on one of the lower benches.

“Uh, Sandy, I know we haven’t known each other that long.” He got down on one knee and fumbled the little box until it fell below the seat. “Wait a second.” He crawled under the bleacher to retrieve the ring box, then got back into position—on one knee.

“Chip are you about to propose?”

“Wait a second, I have to show you the ring.” He opened the little box and lifted out the ring. “Sandy, will you marry me?”

Sandy took a deep breath and said, “Yes, Chip, I will, and that ring is spectacular.” Holding out her left hand. “It goes here.”

Chip put it on her finger and gave her a long kiss. “Whew, I did it.”

“No, Chip, *we* are doing it.” Sandy stood up and took both of Chip’s hands, “Come on; let’s celebrate. We have a fair to enjoy.” With a bounce in her step she said, “Oh, Chip, I’m so happy. I can’t wait to tell everyone.”

Beaming with excitement, Jo Lynn was anxious to tell Eddie and Cole about Dayton & Mauby and their five-thousand-dollar offer for her recipes. Propelled by the exciting news, Jenna and Jo Lynn scurried through the crowd in search of the other Dormans. “There they are, Mom, by the games,”

“Five thousand dollars! Did you get any ribbons?” Eddie asked.

"Three blue ribbons!" Jo Lynn said. "And because I won the ribbons, Dayton & Mauby offered me an extra five thousand dollars! I won't know about the grand prize ribbon until tomorrow morning. Oh, Cole, it's a good thing we're staying here tonight in that motor coach. I want to know as soon as the judges make an announcement, but my three blue ribbons have pleased Dayton & Mauby!"

"Jo Lynn, I don't believe you'll get a wink of sleep tonight," Jenna said.

"Oh, Cole, my heart sunk when I saw a note the judges left at my table. I thought for sure I was disqualified, but it was nothing. I forgot to include our email address on the entry form. That's all—a quick fix."

"Say, everyone," Eddie said. "Hudson wants to try his luck at this game. Show your mom and dad that you can knock over those milk bottles and win a prize."

Cole, Eddie, and the carnie didn't think Hudson had a chance, but fairs aren't always about winning prizes, it's about having fun with family and friends.

"Here you go." The carnie handed Hudson three baseballs. "You get three tries to knock them all down. Knock them all down on the first try, and you get the grand prize."

Hudson had no baseball experience, but he was certainly strong. As luck would have it on the very first pitch, he hit the sweet spot, and they all fell to the ground.

"Well, that was some pitch," the carnie said. "Which one of these stuffed animals would you like?"

Hudson's eyes lit up, and he selected a panda bear that was almost as big as he was.

The family continued to stroll along the fairgrounds until they found Chip and Sandy.

"Hey, everyone!" Chip beamed with excitement as he held up Sandy's left hand. "We are engaged!"

"Well, Sandy," Jenna said, "this deserves a big hug from all of us."

"Congratulations!" Cole said. "Do your mom and dad know? More importantly, does Grandpa know?"

“They’ll all know, and before I take Sandy home, we’re stopping by the house.” Looking at Hudson’s stuffed animal. “And did you win that big teddy bear?”

“He did,” Cole boasted. “I guess now I’ll need to sign him up for little league.”

“How many rides have you been on?” Sandy asked.

“About ten,” Jake said, “and I rode my favorite three times.”

“Have you seen the little pig races?” Sandy asked.

“Pig races?” Jake said.

“They’re starting in fifteen minutes,” Chip said.

“Daddy, I want to see the pigs,” Jake said.

Cole picked up his son. “Then let’s go!”

CHAPTER THIRTY-SEVEN

Visiting Aunt Millie – Late September

Dave sat on the front porch with Eddie and Jenna enjoying the morning air while sipping their second cup of coffee. All their luggage rested on the top steps, waiting to be loaded into the car that would take them to the airport.

"That was quite a breakfast we had this morning," Dave said, "and it was wonderful to have our entire family together around the table. If there is one thing Tim Higgins taught me, it's that family means more than a last name. I can speak these words that love and family are important, but Tim actually demonstrated it by giving Roy a second chance for life."

"Daddy, I'm glad you're going with us to Denver," Jenna said. "I don't want you or any of us to lose contact with Aunt Millie and her kin."

"You're right, Jenna. I can't wait to see my sister again, but I'm not looking forward to this plane ride to Denver."

"It's only a few hours and before you know it, we'll be there."

"That's good!" Dave looked down their lane. "Here comes the mail truck."

Jenna stood up. "I'm expecting a package from a shop in Annapolis. They do remarkable work framing photographs and art."

Dave chuckled, "What sort of art did you have framed?"

"Oh, you just wait and see, that is, if it comes in this morning's mail."

The mail carrier pulled up to the house and parked in the driveway. "Miss Jenna, I have a package for you, and a few letters."

Jenna beamed as she accepted the package. "This is it, Daddy." She called into the house. "Jo Lynn, I need you to come out here on the porch. The dishes can wait. I have something very special for you. You come too, Cole."

Cole and Jo Lynn stepped outside. "What is it, Mom?" Jo Lynn asked.

"This is for you."

"Go ahead, open it," Cole said.

As Jo Lynn unwrapped the brown paper package, she revealed her Grand Prize Rosette Ribbon from the Delaware State Fair, wonderfully displayed in a shadow box frame. "Oh, Mother, it's beautiful." Jo Lynn hugged Jenna. "Look, Cole, it's the nicest thing I've ever won, and it's here for everyone to see."

"I didn't think the drawer in our hall secretary was the proper place to store a family heirloom, so I had it framed."

"Where are you going to hang it?" Cole asked.

"Put it in the kitchen," Dave said. "That's where you did all the work to win that grand prize, and we can all enjoy it every morning at breakfast."

Cole took Jo Lynn's hand. "Grandpa, Mom, Dad, we have a surprise for you. We're expecting again."

"Oh, how exciting!" Jenna gave Jo Lynn a tender kiss on the cheek.

"This means another little Dorman!" Dave said.

"Yep, in April," Cole said. "And if it's a girl, that small fourth bedroom upstairs can no longer be used for storage."

Eddie shook his son's hand. "Congratulations! Have you told the rest of the family?"

"No, not yet," Jo Lynn said, "but I think it's time."

Eddie hollered into the house and asked that everyone step outside onto the porch.

Jenna whispered in her father's ear. "If the baby is a girl, please remember that girls are farmers, too."

"Yes, yes, you've finally convinced me," Dave said. "Jenna, you're just as much a Johnson and Evans as your brother Robert, and it's all that's needed to keep the farms in the family. In the end, it doesn't matter what the farm sign says. It's all in the blood. If Chip never has boys, it won't hurt to see the Johnson Farm have a name change."

Jenna kissed her father's cheek. "That's all I ever wanted to hear."

As the rest of the family filed out onto the porch, Eddie insisted that Roy take his chair. Their father-son relationship had become close, perhaps the closest it had ever been. Eddie finally realized that his son just wanted to be a farmer, and his organic farm in partnership with Jasper would be perfect as he gained strength.

"Please take the seat, Roy," Angela insisted. "I don't mind standing here next to you."

Little Jake looked up at Eddie. "Grandpa, are you really going to ride on an airplane?"

Eddie picked him up and said, "Yep, we're driving to Baltimore and flying to Denver."

Dave gazed at his entire family, and seeing everyone together gave him a great sense of pride. "I want all of you to know that I feel truly blessed. We love one another, and most importantly, we all love Jesus. We have all worked hard to make our family strong and our livelihood a success."

"Thanks be to God," Eddie said.

Roy stood up and hugged Eddie. "Thank you for saying that, Dad, because I feel very blessed to have a family that stood by me, even when I couldn't stand up."

Eddie's eyes started to well up. He was overcome with emotion when he said, "Okay everyone! Listen up. Jo Lynn and Cole have a big announcement to make. They're going to have another little Dorman!"

"Eddie!" Jenna scolded her husband.

"Oops, that wasn't for me to say. Oh, well can you blame me? I'm going to be a grandpa again—three little Dormans—what a legacy!"

"That's all right, Dad," Cole said. "I'll probably blurt out the same thing when I'm a grandpa."

"Me too," Rob said. "Dad, when was the last time you saw Aunt Millie?"

Dave thought for a moment. "Years, it's been several years. I'm sorry to say, it's been too long."

Rob put his hand on Dave's shoulder. "Dad, remember when you and Grandpa Johnson planted a redbud tree in our front yard when Marylou and I got married?"

"Of course—your love tree, the tree of committed love and devotion."

"Well, Dad, I think you and I ought to plant another redbud tree over at the Johnson Farm—by the right corner of the house in honor of Chip and Sandy. It would look good if my tree and Chip's tree were to flank our house."

Dave smiled. "Yes, of course. Order one from the nursery, and as soon as I get back, we'll get our shovels out and plant it."

A few moments later a Lincoln SUV pulled up to the front porch. Dave stood up, knowing that it was now time to leave. The chauffeur got out and opened the door for Tim, who stepped out and onto the porch.

"Uncle Tim!" Roy shouted.

"Hello, everyone!" Tim walked over to Roy and Angela and took their hands. "Just seeing you and Angela so happy is truly wonderful."

Angela gave Tim a tearful hug. "Look at you, Uncle Tim! You're looking fit."

"Thank you, and I'm feeling much better. Roy, how's that organic farm coming along?"

"The old Bennett house is currently getting a facelift and a large modern addition in the back. It's going to become our store."

"Have you got a name for your new business?"

Roy smiled. "Oh, yes! The Corinth Organic Vegetable Market. Our land will take a few years to get certified, but in the meantime, Jasper has already installed three huge greenhouses so we can sell organic starters for anyone wanting a garden in their yard."

"Gracious, Brother Tim!" Rob said as he gave him a welcoming hug. "All of us are glad to see you again. You've gone out of your way to stop in Corinth from Missouri only to crisscross the country again and head to Denver."

"I had to return and get this great sendoff from all of you, but most of all, I wanted to see you and Marylou again. You were wonderful hosts while I was recovering, and I had the very best nursing care."

"That's because you belong to this family," Rob said.

Marylou placed a tender kiss on Tim's cheek. "That means you're always welcome. Isn't that right, Jenna?"

Jenna nodded.

Tim looked around at everyone on the porch and gave them a warm smile. "Thank you. I want to thank all of you. Your acceptance of me has been a great gift. I came here today with an open heart because you mean so much to me, and I promise to be back for Christmas with my two daughters and their families."

After a hug from Chip and Sandy Tim asked, "When is the wedding?"

"Saturday, January 6, in San Antonio. It will be a destination wedding at the Historic Menger Hotel." Chip said.

Sandy curled her arm around Tim's. "And, of course, we want you to attend. I want you to meet my Texas family, and you'll love the Victorian hotel. It's located next to the Alamo and the famous San Antonio Riverwalk."

"I can't promise you right now. You'll have to pardon me if you I'm not up to that much travel in one year, but I'll do my best to be there." Tim turned to Dave. "Well, are we all ready to fly to Denver?"

Dave gave Tim a bear hug and smiled, "Yes, we are, and your Aunt Millie will be very surprised when I introduce you as my son."

CHAPTER THIRTY-EIGHT

A Quiet Visit

It's been said that time heals all wounds, but when the wound strikes deep into the soul, time is merely a Band-Aid that partially covers the pain. It's especially true when you lose a close loved one. That's when it feels like our humanity has played a mean trick on us.

Dave Johnson parked his white pickup at the entrance of a long dirt path where several headstones poked out of the ground in perfect rows. He grabbed the folding chair from the back of his truck, walked down the narrow path, and placed it next to a particular monument which read:

Audrey Evans Johnson
July 11, 1941 – November 9, 2021
Beloved Wife, Mother

"I'm here Audrey, and we're all alone. I got back from Denver last month. Yeah, you guessed it. I was visiting my sister Millie. Oh, she's doing fine, and I was pleased to see her in good health, but I was a bit tuckered out from the trip.

Do you realize, Audrey, that today we've been apart for exactly one whole year? It seems much longer. I guess it's because we grew up together and were married for sixty beautiful years. I just got so used to you being in my life that when you left me, a big part of my heart died, too.

I bought you some flowers. It was the best-looking bouquet I could find in the grocery store." Dave laid the flowers on the monument and sat in his chair.

"Audrey, you won't believe what has happened since you've been gone. Chip found himself a mighty fine woman with my help, of course. Her name is Sandra Moore, but we call her Sandy. You'd love her. She's kind and thoughtful. She grew up on a Texas ranch, has a degree in agriculture, and is she a real beauty! They're getting married in San Antonio on the sixth of January.

Oh, I understand; you want to know where they'll settle down? Well, after much thought, Chip and Sandy decided to take the three upstairs bedrooms at the Johnson Farm, just like we did when we got married. Aren't you glad we installed those two full bathrooms upstairs? Robert and Marylou will take our downstairs primary bedroom, and you should see how Marylou has redone that room. The bathroom has been completely remodeled and she enlarged the closet so it's now one whopper of a walk-in. Marylou wanted to get all that downstairs construction done while she and Robert were still using the upstairs primary, but then they were hit with a big financial surprise. While working downstairs, the plumber discovered that the upstairs two bathrooms, which we put in sixty years ago, also needed a re-pipe. I helped with the added costs because, Audrey, I think you'd agree, it was all for a good cause. The water pressure is fine, all the toilets flush, and everyone is happy.

But here's the biggest news of all, and it's serious. It's also embarrassing for me to tell you, but you see, I had an affair with another woman before we were married. I probably should have told you about this before we were married, but I saw no reason to upset you, and now there's more to this story. I fathered a son with that woman. His name is Timothy Higgins. Audrey, I honestly didn't know he existed until this summer, but the situation took an interesting turn. Our Grandson Roy became a real drunk losing jobs left and right, which naturally worried Eddie and Jenna to death. Well, maybe I shouldn't use that word *death* around here, so let's just say it was a difficult time for our daughter and her husband. Roy's demeanor changed. He became angry and bitter toward his family. He was getting meaner by the day, and what's worse, his kidneys failed. Now, here's the unbelievable truth. My son Timothy gave up one of his kidneys and saved our Roy's life. Quite a story, isn't it? Naturally, you want to know how Roy is doing. Well, his health is improving, but here's the exciting thing. Roy met this young whippersnapper named Jasper, a real character he is. If you were to meet him, the first thing he'd ask you is whether Jesus is your Lord and Savior. I can't fault him for that, even though his technique is a bit aggressive. Anyway, Roy and Jasper are going to start an organic vegetable farm. I'll tell you more about that later.

Oh, and I know you're wanting to know the latest on Grandson Cole. He and his wife Jo Lynn are expecting another baby in April. Number three and quite exciting, isn't it? You know how we love babies, and it also means that our two farms will be well supplied with farmers. Praise the Lord, everyone else is doing just fine. Yes, siree, it has been one big year for our family. Well, Audrey, that's about all I have to tell you for now, except… I sure do miss you."

Dave wiped his eyes, picked up his folding chair, and walked up the dirt path to his pickup, tuning back one last time toward Audrey's grave. "Don't worry, darling. I'll be back for our wedding anniversary."

He knew Audrey couldn't hear his words, but expressing his innermost thoughts gave him solace and some relief as he continued to mourn the loss of his beloved wife.

CHAPTER THIRTY-NINE

Late November

The golden leaves of autumn gently found their way to the ground as Audrey's best friend Carrie Russell drove up the Dorman driveway to their stately house. She was on a mission to convince Dave to join the church choir.

After Carrie's family bought the Evans Cannery from Audrey's parents, Carrie and Audrey met and became close friends. Soon thereafter, Carrie married Martin Russell, who was always boasting that he would eventually take over the cannery. Of course, he had to learn the canning operation, which he did.

Martin had striking good looks which swept Carrie off her feet, otherwise no one in Corinth thought the two had much in common. Regardless, she married Martin, and ever since their wedding, they fought like cats and dogs.

Dave welcomed Carrie on the front porch and held open the door. "Come in, Carrie! It's chilly outside. I'm glad you stopped by, 'cause I sure love your company."

Carrie removed her fur coat and laid it across an entryway sofa.

"Let's head back to the kitchen, where I have a roaring fire going in the fireplace."

"That sounds delightful, Dave. Where is everyone?"

"All the ladies and the children are working over at the Johnson Farm today, so it's a little lonely here."

"Oh, I guess I've shamefully neglected visiting you since Audrey died. I enjoyed reading to her when she was bedridden and sharing old times, but after she passed, it seems like she took a piece of me with her."

"But you're here now, and I couldn't be happier."

"Wait until you hear the two favors I need to ask of you."

Dave pulled out a kitchen chair for Carrie. "This sound serious."

"Not really. You know how much our congregation has decreased over the years, so I'd like you to join the church choir for the Christmas concert. We only have one tenor, Marlin Jones. He's such a nice man, but he can't carry a tune, and it would be a great help if you would join us. I'm only asking for the Christmas season."

Over coffee and a slice of sweet potato pie, Dave agreed to sing because he considered it a duty, and he knew his wife Audrey would have insisted.

"Carrie, I got to thinking how times have changed over the decades, and yet, I feel we have a responsibility to teach the next generation the joys of our simple way of life like singing in the choir. I want my children and grandchildren to always consider community and kindness, and for the most part, they do. But so many young adults are wrapped up in their cell phones, concerts, and electronic games that I fear the joy of human conversation and interaction will become lost."

"I think it's lost now. You should hear the arguing among the young workers at the cannery. Many despise anyone who belongs to the wrong political party or religion. They simply cannot respect the beliefs of others."

"It's shameful when they don't know how to disagree agreeably."

Carrie gently fluffed her hair. "And I doubt they'll listen to this snow-white senior."

"Well, don't stress over it. Carrie, you mentioned you had favors. Was something else on your mind that you wanted of me?"

"Yes, very much. I need a trusted friend to witness a troubling situation that involves Martin, Sheriff Stewart, and the Jenkins family. Dave, you are friends with all the parties involved, and you have a very calming demeanor. You'd be perfect!"

Thanksgiving was over, and the shops along Main Street wasted no time putting up their Christmas decorations. Colorful lights, wreaths and wrapped boxes under Christmas trees adorned the storefront windows. In addition, the town had hung its snowflake and candy cane lights on all the utility poles. The rural town of Corinth, Maryland, was ready to celebrate the holiday season. As clerks swept a light dusting of snow off the sidewalks in front of their stores, they waved to all passersby. Even those whom they didn't recognize received a friendly wave because it was a centuries-old tradition.

It was on this day that Dave stopped by the Sheriff's office just before regular office hours had begun. Sheriff Stewart expected him this morning for coffee.

"Is there anything new in your department?" Dave asked as he poured himself a cup from the nearby coffee bar.

"Dave, as unbelievable as it may seem, I finally got another deputy. She starts this morning. Council President Martin Russell finally agreed to spend the money for the position." For years Sheriff Stewart had been asking the County Council for another deputy, and after some arm twisting by fellow councilmen, they voted to fund and hire another deputy. "Her name is Helen Ward. She and her husband Darryl bought the house next door to Roy and Angela."

"Yes, I believe they mentioned that."

Newlyweds Helen and Darryl Ward had recently moved to the Eastern Shore from Western Maryland. Darryl accepted a job as Corinth's town manager, and Helen, a recent graduate of the police academy, accepted a job with the County Sheriff's Department. On this Monday morning Deputy Helen Ward pulled into the parking lot of the jail. Her short brown hair was neatly styled to accommodate her new deputy hat. Slightly nervous on her first day, she entered the large brick building where she was met by a uniformed receptionist.

"Hello, I'm Kelsy, and you must be our new deputy."

"Yes, I'm Helen Ward here to see Sheriff Ken Stewart."

"Of course, we've been expecting you. Follow me."

Kelsy walked Helen down a long hall to the Sheriff's office. She knocked on the open door. "Sheriff, Helen Ward is here to see you."

"Come on in. This is an old friend of mine, Dave Johnson. He's your neighbor's grandfather. I hope you don't mind his presence."

"Not at all." Kelsy smiled demurely. "Pleased to meet you."

Sheriff Stewart pulled up a chair. "Have a seat."

Kelsy grabbed the doorknob as she turned to leave. "It was nice meeting you, Deputy." She left closing the door behind her.

"Coffee, deputy?"

"No, thanks."

"I saw on your application that you're from the Garrett County."

"Yes, sir, the western end of the state."

"Don't let our local prejudices bother you," Dave said. "Even though you're from Maryland, you'll hear folks say in a condescending way—*you're not from around here*—but don't let that worry you. They don't always believe that the land west of the Chesapeake Bay is still in Maryland, but I know you'll fit right in."

"Of course, she will and her husband, too," Sheriff said. "I've met Helen's husband. He's a friendly sort and should do well as our new town manager."

"Thank you," Helen said. "We've already felt Corinth's gracious hospitality. We have lovely neighbors, your kin, Mr. Johnson, Roy, and Angela Dorman. Darryl and I have been invited to their Christmas Eve buffet. They are so thoughtful!"

"That's the kind of folks the Johnsons and the Dormans are," Sheriff Stewart said. "Believe me, our deputies have been invited to plenty of those special holiday meals, but now we need to get down to business. Deputy, there are many satisfying jobs we perform in our department, but serving papers or evicting folks from their homes can be a heartbreaking and dangerous task, but as you know, it's part of our job."

"I understand."

"Good, because we have one of those unpleasant jobs this morning." Sheriff Stewart began to give Helen some background.

"Christmas is a joyous time of year, but not for Paul Jenkins, his wife Doris, and his mother Miss Mae, who is wheelchair bound. The court has assigned our department the task of evicting them today."

"But why so close to Christmas?"

"About two years ago, our largest factory in Corinth left town abruptly, leaving several hundred people scrambling for work. When the layoffs occurred, Mr. Jenkins was one of the unfortunate folks."

"How old are the Jenkins?"

"Paul is about sixty and his wife Doris a bit younger, but Miss Mae must be close to ninety. Paul had a steady job for about eight years, just long enough to believe it would last until his retirement. That's when he bought a new van with a special lift so he could take his mother to her medical appointments. He purchased the van not realizing he'd soon be unemployed."

"Is he employed now?"

"Yes, two part-time jobs, but together they aren't as lucrative as the one he lost. That good job paid for his family's health insurance. Today his main concern is keeping up the payments on his rent, utilities, his specially equipped van, plus covering his health insurance. Miss Mae needs full-time care, which keeps Doris from working outside the home."

"That's an awful shame when they need the money," Helen said.

"But here's the worst part," the Sheriff continued. "Paul and his wife bought their furniture on time from their landlord, so they're not just losing their rental home, but all their furniture, too."

"Where will they go?"

"Reverend Hayworth offered to let them stay at the parsonage until the end of the month. It's Christmas, and Doris and Paul's situation is desperate."

"Sheriff, I know renting property is a business, and the landlord has every right to reclaim his property, but it seems cruel to turn them out now."

"To make matters worse," the Sheriff inhaled a deep breath and released it with sadness, "Jenkins and his landlord Mr. Martin

Russell are members of my church. That's why this job today will be difficult for me."

Dave chimed in. "This whole eviction matter has upset Mr. Russell's wife, so as a personal favor to her, do you mind if I tag along to make sure there's no upset between her husband and the Jenkins."

"Please do, and I'm grateful for that." Sheriff Stewart put on his hat. "Well, I have a job to do. Deputy, I'd like you to come along. It will be your first lesson in our local politics. I'll drive, but Dave, you'll have to meet us at the house. Protocol, you understand."

As they walked out to the parking lot, Helen turned to Sheriff Stewart. "What can you tell me about Mr. Russell?"

Sheriff Stewart stopped abruptly. "I can only tell you what's public knowledge. Mr. Martin Russell and his wife Carrie own the Evans Canning Company. Carrie's parents bought the factory in the early sixties from Mr. Dave Johnson's father-in-law Arthur Evans. Naturally, when Carrie's parents died, Martin and Carrie became the new owners. Martin also owns several rental properties, and just so you know, he's also the President of the County Commission that controls our budget."

"That doesn't sound good."

"It's not. The sheriff's department and our county have many needs, and yet the County Commission cries that they have no money. I testified last spring that our budget shortfall could harm public safety, but it fell on deaf ears. Many folks will tell you that Mr. Russell keeps the tax rate low to improve his bottom line at his canning factory. Those low-tax bragging rights are good for him when he's electioneering, but of course, that motive is pure speculation. I've never heard him say that's his reason for his tight reins on the budget."

"I can see it would give him greater profits."

"Exactly. Every penny the tax rate goes up, it adversely affects Martin's bottom line. And since his factory is up for sale, his bottom line must be front and center on his mind these days."

"Where is Jenkins's home?

"Just outside of town and across the creek which separates the town from the county limits."

"That's quite an old bridge at that crossing."

"Yep, and it's the county's responsibility to keep it in good repair, but don't bother to ask Mr. Russell to put one penny into the repair of that hundred-year-old bridge. Mr. Russell will tell you that it's a strong and safe because it was built in the 1920s when folks knew how to build quality."

Helen breathed in deeply and exhaled. "I don't like this bridge."

"Well in order to get to the other side we need to use it." As the Sheriff's SUV crossed the bridge, it vibrated with a fierce shaking until they neared the other side. "Well, Deputy, we made it, and the Jenkins home is that white bungalow on the left. If you continue down this road another half-mile, you'll see the Russell's stately property."

When the Sheriff pulled up to the Jenkins home, Dave had already arrived, and Mr. Russell was standing next to a large panel truck in the driveway. Several burly men could be seen hauling furniture from the house. The Jenkins family decided to leave before Mr. Russell and the Sheriff showed up to avoid embarrassment and heartache as the house was emptied piece by piece and bit by bit.

"This is painful to watch," Dave said, "but I'm sure you're relieved that we won't be witnessing a scene between landlord and tenants."

The Sheriff nodded, and his face showed great relief.

"Is that everything?" Mr. Russell asked of his men.

"Yep," one of his workers replied.

"Then follow my car. I'll unlock the gates to my warehouse so you can unload."

CHAPTER FORTY

Priorities

Situated on several acres on the north side of town, Martin and Carrie's long tree-lined entrance, sweeping curved driveway, and manicured grounds boasted great wealth. Their huge midcentury house deserved many bragging rights in the 1960s, but today it would be considered quite ordinary.

That evening over dinner, a car pulled into their driveway near their front steps. Mr. Russell explained to his wife that he would be leaving on business after their meal. His luggage was in the car, and his driver was waiting to take him to the airport.

"I could be gone for several days to finalize the sale of our factory," he told his wife. "We have a few more negotiations to iron out, so this contract could take as long as a week."

Carrie was not happy. "Martin, it's the Christmas season. Do you really believe these buyers will be in a mood to do business this time of year?"

Martin raised his angered voice. "Anytime there's a willing buyer it's a good time to sell a large enterprise like Evans Canned Foods, and selling our company is what we should want!"

"But, Martin, why would you leave me alone this time of the year?"

"I can finalize this sale quickly because I'll stress the fact that the buyer will be able to reap the benefits of the spring canning season. That, my dear, is called sweetening the pot, and it's a good incentive for the buyer to settle now. I've also kept the tax rate lower than any other county in the state, which has made it possible for us to sell and get a very handsome price."

"Oh, I see. You cheat the people of our county by denying them proper wages and needed infrastructure repairs, so you can get a higher price for our factory. That bridge that I drive over every day is in deplorable condition. Martin, denying folks of safe roads and bridges may be legal, but it's certainly not ethical!"

"My dear Carrie, you worry too much. Once the Evans Company changes hands, I'll resign from the County Commission, and the other board members can do whatever they wish with the tax rate."

"I hope you're satisfied with your greed, because I'm not!"

Mr. Russell gave his wife an obligatory kiss on her cheek. "Carrie, that home where the Jenkins once lived is empty and back on the market. While I'm gone, if you should learn of anyone who would like to rent it, make sure you let them know that they can have immediate possession, and I'll settle with them when I return."

Almost in tears, Carrie said, "Martin, the Jenkins are members of our church. Why did you have to kick them out so close to Christmas? In fact, why did you have to evict them at all? Certainly, we could have worked something out with them."

"Carrie, as a landlord, I can't be giving out charity, or we'd go broke."

"Broke! Ha!" She stood up and threw down her napkin. "We are not about to go broke. We have plenty, and after the sale of our cannery we'll have millions more. In the meantime, Paul Jenkins is now working two jobs trying to make ends meet, and I don't know how Doris has the energy to take care of Miss Mae with the added stress of homelessness."

"Let's talk about it when I return. My driver is waiting."

"Martin, if Paul hadn't lost his good job, he could make his rent, and that goes for many people who live in the area. Besides, real estate is only a small part of our total income."

Martin's steely eyes were a window on his cold heart. "Well, needless to say, the house is empty and available for rent." Martin turned and stormed out the front door.

Every Wednesday evening the Corinth Methodist Church meets for choir practice. On this evening Reverend Hayworth brought Mrs. Doris Jenkins with him. She needed a break from being a caretaker to Miss Mae, so both the pastor and his wife insisted that she go.

"Good evening, Doris." Carrie smiled sweetly as Doris and the pastor entered the narthex. "I'm so glad to see you."

Doris's back straightened. She trembled. "What could you possibly want from me that your husband hasn't already taken?"

"Oh, Doris, that entire ordeal has upset me greatly, and I would be pleased if you would join the choir in song this evening. We're practicing for our Christmas concert."

She relaxed slightly and smiled through her grimacing lips. "I'm not a good singer, but I'll enjoy listening."

"Good. I hope you'll enjoy the music. How is your mother-in-law?"

"The Reverend's wife is staying with Miss Mae tonight so I could get away for the evening."

"I'm glad, Doris, because you deserve some nights off." Carrie caught the attention of the Reverend, and gently tapped his shoulder. "Good evening. May I have a word with you in your office before our choir practice begins?"

"Of course."

Carrie returned her attention to Doris and smiled. "We can talk more after practice."

In the pastor's study, the reverend and took a seat behind his desk. Carrie sat across from him and pulled an envelope from her purse. "Reverend, I want to donate this cash to the church for the care of the Jenkins family. It's ten thousand dollars. This will allow the Jenkins to pay all their debts and have some left over."

"Mrs. Russell, that's so generous, but what about Martin? Won't this sort of contribution upset your husband?"

"My husband won't complain because it's technically a church donation. To him, a big church donation is a way to stay in favor with our county. Even though the church won't make his donation public, Martin sure will. I'm so sorry, Reverend, but the way Martin mistreated Mr. and Mrs. Jenkins was unconscionable, and I need to make things right. Their house is now vacant, and I'd like them to move back in."

The reverend leaned forward. "I can hardly complain about this. My wife and I have been happy to host the Jenkins, but it's good to know they will have a permanent place to live."

"Another reason to help the Jenkins move back into their house."

"I agree there."

"Please tell the Jenkins that this money came from anonymous members of the church, and it's true. My husband and I are both members, and that makes it so."

"But won't Martin object?"

"Martin will be a challenge, because he refuses to believe our wealth is a gift from God. When he sits in a pew, he has no problem singing, *Praise God from whom all blessings flow*. I just wish he'd believe those words."

"Oh, Carrie, there are many others I'd like to convince about blessings."

"When Martin and I were married he was penniless, and it was my parents who gave him wealth. This money will make it possible for the Jenkins to have a real Christmas, and the truth is, Reverend, I'm only recycling my family's money. I just wish my husband would believe as I do and be more charitable and pay forward."

"I tell you what. The day that Martin returns home, invite me to dinner. Perhaps I should have a little time alone with him after our meal—a little coffee in your den after we eat. Opening a person's spiritual eyes is God's job, but you and I are commanded to point him in the right direction." Reverend Hayworth stood up and started for the door. "Carrie, no one changes overnight, but there is always a starting point."

"Reverend, my husband and I are advanced in years. I'm afraid there's little time left for Martin to change."

"You leave that up to God, Mrs. Russell. The Lord works with us individually to lead us to salvation. Martin is not the first stubborn man to find Jesus late in life. Let's trust in God's plan for Martin. He knows what it will take to open his spiritual eyes."

Carrie stood up. "I fear God will need a heavy hammer and a crowbar."

"I prefer to think that God will be gentle with Martin."

"Thank you, Reverend."

"Carrie, I know you have fears in this regard. Why not give those fears to God. He wants you to."

As Carrie left the Reverend's study and entered the sanctuary, she pulled Doris Jenkins aside. "Doris, I understand you need a nice place to stay and lots of furnishings. Well, I happen to be the sole owner of a darling house that is available for the purchase price of one dollar, and it happens to be the very place you just left."

"One dollar! Mrs. Martin, you can't be serious."

"Very serious, Doris. My parents left the house to me, and they would be very pleased to know that your family will be the new owners. I've replaced all the carpets, refreshed all the walls with new paint, and installed new appliances—a washer and dryer, too. If you could meet me at the factory warehouse tomorrow, say around ten, I believe there are many lovely items which you may have without obligation that will furnish this house nicely. I'll also provide a large truck to transport anything you'd like to have."

"I don't understand."

"Oh, Doris, you have many friends in this town, including me, and don't forget that. Our heavenly Father tells us that He takes care of the smallest sparrow, and He promises to take care of you and me. In my small way, I'm just one of God's tools charged with helping others."

Doris took a seat in the rear of the sanctuary while Carrie walked toward the altar and took her position with the other altos in the choir. She turned around and looked at Dave. "Dave Johnson, I know that smile of yours."

He leaned forward and whispered to Carrie. "I saw you walking out of the pastor's study and talking with Doris. I know you, Carrie, and I know you just did a very good thing."

Carrie whispered back, "What do you know about it?"

"I know it was a great act of courage and kindness."

"We'll talk later after practice." Carrie smiled, turned around, and faced the choir director.

CHAPTER FORTY-ONE

Mid December 2022

Jasper's New House

Dave sat in the den reading the morning newspaper and sharing parts of it with his daughter Jenna. His reading was interrupted by an important thought which caused him to put down his paper.

"Jenna, Roy's wife is truly a wonderful woman. Angela works hard for our farms keeping the books, doing payroll, calculating our taxes, and keeping a close eye on our expenses. She does all that in addition to taking care of Roy through the worst of his trials."

"Angela is remarkable," Jenna said. "She shared some interesting news about Roy's business partner Jasper Collins. Angela is going to help him buy a house today right here in Corinth, so he won't be needing our bunkhouse much longer."

"That makes her even more remarkable."

"Jasper gave her power of attorney to sign the documents and to make sure they're in order. I'm sure everything will be fine since my dear friends Cathy and Larry are handling the settlement."

"Why isn't Jasper going to the settlement?"

"He's spending Christmas with Mr. Gordon and his family. Mr. Gordon is the instructor at Mapledale, who introduced Jasper to Jesus, and now Jasper considers them as family."

~ ~ ~

That afternoon Angela sat across from Attorneys Larry Dunn and his wife Cathy at their office. Larry, a distinguished looking gentleman, and Cathy an elegant middle-aged lady had been married since they graduated from law school many years ago. The semi-retired couple were charged with Jasper Collins's settlement on the house he was about to purchase.

"This shouldn't take long, Angela," Larry said. "I know you probably want to get back to your husband. Jasper must be a close friend to entrust you with this job."

"He's actually Roy's friend and soon to be business partner, but I'm glad to pitch in and help him acquire this house."

Cathy smiled at Angela. "I don't know if your mother-in-law ever mentioned it, but Roy's mother and I were in the same class at Corinth High School and have remained close friends. We've had Jenna and Eddie over for dinner a few times, but not since Roy's illness. I understand he's doing quite well since the transplant."

"He is, thank you, and progressing as well as to be expected. I insist that he avoid anything strenuous without spoiling him."

Cathy placed her hand on Angela's forearm. "And I'm sure you've done a marvelous job as caretaker these past few months. It's been almost a year since we last saw your family. Larry, let's talk about having Eddie and Jenna over for dinner again."

"Of course," Larry said. Great idea, and maybe when the weather is warm, Eddie, Roy and I can go fishing again on our boat, but in the meantime, let's not keep Angela. I'm sure she has other things she'd like to do. Angela, we need you to sign these documents next to the yellow arrows. We have Jasper's cashier's check, so as soon as you sign in all these places, you may have the keys."

"I'm home, Roy!" Angela's cheerful voice echoed down the entry hall.

Roy popped out of the kitchen, drying his hands on a towel. "It's almost three. I'm surprised you've been out so long."

"Just a couple of hours to run a few errands, and it looks like you're doing the dishes—something different for both of us."

Angela hung up her coat in the hall closet. “I also had an important task to accomplish for Jasper.”

“Yeah? Where is that guy?”

“He’s gone up to Cecil County to spend time with the Gordon family.”

Roy looked puzzled. “Jasper told me that he was going to spend Christmas with his parents, and he didn’t want to miss one minute of their time together. I guess that plan fell apart.”

“Apparently, and that was why he gave me power of attorney to sign some important documents for him. I didn’t think it would take this long, but it’s why I’m late.”

“So, what exactly did you do for him?”

“Jasper bought a house off the internet, sight unseen, and wanted me to sit in on the closing. Apparently, his parents’ attorney was too busy with other family matters, so Jasper asked me to do the signing and to make sure the numbers were correct.”

“Which house did he buy?”

“The old Carroll house—next door to your new joint venture. I believe that’s why he wanted it so much. Jasper will be able to see your organic farm from his dining room window. When I drove by your store this afternoon, the contractors were busy converting the old house into a business. By the looks of things, it will make a wonderful storefront.”

“Jasper told me he wanted to live close to our new operation, and there’s nothing closer than the Carroll house. There’s some land with that property. I guess about two acres.”

“Closer to three. After I signed all the papers, I was handed the keys. If you’re up to it, would you like to ride over there and inspect his house?”

“Sure, but we should leave before the sun sets.”

When Angela and Roy drove up to the house, the exterior appeared to be in good condition. There were no cracks in the foundation, and it had a new metal roof, but the faded exterior clapboards and trim were ready for lots of fresh paint.

Roy unlocked the front door and looked around the living and dining rooms. "The Carroll's took good care of the place, but I'm sure Jasper will want to remodel."

"That's understandable. It's been unoccupied for at least a year."

The two-story Carroll house had two upstairs bedrooms and a full bath. The downstairs had large spacious rooms for entertaining, a powder room, plus two kitchens—one off the dining room and a summer kitchen on the back porch.

"Angela, walk over here and look out this back window. The gardens are overgrown, but it's obvious that at one time the place was a beautiful spot to sit and enjoy the outdoors. I can just picture Mr. and Mrs. Carroll relaxing in that screened garden gazebo."

After walking through the entire house, Roy and Angela concluded that Jasper would probably want to upgrade many things, but the overall condition was good enough to move in after a thorough cleaning and airing.

As they walked back to the car, Angela took Roy's hand and gave him a sweet kiss on his cheek. "Why don't you call Jasper and tell him that he made a very wise purchase. I think he'll be pleased and relieved to hear the news, and he'll be glad to hear from you."

CHAPTER FORTY-TWO

Martin Counts His Money

Late one morning about a week before Christmas, Martin Russell entered through the front door of his home, and after he hung his coat and hat in the hall closet said, "I'm back, Carrie, and just in time for brunch. Have I got exciting news for you!"

"I'm in the kitchen. Let me dry my hands, and I'll join you."

"Carrie love, after taxes, we will be three million dollars richer! Start looking for places in Florida because that's where we're going to live." Martin always thought of himself first and never considered his wife's preferences, and since the Florida tax rate was much more favorable than Maryland's, he decided they should move there.

"Money, is that all you think about? It sounds like our factory sale was a success, but success can be measured in ways other than money."

"Oh, Carrie! Don't spoil my victory."

"What if we don't like Florida?"

"Honestly, wife, what has this state ever given you?"

"I like Maryland. I love my church and its people. In fact, when you told me that you were coming home today, I invited Reverend Hayworth and his wife for dinner."

"Now, why in the world would you do a thing like that? I have nothing in common with that old coot. Oh, yes, on Sundays I put on my polite face, but that's the full extent of my churchiness."

"Well, I'm not going to un-invite them, so you'll have to wear that polite face again for dinner tonight."

Martin huffed, put on his slippers, sat in his overstuffed chair, and hid his face in the morning paper.

"It won't do any good to pout, because I've already started working on dinner."

"Have you found someone for the old Jenkins place?"

"Yes, I sold it to Paul and Doris Jenkins. The house was totally in my name, and now it belongs to the Jenkins."

"You did what! How about the back rent they owe us and payment for the furniture?"

"For your information, the church provided Paul and Doris with the back rent, and I gave them back all of their furniture!"

"Carrie, why did you do a fool thing like that?"

"Because people sleep in beds, eat at tables, and watch TV on their couch, and, yes, I gave them back their television, too. Martin, don't talk to me about money when we have plenty, or that I made a poor business decision out of compassion. I'll hear nothing of it."

"Carrie, you'll be interested to know that the buyers wanted the *Evans* brand more than the land and the equipment. The brand turned out to have the highest value to the buyers. Of course, they will dismantle the newest machinery and ship it to Mexico. Who knows what they will do with the old equipment, the land, and the buildings."

"Mexico! Are you telling me that our cannery here in Corinth will be closed? I thought the buyers were American."

"They are, but the canning operation will be in Mexico. It's progress, my dear."

Carrie felt sick. This would mean more layoffs in Corinth, and there was nothing she could do to prevent it. Martin returned to his newspaper, and Carrie to the kitchen, where she had worked most of the day preparing dinner.

That evening after dinner, Reverend Hayworth and his wife were both appreciative of the work that went into preparing the fine meal and gave Carrie overwhelming thanks.

"Oh, Carrie," Mrs. Hayworth said. "I must have your casserole recipe. It was so delicious."

"If you like, you may take the leftovers with you."

"That would be much appreciated, Carrie."

Carrie stood up and walked over to the buffet. "Gentlemen, I've prepared coffee and several Christmas cookies. I'll put this tray in the den for you to enjoy while Mrs. Hayworth and I clear the table."

"There you go again, wife, always ordering me around."

Reverend Hayworth placed his hand on Martin's back. "Come now, Martin, look at all these lovely, sweet treats your wife has set out for us. Certainly, we can make Carrie feel special by sitting in the den by the fire while sipping on hot coffee and sampling the cookies?"

Martin and the reverend finally headed for the den and sat in facing wingback chairs by the gas fire.

"I suppose you wanted to pull me aside to ask about a tithe now that my factory has sold."

Once settled, Reverend Hayworth said, "Martin, your newfound fortune is the furthest thing from my mind. You and I are old. We've had a good life, but there's one thing that I'd like to ask of you. Do you know for certain that you'll be spending eternity in heaven with our Lord? Or will you take up a permanent residence in hell?"

"What sort of a foolish question is that? Pardon me, Reverend, but you and my wife have different notions about life and death. It's, quite frankly, an absurd question."

"Absurd? How so?"

"You don't expect me to believe in that skullduggery? I'm sorry, Hayworth. I realize we all must make a living, but I equate your church occupation with palm readers and motivational speakers."

"Martin, you have the opportunity today, right now, to open your heart and mind and accept Jesus Christ as your Lord and Savior. Ignore this gift from the Almighty, and one day you could face the dire consequence of eternal damnation. That's when you'll realize that you can no longer beg for His mercy. So, the question becomes, do you want to pick a fight with God until the bitter end, or freely turn your life over to Him? It's up to you. Once you surrender to Jesus as our Lord and Savior, you are guaranteed everlasting life, and I know that Carrie would want you to make that commitment."

"She would because she has bought into your craziness, but not me." He passed the plate of cookies. "Here try one of these chocolate coconut bars. They're my favorite."

CHAPTER FORTY-THREE

Christmas Eve

The Christmas Eve buffet was a tradition that started during the Depression by Audrey's grandparents. All the first responders on duty in Corinth were invited so they could begin their overnight shifts with an outstanding meal. The idea had been well-received over the decades, and when Audrey was no longer able to cook, Jenna and Robert promised their mother that they would continue the Christmas tradition.

They remembered how their mother and their Grandma Evans would work hard with a few friends for days to make sure the men and women had a memorable dinner before working late shifts at the firehouse, hospital, ambulance, police and sheriff's stations.

This year Robert and Marylou hosted the meal. Dave stopped by early in the evening and watched as Marylou and Robert filled the dining room table with holiday fare: crab dip and crackers, an array of homemade rolls, piles of smoked salmon, chicken liver pate, beautiful slices of roast beef, ham, various cheeses, pickled herring, and local oysters on the half shell. Except for the large array of snacking vegetables, it was a cholesterol feast to behold.

Chip grabbed a plate and piled it high with various foods. "Don't worry, Mom. It's for our workers. I know Aunt Jenna had fixed them dinner, but this food is special, and it is Christmas Eve."

"I'm not worried; just grateful for remembering the men. Your Aunt Jenna told me that Walter, Darcy, and Joe will be joining us tomorrow for Christmas dinner. They're part of our family now. Before I forget, I want to thank you again for giving up your bedroom for a couple of nights and sleeping over at the bunk house."

"I don't mind a bit. I'll drop off this food and be back before Uncle Tim and his family arrive."

Marylou peered out the kitchen window. The glow of headlights could be seen in the distance. "Rob, I think that's Tim coming up the driveway!" She looked again. "No, it's your sister Jenna and Eddie. I suppose Cole and Jo Lynn will drive over separately with the boys."

Rob stepped outside to meet Jenna and his brother-in-law in the driveway. "Merry Christmas, Sis. Can I help you with anything?"

"No, I think we can manage," Jenna said. "It's just two large platters of cookies and brownies, but you can hold the back door for us."

"I would, but look, Marylou has beat me to it."

"Merry Christmas, Marylou! Where would you like Eddie and me to put these dessert platters?"

"In the living room on the coffee or console table will be fine."

As Jenna entered the living room, she was overjoyed to see her son Roy and daughter-in-law Angela. "Don't get up, Roy. I'm just thrilled to see you here for Christmas Eve."

"Oh, but we always look forward to our family's Christmas Eve celebration," Angela said. "You just missed the Deputies and a few nurses. They were all here for their annual Christmas Eve buffet, in uniform and ready to start their night shifts. You also missed Corinth's new town manager Darryl Ward and his deputy wife Helen. They're our new neighbors, and they're very nice."

"It pleases all of us when the deputies know they are welcome in our home. How long can you and Angela stay?" Jenna asked.

With stretched out arms and a long yawn, Roy said, "Not long, Mom. I want to save some of my strength for Christmas Day."

Jenna gave Roy an extended motherly embrace. "I understand, and I don't think anyone will stay late tonight. We have beds to assign, and we want everyone to settle in comfortably."

"By the way," Angela asked. "When will Uncle Tim be here with his family?"

"He's almost here," Rob said. "He called me from his car after he crossed the Bay Bridge." Rob put his arm around his sister Jenna. "What a special time for us. We're having our first Christmas with our new brother Tim."

"Oh, Rob, I get a lump in my throat every time I see our house at Christmas. I'm glad you and Marylou use the same corner of the living room for the tree. I often think about how we would peek down the stairwell in our pajamas to see if Mom and Dad had placed our presents under the Christmas tree." Jenna hugged her brother. "You know, Rob, there really is no place like home."

"And I feel the same whenever we have Christmas dinner at our grandparents' house, which is now your home," Rob said. "We can have countless meals at both places throughout the year, but when our entire family gets together for Thanksgiving and Christmas dinners at our Grandma Evans house, it's magical."

"I agree, and it's up to us to keep this tradition going for our children and grandchildren." Jenna's eyes welled. "Merry Christmas, Rob."

"It looks like the rest of the Dormans are here," Marylou said.

Jenna's son Cole entered with his wife Jo Lynn and their two sons Hudson and Jake. "Merry Christmas, Aunt Marylou. Merry Christmas, Uncle Rob."

"Aunt Marylou!" Eleven-year-old Hudson proudly proclaimed, "I have a present for you and Uncle Rob!"

"How wonderful!" Marylou said. "Find a spot under our tree, and your uncle and I will be excited to open it tomorrow morning."

"Ah, don't you wanna open it tonight?"

"Oh, maybe."

"It is a very Merry Christmas," Rob said. "Dad, take a seat in the recliner. You've earned the best seat in the house, and I'll get you a plate of food."

"Here comes another car," Angela said. "I hope it's Uncle Tim."

Roy looked out the window. "It's two cars. No, it's one car and Chip's truck. That means Uncle Tim is here!"

"Merry Christmas," Rob greeted the crowd. "Please, come in, come in!"

Tim, his daughters Robyn and Julie entered with their spouses and children, followed by Chip.

"Let me take your coats," Rob said. "We're all so excited to see you. How was that Western Maryland ski lodge?"

"Tremendous fun," Tim replied. "My girls and their husbands took to the slopes, and I stayed with the grandkids in the children's play section. I love being Grandpa. I'm sorry that my daughters will be returning to work right after Christmas. Their dental practice can only be put on hold for so long."

Rob hugged Tim. "Merry Christmas, brother."

"And now, it's my turn," Jenna said as she hugged Tim.

Julie leaned over Dave, who was seated in his comfortable chair, and gave him a kiss on top of his head. "Robyn and I decided that we'd like to call you Grandpa Dave, if that's okay with you."

"Of course, and it will be a great honor if you do."

Robyn couldn't take her eyes off her father and Rob. "Dad, the resemblance of you and Uncle Rob is remarkable. I can now appreciate that amusing Denver story you told us about meeting Aunt Millie. The moment she first saw you, she kissed you on the cheek, thinking you were Rob."

Dave smiled. "Needless to say, my sister was quite surprised when I told her that the man she just kissed was not Rob but her new nephew Tim. Oh, well, I had fun explaining how I wound up with two wonderful sons."

Rob put his hand on Chip's shoulder. "This is my son, Chip, and my wife Marylou. Of course, Jenna is my sister, and Eddie Dorman over there taking home movies is my brother-in-law. Their son Cole is married to Jo Lynn, and their younger son Roy is married to Angela."

Julie immediately went to Roy's side. "Oh, Roy, how are you feeling? You're the one who has my dad's kidney."

"Yep, and I promise to take good care of it. Your father saved my life. He's an incredible man."

"That he is," Julie said.

“Allow me to explain the sleeping arrangements,” Jenna said. “Tim and his grandson will be sleeping over at the Dorman Farm.

Robyn and her husband can have the upstairs primary bedroom here. It has its own ensuite, and then there are two more bedrooms upstairs connected by a bathroom for Julie and her husband, and their daughters can share the other bedroom.”

“This means no one needs a hotel,” Rob said. “Our home is your home.”

Marylou extended her arm, directing everyone to the dining room. “Please, don’t forget to grab a plate and enjoy all this food. We also have punch and fresh coffee. Don’t be shy. I’m sure you’re all hungry.”

While standing in line for food, Robyn said, “Chip, tell us about the wedding plans and about your fiancé, Sandy. Dad said she’s lovely.”

“She is. Next week we’ll be tying the knot in San Antonio, Texas, at the Historic Menger Hotel. It’s a very stately place, very palatial and across the street from the Alamo. Sandy picked San Antonio because it centrally located for her immediate family. Two of her brothers live in Austin, and she has cousins all around that part of the state.”

“I know that my father wanted to attend the wedding, but after his surgery and travels to Denver and back, my sister Julie and I thought that this Christmas trip should be Dad’s last bit of travel for a while. It’s just that we don’t want him to push himself too much.”

“I understand. I know that we wanted Tim to meet my future in-laws, but we are all very concerned for this health.”

Rob interrupted, “Dad, now that everyone has a plate of food, would you please say the blessing?”

“I’d love to.”

Tim chimed in, “Before we bow our heads in prayer, I’d like to say a few words especially for our little ones. Prayer is a serious conversation that we have with God. It’s a great privilege to be able to speak with our Lord, and it’s important that we all stay connected to God. So, I’m asking that when you pray, you do it with your strongest loving thoughts of Jesus, because he is the reason we celebrate Christmas."

"Wow, Tim!" Rob said. "I'm sure glad you're my brother. That was a perfect introduction. And now, Dad, may we have the blessing?"

> "Of course. This year has been a special blessing for all of us, and especially for me. I thank the Lord for his mercy and generosity. I learned that I had another son, Tim, and he generously donated a kidney to my grandson Roy when he was in a desperate condition. We had record-breaking profits on the farm, and Jo Lynn's peach recipes made her the grand prize winner at the State Fair. Chip was this year's *Farmer of the Year* and engaged to a great lady. My great-grandson, Hudson, figured out how to start the old dump truck when none of us old folks could. We were able to hire another hand to work on the farm. Best of all, we are all here together, my two sons and daughter, my grandsons and granddaughters, their spouses, and children. Yes, having all my family together, both old and new, makes this a very blessed year. So let us pray."

Everyone bowed their heads in reverence to God, and Dave continued.

> "Dear Heavenly Father, Christmas is a special time when we can praise you and thank you for all that you have provided. Christmas is when we celebrate your miracle birth, that you Almighty God would come to earth as a person to save humanity. For that we thank you, dear Lord, along with the many blessings we have enjoyed throughout the year. We ask that you bless our family in the coming year and bless the wonderfully prepared food that we are about to eat, in Jesus' name we pray, Amen."

Rob placed his hand on Dave's shoulder. "I don't think anyone could have summed up this year's blessings better than you, Dad."

After most had finished eating and chatting, Jo Lynn said, "Let's sing some carols like we did when Grandma Audrey played the piano. Tim, do you or your daughters play?"

"I'm sorry," Tim said. "My daughters are great dentists, but as musicians, I'm afraid my whole family comes up short."

"It doesn't matter, because we know the songs," Julie said, "and we can sing without the piano, can't we?"

"Of course, we can," Rob said. "How about, *Oh, Little Town of Bethlehem*? Wait a second. I just saw some headlights in the driveway. It looks like a white pickup." Rob stepped out onto the front porch to welcome another visitor. He returned indoors with Sandy. "Guess what? We now have a piano player!"

"Sandy!" Chip rushed to the front door, took her in his arms, and gave her an extended kiss.

Dave chuckled. "Well, I'm sure glad these two are getting married next week."

"Sandy, this is a great surprise. Mom, Dad, did you know about this?"

"Yes, Chip, we did," Marylou said. "We worked out the surprise with Sandy's parents, and your Aunt Jenna has made a bed for Sandy on the couch in their den.

The best news is, you're both booked on the same flight back to Texas."

Chip couldn't take his eyes off Sandy. "I think a couple of nights on the den sofa won't be as bad as my two nights on a bunkhouse cot."

Sandy smiled and walked over to Roy and Angela. "How are you feeling, Roy?"

"It's unbelievable how much Uncle Tim's kidney has done for me, but I'm sorry that I'm not going to make it to your wedding. I have to take it easy for the next few months."

Sandy grabbed Angela's and Roy's hands. "Roy, I'd rather you miss our wedding ceremony than endanger your health. Angela, how are you holding up? You've had so much on your shoulders, too."

"Actually, I'm doing quite well. When Roy first went into Hopkins, those were trying times for both of us, but renewed prayer and meditation carried me over the hump and refreshed my spirit. Roy and I now share daily quiet times in prayer."

Dave clapped his hands. "Say, now that we have a piano player, we should sing Oh Little Town of Bethlehem. Do you mind playing for us, Sandy?"

"I'd love to." Sandy sat at the piano and before she began to play said, "Everyone knows the first verse, so when we get to the end, let's repeat the last line. Are we ready?" She played the introduction, and everyone joined in.

Oh, little town of Bethlehem, how still we see thee lie

Above thy deep and dreamless sleep the silent stars go by

Yet in thy dark streets shineth, the everlasting light

Our hopes and fears of all the years are met in Thee tonight.

"Repeat!" Sandy said as she slowed the meter.

Our hopes and fears of all the years

Are met in Thee tonight.

CHAPTER FORTY-FOUR

A San Antonio Wedding

Other than the bride and groom, no one was more excited than Dave to see Chip and Sandy tie the knot. He had longed to see his grandson marry and have a son so the Johnson Farm could keep the Johnson family name. Dave tried not to `hold onto those old familial traditions, but it was the way he was raised.

Robert and his wife Marylou escorted Dave on the long trip to San Antonio for Chip's wedding. They landed in San Antonio just before noon, and from the airport took a cab to their hotel.

The historic Menger Hotel lived up to all its exquisite descriptions. Sandy and Chip booked the Victorian lobby for their ceremony, which was in the oldest section of the hotel. Its pale blue and cream colors were a perfect complement to its original mosaic floors that dazzled the entrance and beyond. Looking up toward the soaring ceiling, white marble columns with gilded Corinthian capitals reached up beyond the first balcony to the second one, creating two galleries for viewing. Both were framed with elaborate gilded balustrades. The antique furniture and electrified period light fixtures were the finishing touches that transported modern visitors back in time.

Dave, Robert, and Marylou stood in the majestic historic lobby and looked up at the massive stained-glass skylight. Marylou slowly pivoted to take in all its splendor. "This place is breathtaking."

"There's nothing like this in Corinth," Rob said.

"I'll say!" Dave said, "And I cannot wait to see the Alamo. It's right next door."

"Dad, there's plenty of time for touring the town. Let's find the front desk and get checked in. Folks will soon be gathering around in the garden for lemonade and sweet tea, and if anyone wants a cocktail, they can walk across the hall and belly up to the bar."

The staff began to set up chairs in the Victorian lobby along with large stands of white flowers dotted with a few Texas yellow roses.

"We need to move along," Marylou said, "so the staff can do their jobs. After the vows, there will be plenty of time to linger, dine, and dance to live music in the Minuet Room."

"Clay and Shirley Moore have gone all out for their daughter, Dave said."

"Yes, darling, they have, but now we need to get ready. Do you mind going with Dad to his room? You'll probably see Chip. He told me he'd wait in his grandfather's room until we arrived. That will give me extra time for a nice hot bath."

"Okay, Dad, I guess you heard Marylou. We're both getting ready for the big day in your room."

Guests began to gather in the garden for light refreshments before the ceremony, while the bride and her mother were getting ready in the bride's dressing room. Sandy's four brothers joined their father in his hotel suite.

Clay looked at all his sons. "Sandy's wedding is much more expensive than when you got married. Of course, walking down the aisle is new for me. I'm wondering why we didn't rehearse this important of event."

"Oh, there's nothing to it, Pop," Mark said.

"That's what you say, son!"

"Wait until your daughter gets married. I bet your nerves will be a tangled mess, too."

Mark took Clay's arm as if his father were the bride. "You'll enter the lobby from the sidewalk with Sandy and walk her into lobby where you'll stand in front of the pastor. He'll ask, *who will give this bride away*? And you'll answer, *I, her father*. See, it's easy. Then you'll take a seat next to Mother."

"I'm glad that we don't have to be ushers," Jeff said. "One tux rental for Dad is plenty."

"Sandy wanted it this way—a simple, sweet, and Godly ceremony," Clay said.

Jeff looked over his father's outfit. "Let's get you unpacked, Pop. You can't wear blue jeans and your old dirty work boots to a wedding, even though they are fitting for a Texas rancher." As he opened his father's luggage he asked, "Where are your dress shoes? Did you leave them in the car?"

"I'm not sure. Here, take my keys, and check the trunk, too. I'll call your mother to see if she knows where my shoes are." As Jeff was about to walk out of the room, Clay called his wife. "Hello, Shirley. Where did you pack my dress shoes? ...Oh, you didn't? Well, then, I'm in a real pickle because I certainly didn't pack them. ...What, use one of the son's pair? That's a good idea."

Clay poked his head out the door and hollered down the hall. "Jeff, please come back. The shoes aren't in the car. Can borrow a pair of black shoes from one of you boys just for the ceremony and the photographs?"

Sandy's brothers looked down at their casual shoes and shook their heads. "Sorry, Pop." Mark spoke up. "It looks like you're out of luck. Besides none of us wear your size."

"Wait a second!" Don said. "You can wear my loafers. They're broken in and freshly polished. I can wear my black running shoes."

Mark comforted his father. "There you see, Dad. Don has saved the day with his extra pair of shoes. They may not be formal, but it's the best we can do."

Don removed his shoes and handed them to his father. "Here, they may be tight on you, but you'll only have to walk about thirty feet in them. Then, after you give Sandy away and you'll sit down next to mother and ease the pain."

Clay sat on the side of the bed and struggled to put on Don's left shoe. "Oh, it's way too small. I'll have a blister just walking downstairs to the lobby. I suppose I can wear my old brown cowboy boots downstairs and put these on just before Sandy and I enter the lobby."

Don put his hand on his father's shoulder. "Don't worry about this, Pop, just hop in the shower, and you'll see. Everything will be fine."

It was almost five, and the ceremony would soon begin. Eighty-four guests filled the lobby and part of the first balcony where they could watch from above. Clay entered the bride's dressing room and saw Sandy standing in front of a full-length mirror in all her splendor. Her ankle length, long-sleeved silk gown gently flared below the waist, and the pearl studded bodice accentuated her lovely figure.

"Shirley, we have the most beautiful daughter in all of Texas. My dear Sandy, you cannot imagine how much your mother and I love you." Clay reached into his breast pocket. "In fact, we have something for you." He handed a jewelry case to Sandy.

Shirley's eyes welled up. "We thought this string of pearls would look lovely with your gown. Here, let me help you put them on." As she unlocked the clasp, she noticed her husband's feet from the corner of her eye. Clay, why are you wearing those old dirty boots? You'd better put on your dress shoes. Once you walk out this door, the photographer will capture your every move."

"I know. He's already photographed me walking down the hall in my stocking feet."

"Really, Clay! This is your daughter's big day, and appearances will be captured in pictures to be enjoyed for generations. Sandy, let me help you put on the veil. It should cover your face until you're standing in front of the minister. Your father will help you lift it over your head."

Clay wiped his brow with a kerchief. "Oh, dear heavens, another step for me!"

"Yes, Clay, another step. Okay, I believe we're ready." Shirley gave her daughter a final hug. "I'm going to take my place, and I'll meet you downstairs."

Clay escorted his daughter outside, wearing his old boots and carrying his son's dress shoes. They approached the entrance of the

Victorian lobby, where he took off his boots, jammed his feet into his son's black shoes, and handed his boots to a staff member. "Would you please take my boots up to my room?"

"Of course."

"How are your feet, Dad?"

"Sandy, today is such an honor for me that I don't want to think about my crushed toes or blistered heels. But don't worry, I'll not grimace."

"Dad, can you see Chip?"

Peering through the glass double doors, "Oh, yes, he's there next to the minister, looking quite dapper. Oops there's the music, and look, everyone is standing."

Two hotel staff members held open the glass doors for Sandy and her father, who took a short walk through a small lounge and into the main lobby, where Chip looked at his bride with adoring eyes. Clay did his fatherly duty with great aplomb, as he walked his daughter up to the preacher and Chip, lifted her veil and gave his lovely daughter away.

The moment Clay took his seat next to his wife, he let out a sigh of relief, and then whispered in Shirley's ear. "Can I remove these foot clamps now?"

"Just slip your feet out slightly to relieve the pressure."

"How far away is the reception?" He whispered again.

"Not far—just a few steps down that hall and then to your right. Please, Clay, pay attention, or at least look like you are, and smile."

After they exchanged vows, and after Chip kissed his bride, it was time for dinner, served in the Minuet Room. Clay managed to walk the short distance by folding in the heel portions of his son's shoes. It was an obvious strain.

The large dining room was also a part of the oldest section of the hotel with all its Victorian charm and with a similar décor to the original lobby. The staff had set up a dance floor and an area for the live music.

Clay and Shirley were seated with Dave, Rob, Marylou, Eddie, and Jenna. As Dave scooted his chair forward, he stepped on something unusual. "Is anyone missing a couple of shoes?"

Clay, with a guilty smile on his face said, "They're mine, or rather my son's. I left my dress shoes at home and had to borrow a pair. These shoes are so small that it feels like medieval foot torture. Dave, I'm sorry the shoes were in your way."

Dave looked at Clay's woeful face. "Well, you made it through the ceremony."

Rob half chuckled, "Clay, your fatherly duties are not completely over. What will you wear for the father-daughter dance?"

"Oh, Shirley, must I do that?"

"Of course."

"What shoe size do you wear?" Eddie asked.

"A twelve, extra wide."

"Then you're in luck because that's my size." Eddie removed one of his shoes. "Here try on this. We can't have the father missing his daughter's dance."

"Ah, this shoe feels great."

Eddie smiled. "That's because it's broke in real proper. They've had a couple of weddings and a few funerals. So, Clay, if they fit, wear them the rest of the night. I'm not part of the wedding party, so the photographer won't be snapping my photo. And when it comes time for me to dance with my beautiful wife Jenna, well, it will be sort of a sock hop for me."

"I can honestly say that my daughter has married into a truly wonderful family. Thank you, Eddie. You saved the day!"

"And I'm glad to do it. Now take my other shoe and smile for all the cameras. No more grimacing tonight."

Shirley smiled wide, "Sandy told us that when she fell in love with Chip, she also fell in love with the Johnsons and the Dormans. I can clearly see why."

"Well, rest assured, we all love Sandy, too," Jenna said. "Our son Cole is also here with his wife Jo Lynn and their two sons. I'm sure they will be stopping by our table to meet you."

"And you have another son who couldn't make the trip?"

"Yes, that's Roy," Eddie said. "He's getting stronger every day, and he's looking forward to opening an organic farming operation with a partner. His wife Angela is a CPA and an important part of our farming operation. She not only keeps our books, but she keeps us straight with our taxes and investments."

"Dave, that's some family you have," Clay said. "I'd like for all of you to stop by our place before you leave Texas. Shirley and I thought it would be nice if you could stay a couple of nights and have some very fine barbecue out at our ranch. It would be our pleasure to host you."

"That would be lovely," Marylou said. "And it would give us a chance to really get to know you."

The waiter began pouring the toasting glasses. "Champagne or sparkling grape juice?"

Dave looked at the head table. "It looks like we're about to have the toast."

The tapping of glasses quieted the room, and Chip stood up and looked over the room, and adjusted the microphone.

"If you look at a wedding ring, you'll see that it's a complete circle. It's a circle that means much more than Sandy and me spending the rest of our lives together, building a future for ourselves and our children. It's a family circle that has expanded, today. I not only have a lovely wife, but I have two more parents Clay and Shirley, and four new brothers. And today, Sandy has two more parents Robert and Marylou and the most wonderful grandfather David Johnson. Of course, we cannot forget all the wonderful Dormans that Sandy can now call family. I also won't forget my generous Uncle Tim Higgins and his family, who couldn't be with us today. There is so much love among our families, including all my Texas cousins here today. Most importantly, Sandy and I want you to celebrate that our two families have now become one. May we all lift our glasses and toast to this love, to our expanded family, and to this marriage of Sandy and me.

"Here, here!" The crowd applauded and shouted.

Dave looked at everyone seated at the table. "Chip is so right. Today we are an expanded family with a moral obligation to this new couple. We have a responsibility to support and defend this holy marriage."

"As a God-fearing family, Shirley and I heartily agree," Clay said as his eyes welled up. "Shirley and I prayed daily that our Sandy would meet a nice farm boy from a Christian family. Today that prayer was fulfilled."

"Thank you for the acknowledgement," Dave replied.

"Now, here's the best part," Eddie said. "Dinner is being served."

Later when the band began to play, and the lead musician announced, "We'll begin with a special dance with Chip and Sandy, and then sometime during the song I'll announce the father-daughter dance."

The moment Chip and Sandy took to the dance floor, Marylou grabbed Shirley's hand. "Oh, Shirley, I feel so blessed to have such a sweet daughter-in-law."

"And I, too, feel blessed. Chip is a marvelous man. Clay and I could not be happier."

"Mr. Moore, will you please join your daughter Sandy on the dance floor?"

Shirley grabbed a hanky and wiped her tears as she as Clay took his daughter in his arms. "I didn't think I'd cry, but watching Clay and Sandy dance at her wedding, well, it's emotional for me."

"It's a very precious moment," Marylou said, "and your tears are quite beautiful."

"Okay, all you fathers out there," the lead musician said. "It's your turn. Please find your daughters and join Clay and Sandy on the dance floor."

Jenna stood up. "Daddy, I'm not going to miss this opportunity to dance with you."

"I agree," Dave said. He stood, and the two of them walked arm in arm to the dance floor, where the two hearts melted in admiration. "I remember how you'd stand on the tops of my shoes, and you'd reach up and take my hands as we danced around the living room."

"Yes, as Mama played the piano."

When the song ended the lead musician said, "Okay, y'all! My band and I are going to play one more slow-tune for you old folks, and then it's time to kick up our two-stepping heels. So, if there's a special gal you'd like to slow dance with, this is your final call."

Eddie looked at Jenna. "This is our dance, my sock-hop." He took Jenna's hand and led her out to the dance floor.

Jenna looked down at Eddie's feet. "Eddie, your big toe is poking clean through your sock, and that toenail looks like a swashbuckler's sword! When was the last time you clipped your nails? I wish you would have told me that your sock needed darning."

"Come now, Jenna. Where's your sense of humor? Life is always perfect when you're in my arms."

"Click, click." The photographer got a close-up of Eddie's big toe.

CHAPTER FORTY-FIVE

A New Friend

After being released from the hospital, Roy went into partnership with Jasper. Although Roy had orders from his physician to take it easy, he was anxious to get started. Jasper fully respected the doctor's orders, but as his friend, he insisted Roy not do anything strenuous. Both had shown a great appreciation for the land and wanted to grow organic fruits and vegetables, and naturally Dave wanted to see his grandson's business succeed.

The last bit of interior paint was finally dry on Jasper and Roy's old two-story house that was being converted into a storefront. Robert and daughter Jenna bought the property last year because it was adjacent to both the Johnson and the Dorman Farms. Little did they know at that time what a blessing their purchase turned out to be.

Excited to show off the progress, Jasper called Roy and Angela and invited them to see their new and improved store.

"We'd love to see the place," Angela said. "Roy's grandfather is here visiting, and I'm sure he'd like to join us."

"Great! Bring Grandpa Dave along. I think he'll be impressed."

The front rooms of Jasper and Roy's business had been completely refurbished to accommodate a modern coffee bar and check-out stands, yet it still maintained its old farmhouse appearance. As per the architect's plans, the exterior of the 1910s era gem had been restored to bring back its historic charm, and in the rear, contractors were busy working on the new addition that would enlarge their store by four times. The new section would eventually provide a modern space to store and display all of their organic fruits and vegetables.

When Dave, Angela and Roy arrived, they were stunned by the unexpected illuminated sign along the highway mounted on a tall pole. The sign displayed carrots, tomatoes, lettuce, and squash and the brightly colored words that stated: *Coming Soon! Corinth Organic Market.* It was only moments later when they noticed that the sign changed to read: "Free wake-up coffee to all first responders in uniform 6-10 a.m."

"Now doesn't that beat all?" Dave said.

Roy gasped. "Jasper told me that the architect had a great idea for a sign, but I didn't expect something this big or expensive."

"He's sure burning through his ten-million-dollar trust fund," Angela said.

"Ah, he's having fun," Dave said. "Let's not spoil his accomplishment with negative thoughts or words."

"Fair enough, Angela said, "but he has also hired a professional decorator for his new house, and he has begun going over plans with a landscaping company to refresh his gardens and that large gazebo in his backyard."

Jasper met them on the front porch. "Come in! Come in where it's warm. What did you think of the sign? Really something, isn't it?"

"All say," Roy said.

"Just wait until you see the inside." Jasper led the way.

"My, oh my!" Dave said. You've eliminated most of the downstairs walls."

"Yep. The contractors put in these long steel beams to support the upstairs."

"It's stunning!" Roy said. "This is the nicest coffee lounge I've ever seen."

"Our architect wanted to keep much of the original elements of the house and blend them with the new."

"I can see that!" Angela said. "The cozy seating around the fireplace is a nice touch, and it looks like the original mantle and surround."

"Yep! It sure is, but the bookshelves on both sides are new. They were made with old wood to look like it was part of the original house. Do you want to see the upstairs?"

"Of course," Dave said.

Roy turned to his grandfather. "It's going to be our office."

"It will be, Ol' Buddy, but the electricians need to finish all the wiring, and the carpeting hasn't been installed."

"When do you expect to be open for business?" Angela asked.

"We have all of our licenses and permits. We're just waiting on our final inspections. I've ordered a thousand bio-degradable seed cups, and as soon as the seeds start sprouting in our green houses, we can start selling."

"That's after our soil and seeds are delivered, and after we fill the cups," Roy said. "Rest assured I'm strong enough to do that!"

Angela asked, "Roy, would you like to join us for dinner?"

"I'll take a raincheck. I'm eating with your Aunt Marylou and Uncle Rob tonight. With Sandy and Chip still on their honeymoon, I guess they aren't used to eating with an empty chair at the table. Besides, I can walk to their house, though it's a bit of a hike, and Uncle Rob said he'll drive me home."

"I don't have a license or a car but I make do."

The following Friday was the thirteenth, when bad things happen for the superstitious and satanic worshippers, but not for God fearing Christians. This morning was very cold, and the sun wouldn't rise for another hour. Jasper dawned his heavy coat, gloves and knit cap, and with flashlight in hand walked next door to the Corinth Organic Market. This was his daily morning routine before six. He would make coffee for the construction workers and for any first responders who happened to stop by in need of a hot drink.

As he neared the store, he noticed an old Ford Taurus parked in front of the store. It was odd, because the workmen always parked their trucks and vehicles in the rear of the store, and never showed up before daylight. Even more strange, the motor was running. Jasper walked up to the car and shined a light though the passenger window and saw a young lady shivering in the front seat.

The window rolled down, and the lady said, “I’m sorry I’m not a first responder, but I’d like a cup of coffee, if you can spare one.”

“Absolutely! We can’t have you sitting out here in the cold. You come on inside and warm up. I’ll get you some coffee, as soon as it’s ready.”

Jasper unlocked the store, and the young lady got out of her car and followed him inside.

“The temperature in here is only fifty-five degrees because I don’t crank up the heat until morning, but I can turn on the gas fireplace with just a click of a switch.” Jasper turned on the lights and then the fireplace. “See, it’s an instant flame, and I turned the room thermostat up to seventy. Go sit by the fire while I start the coffee. It won’t take long. I have these two urns, and I get them ready the night before so all I have to do is plug them in. On cold days like today, the workmen will empty them both before the day is out, but don’t you worry. We’ll get you thawed out with a hot cup of coffee and a warm fire.”

“Thank you, sir,” the young lady held out her hands by the fire before she sat on a nearby club chair.

“Oh, you don’t have to call me sir. Call me Jasper. What’s your name?”

“Pamela Rose. Rose is my last name.”

“That’s a pretty name. The coffee won’t take long. Do you use cream and sugar?”

“Yes, please.”

“Then that’s what you will get—cream and sugar.”

Pamela was tall and quite thin; most would say too thin. She had tape on her glasses to keep the temples in place and holes in her sweater. In addition, her teeth were so crooked that her uppers didn’t point south, and her lowers couldn’t find north. In addition, her two twisted front teeth had a wide gap. Her long stringy brown hair draped down below her shoulders, and when she removed her knit cap, it was obvious that her hair needed a good shampoo, and her body shouted for a bath. Anyone who saw her would say her best feature was the small rose tattooed on her right cheek.

Jasper sat down on the opposite club chair. "My workers will be here soon to fill up their thermoses, but in the meantime, tell me why you're living in your car."

"When I was fourteen, my dad died. He was sick for a long time. I loved my dad. He left me his car in his will. When I turned sixteen, my mother remarried. I don't have much good to say about my stepdad. On occasion he hits my mother. My dad never did that. Before my mom remarried, she agreed that I was to move out when I turned eighteen. That's because my stepdad said he'd only support me until then. So, here I am, eighteen—penniless, cold, and hungry, but I do have a car."

"And a car is a good thing."

"Jasper, I see you also have a tat on your face. I got this rose tat on my cheek because the lady who put it on me wouldn't do tear drops like I wanted. She said that I won't always feel sad, so she convinced me to make it a rose like my last name. I see you have a lightning bolt on your cheek. Is there a significance to that?"

"Not really. At one point in my life, I just thought it would be cool to have it tattooed on my cheek. I don't think it's cool now, and I wish it wasn't there, but I had it done before I knew Jesus. Tell me, Pamela. Do you know Jesus?"

She thought for a moment. "Maybe. What's his last name?"

"Well, for now, let's just say you haven't met him. You see, Jesus is my boss, but he's much more than that." Jasper paused for a moment and bowed his head in quiet prayer.

Pamela sat puzzled, staring at Jasper during this time.

"I tell you what, Pamela Rose. Would you like a job here? Very soon we'll have a thousand seed cups to fill and keep watered. It's an easy job, and I know you can do it if you're willing to learn."

"I'd love a job, and I really need one."

"That's good, but we can't have you living out of your car. If you agree to work here and be a good employee for three months, you won't have to pay the company back for your three months of rent on an apartment. How does that sound?"

"An apartment! That sounds wonderful. Will I get a paycheck, too?"

"Absolutely."

"Do you need approval from your boss Jesus?"

"I just got it, and you have a job and an apartment for three months. You see, when you believe in Jesus, you have a direct line with the God, the Creator of the universe. It's called prayer."

"Is that what you were doing when put your head down, talking to God?"

"Yes, indeed," he gently patted his chest, "because God is inside all believers. Do you believe there's a God?"

"I don't know. I haven't thought about it."

"Would you like to think about it?"

"I suppose so."

"Good, then you've come to the right place. Now, before you start working for me and Roy, you'll need to fill out some employment forms over at Angela and Roy's house, so I hope you won't mind driving us to downtown Corinth after the workers get their coffee. We'll stop by the diner and order some breakfast before heading over to Roy and Angela's place. Does that sound good?"

"Yes, thank you. I sure would like breakfast."

Jasper sniffed the air. "I think the coffee is ready. Let me get you a cup. The workmen will be here in a minute, so I'll jump to the front of the line just for you. You said cream and sugar?"

"Yes, please."

"Here you are. I hope this hits the spot and warms you while I make a phone call. Please excuse me. I won't be long." Jasper dashed upstairs and closed the door to the office for privacy and called Angela on his cellphone. "Hello, Angela, I just hired a homeless girl. It's a three-month deal. If she works out, we may keep her on. Angela, I want to pay for all of her wages and expenses for the next three months. It's only fair because I didn't ask Roy about this. …I'm going to take her to breakfast and then we'll stop by to sign employment papers. …Thanks, Angela, and would you do me a favor and find out if there is an available furnished apartment in Corinth. …Ah, thanks, Angela. If I had a sister, I would want her to be just like you."

After breakfast, Jasper and Pamela stopped by Roy and Angela's home.

"Come in, come in! It's cold out there. I'm Roy Dorman and you must be Pamela, our first employee. I'd say being first is an honor. Isn't that right, Jasper?"

"Yes, it is, Ol' Buddy."

"Pamela, step in the office and meet my wife, Angela. She keeps the books on my family's farms and will be doing the same for the Corinth Organic Market."

"I'm pleased to meet you, ma'am."

"Thank you, and I am also pleased to meet you. When Angela saw Pamela's condition, she immediately talked about the apartment. "Jasper, here is the address of the place that has an available furnished apartment. I asked them to hold it until noon because it's their last one. Pamela, here is the form that we need, and once it's filled out, then Roy and Jasper can officially welcome you to their business." Angela handed Pamela a clipboard and a pen. "If you have any questions, Roy will help you. And, Jasper, I need to show you something in our kitchen."

Jasper and Angela walked down the hall, through the kitchen, and onto the back porch.

"Jasper, it's as though you have picked up a wounded stray kitten. That poor girl needs lots of help and an apartment is just the beginning."

"I thought so, too."

"Here's a check from your personal account. If you write it for more than twenty-five hundred, let me know and I'll transfer money from your savings account. You can always ask the apartment if they take a credit card."

"Thanks, Angela."

"Does she have any clean clothes? Because what she's wearing is filthy and quite smelly."

"I don't know if she has any clean clothes, but her back seat is full of clothing. She had to make room for me in the passenger seat, so she tossed lots of clothes there."

"Jasper, I'm going to give you a bottle of laundry detergent. Put it in her car while I look over her employment paperwork. I want you to help her find a laundromat if there isn't one in the apartment complex."

Angela walked back inside and returned to her office. "Have you finished filling out the form?"

"Yes, ma'am."

"Great. Pamela, I think having your very first apartment is quite exciting, and I've got a housewarming present just for you as a celebration gift. Wait here and I'll be right back."

Angela gathered many necessities that Pamela would need and returned with a large wicker laundry basket. "In our house, there are spur of the moment occasions when guests spend the night with us, and naturally they didn't bring an overnight bag. In which case, I always keep a guest basket just for this purpose."

Pamela took the large wicker basket from Angela and started crying. "Thank you! No one has ever given me something this nice. I've always been shamed and bullied by people. May I call you, my friend?"

Angela held her breath as she accepted Pamela's heartfelt hug. "Of course, we are all your friends. There are soaps, bath salts, toothbrush and tooth paste, shampoo and conditioner, lotion, a roll of toilet paper, and a full set of towels. Congratulations on your very first home."

"I don't know how to thank you."

"You just did, Pamela."

"But I don't understand. Why is everyone so kind to me?"

"Pamela, we do it for Jesus."

"Your boss Jesus?"

"In many ways He is our boss, but we worship Him as our Lord and Savior. I'm going to give you this card. On one side it has the Lord's Prayer, and on the other side is the Twenty-Third Psalm. Keep it close to you. Read it daily. Here I'll put it in your basket. Now, you need to scoot over to that new apartment before the manager rents it to someone else. I believe Jasper is waiting for you by your car."

CHAPTER FORTY-SIX

Late January

The Birthday Breakfast

Sixty-five didn't feel old to Eddie Dorman, but in a few days, it would be a special milestone for him. He was about to qualify for Medicare, so Dave suggested that Eddie join Cole, Roy, Chip, Robert for an early birthday breakfast at the Corinth Diner.

As they entered the restaurant, the cook behind the counter greeted them with a smile. "Well, Dave, it looks like you have all your boys with you."

"Yep. We're having sort of a birthday celebration for Eddie."

The waitress stopped by their table with a tray of water glasses.

"Thank you, Evelyn," Dave said with his usual charming smile.

"Well, happy birthday, Eddie. You just missed Jasper. He was in here with your new gal Pamela, or maybe it's his new gal." She gave us a suspecting wink. "I see that Pam's now wearing braces and fancy new eyeglasses."

"Evelyn what would we do without you?" Robert said. "I can always depend on you to give me the latest news."

"It's a talent of mine. I won't pass out menus if all of you fellas want the hunter's special."

“Yes, please, the hunter’s special all the way around, and lots of coffee.” Dave turned to Cole. “I’m glad you and your father have of your new field planted in peach trees.”

It’s more peaches than we wanted in one field,” Eddie said, “but if we have some great peaches in the years to come, it will pay off, and we can always divide up that field later.”

Cole looked at his father proudly. “We also planted a hedge row to separate our peaches from Roy and Jasper’s organic operation. Pop, that was a lot of work, so tell us something special you’d like to do today to celebrate your birthday? There’s not much happening on the farms, and our workers can take care of the daily chores.”

“Yeah, Pop,” Roy chimed in. “That’s a great idea, and since we’re all here together, do you have a suggestion?”

Dave said, “It’s supposed to a warm day with a high temperature near sixty degrees.”

“This may sound crazy, but I’d like to drive over to Atlantic Tractor and check out all the new John Deere's and especially their latest combines. Angela wouldn’t want me to even think about any million-dollar pipe dream, but looking over the new farm equipment will make me feel like I was in high school again. Those were the days when I would cut school to see the latest Corvette on display at the dealership. In fact, I was anxious to see all the new models.”

“Uncle Eddie, Atlantic Tractor is a great idea!” Chip said. “I’d like to do that, too.”

“When I married Jenna, I brought with me to the marriage my own combine. It was only a four-year-old machine back then. Today it’s over thirty, and it’s getting harder and harder to find spare parts.”

“Very hard,” Chip said. “I dread having to fix the Dorman Combine for that very reason. I’m constantly looking for used models like yours for spare parts.”

“Then it’s settled,” Dave said. “After breakfast let’s go check out all the John Deeres and drool over their latest and greatest.”

The back lot of Atlantic Tractor was a vast field of John Deere equipment, tractors, combines, and platforms. The trademark green paint with yellow trim was a billboard all by itself. Everyone who drove past the place knew instantly what they were selling.

As the men walked around the sales lot, Eddie spotted an S-790 deluxe combine that came with all the bells and whistles, including a remote diagnostic reading feature. "Isn't it a beauty? A guy can only dream of harvesting with this machine."

"I wonder what it costs," Dave said.

"I'm wondering how to repair a fancy machine like that with all the new electronics," Chip said.

"Whatever it costs," Roy said, "the price tag will give Angela heartburn just to figure out how to pay for it."

"If we were to buy it, last year would have been the year. You know Angela. She wants us to put our bounty back into the farm for tax reasons," Rob said. "That why Jenna and I bought the Bennett farm and planted new peach orchards. We also gave all our out-buildings a needed facelift, and Joe got a bedroom. We'd have to have another record year to buy this piece of equipment."

It wasn't long before a salesman came out to greet the men. "I see you like this S-790"

"Show me a farmer who wouldn't," Eddie said. "May I climb up into the cab? I can dream much better up there."

"Absolutely."

Eddie entered the cab. His smile stretched from ear to ear as he looked down on the other men watching him enjoy the combine.

Cole chuckled. "Dad looks like you and me when we were kids and were pretending to drive a car."

Roy turned to the salesman. "How much is this model?"

"This particular combine with the three platforms you'll need comes to about one point two million."

"Woah!" Roy was shocked.

"I'm glad my dad is still up there in that cab where he can't hear you," Cole said.

"Yes, but she's a real beauty," Dave said, "and I'm going to ask Angela if there is any way we can buy this machine."

"Dream on, Dad," Rob said.

"Well, I can ask, can't I? Soon we'll need to replace our combines."

Chip pulled the salesman aside. "Is there a John Deere school I can attend to learn how to repair these beasts?"

"Sure. Stop by my office and I'll give you some paperwork on that."

When Eddie climbed down from the cab, he was overwhelmed with excitement. "This is the sort of combine I see in my dreams. I'm telling you sons, if you saw what I just saw up in that cab you'd be counting your pennies to buy one."

"Dad, you'll have to count more than that," Roy said. "It's one point two."

"As in—one point two million?"

"Yep. That's right, Dad."

"Well, it was nice of all of you to humor me for my birthday. I guess we better head home."

A few days later, when Eddie turned sixty-five, everyone gathered around the Dorman dining table for supper and birthday celebrations, singing *Happy Birthday to You!*

"Make a wish, Grandpa," little Jake said.

"Yeah, make a big wish," Hudson chimed in. "Mommy only put one candle on the cake so you could blow it out in one breath."

Although Eddie didn't express his wish, Dave, Robert and the grandsons all knew what he really wanted—a new John Deere combine.

CHAPTER FORTY-SEVEN

The Old Shirt Factory Fire

Pamela was up early at her apartment. She had set her alarm for five, but around four in the morning she was awoken by the faint smell of smoke. She jumped out of bed and looked around her apartment. Seeing nothing ominous, she stepped outside and saw smoke billowing out of the old, abandoned shirt factory which was about a half mile away and located just outside the town limits. With no cellphone to call the fire department, she dressed quickly and hopped in her car. By the time she reached the end of her driveway, sirens began to blare all over town. It was obvious that the authorities had been alerted, so rather than drive to the police department, she parked in front of the Corinth Donut shop, ran up to the door, and banged on it until someone let her in.

"There's a huge fire, and I want to buy donuts for the first responders." Pamela was nearly out of breath as she spoke, and by now flames began to light up the sky. "Here's sixty dollars. It's all the money I have, but I'll buy as many donuts as I can."

"I'm sorry. It will be another thirty minutes for fresh," the baker said, "or I can let you have these day-olds for half price."

"I'll take the day-olds, please, sixty dollars' worth."

Sheriff Ken Stewart was notified by radio moments before the first siren blared across the region. Without missing a beat, he dressed, grabbed his coat, hat, and gloves and he headed for his car. He was first on the scene and immediately reported back to the dispatcher. Corinth's two fire trucks, engine, and ambulance were on their way.

A nearby streetlight revealed the billowing black smoke coming out of the out the rear of the building, and it also exposed a silhouette of a large man coughing as he tried to exit the building. He had fallen about eight feet short of the door.

Sherriff Stewart ran towards the downed person who was overcome by smoke.

"Sir, give me your arm," he yelled, "and I'll get you out of here."

Adrenaline was pumping hard as the two left the building. The flashing lights of the first ambulance were a welcome sight as it pulled into the parking lot. A medic rushed to the victim's side and placed an oxygen mask over his face.

"Are there others in the building?" the medic asked.

The middle-aged victim shook his head which gave everyone a sense of relief.

After he was placed on a gurney and loaded into the ambulance, the victim caught his breath and could talk without coughing. Sheriff Steward asked how the fire started.

"I was cold," the victim explained. "So, I started a small fire with some busted up floorboards. I didn't realize how fast it could get out of hand."

Once the ambulance headed for the hospital, Sheriff Steward turned his attention to the conflagration. When the north side of the building collapsed, the fire chief made the decision to let the building burn out and use all the firemen to keep the surrounding buildings out of harm's way.

The loud sirens woke Jasper from a deep sleep. Every out-of-town fire truck that headed to the conflagration passed by his house and his store. Although he couldn't see the fire, he knew whenever several fire companies were involved, he'd need to get the coffee brewing at his Organic Market. He bundled up and walked next door to his store, where he noticed that Pamela had already arrived and had started the coffee urns.

"What's this I see? Dozens of donuts. Did you buy all of this?"

"Yes. I figured at four in the morning, not too many firemen had a chance to get a bite to eat before heading out to the fire. They won't stop here going in, but when they're done putting out the fire, they'll be exhausted and hungry."

"Well, I'll be, Pamela. You just made our boss Jesus quite pleased. Thinking of others was a very nice gesture. I guess I better retype the sign to read, *free coffee and donuts for all first responders*."

"Take a look out the window, Jasper. I've already changed it."

"Wow-wee! When I hired you, I asked you to be a good employee. You have exceeded my expectations."

"Thank you, Jasper. I wanted to prove myself to be worthy."

"Pamela, you are worthy, and I hope no one tells you otherwise. Today or tomorrow, we are expecting a delivery of soil from Gordon's Nursery. He has developed a great soil mixture for all our seed cups. You'll have to fill them and set them up in our greenhouses. That will be your next task, and Roy will help you with that. There's one thing, though. I want you to keep an eye on him. If Roy starts looking tired, tell him to lie down. We have a bed for him up in the office."

"I can do that."

"I know you can, because that's the sort of person you are. Pamela, there's a story in the Bible where all these wealthy men tossed lots of money into the offering plate, but this poor widow only gave two mites. Jesus then said that the wealthy donors gave from their abundance, whereas, the poor widow, who gave two only mites, gave all that she had. That's why Jesus made the point that the widow gave more than the wealthy men because of her great sacrifice." Jasper kissed Pamela on the forehead. "You spent all your money on donuts so that the firemen could have something to eat after putting out that fire. You are very kind, Pamela, and that's why I like you."

"Will you teach me more about the Bible?"

"I'd love to, but there's so much I don't know. What I'm saying is, we both need to be in a Bible study, and maybe that's something we can do together. I know Joe would like us to join him for Bible study over at the bunkhouse, so let's tell him we'll be his new students."

"I'd like that, Jasper."

CHAPTER FORTY-EIGHT

Late April

Heavy rain welcomed Cole and Jo Lynn when they brought their beautiful baby girl home from the hospital. They named her Audrey Elisabeth Dorman to honor both Eddie and Jenna's grandmothers, but it wasn't the only good news for the family. Chip and Sandy announced that they were expecting to welcome their first baby in late November.

"More little farmers," Dave said with a wide smile, as he held tiny Audrey in his arms. "We love our babies, and I'm glad more are on their way. Here, Eddie, it's your turn to hold her."

Eddie sat in his man-sized chair before carefully taking his new granddaughter in his arms. "Jenna and I love being grandparents, and little Audrey is a delight. Hudson, Jake, come over here and visit with your baby sister. I held both of you boys when you were this little, and I believe it was raining cats and dogs just like today when you first came home."

Cole looked out the living room window. "Do you think it will let up soon?"

"I hope so, son. I'm sure this downpour is tearing up our driveway by the barn and the bunkhouse. What do you say you and me take Big Red out tomorrow and pick up a load of stone at the gravel pit?"

"Sounds good to me, Pop."

The following morning the sun cast a warm glow in the sky. It was sure to be a great drying-out day. Cole and Eddie hopped in

Big Red and backed it out of their barn. Eddie drove the dump truck and headed for the bridge on the edge of town.

"You're not going to take Big Red across the Corinth Bridge?" Cole asked.

"It's the shortest way, but don't worry. I'm not too crazy. I'll go the long way around when we're loaded with stone, even though it's twenty miles longer."

"I don't mind the extra distance, Pop."

Eddie had just started across the bridge when he saw the front end of an approaching car suddenly sink into the bridge's decking.

"Cole, did you see that?"

"Stop the truck, Pop! There's a problem with this bridge. Can you back up?"

"I can't. There's a pickup behind me. Cole, that car up ahead looks like Carrie Russell's Lincoln. You better go see if she's okay while I call 9-1-1."

Cole hopped out of the truck and ran toward Carrie's car. Seeing that her airbags had been deployed, he opened the driver's side door. Carrie was visibly shaken. "Mrs. Russell, can you hear me? It's Cole Dorman."

"Yes, Cole." Her weakened voice signaled trouble. "Can you help me?"

Cole noticed that she would need immediate medical attention. He looked toward the town and saw Deputy Helen Ward standing on the bridge urging cars to back up.

"We are condemning this bridge," she yelled. "You must back up toward the town."

The town police were also frustrated by the motorist not heeding their instructions to turn around so that the bridge could be cleared. Even town manager Darryl Ward, who was drawn out of his office by the commotion, was on the scene.

Cole vigorously waved his arms to get Deputy Ward's attention as he called out for help. She ran towards Mrs. Russell's car.

"Helen! Mrs. Russell needs an ambulance."

"We can't risk any more weight on this bridge with an emergency vehicle," Deputy Ward said. "There's an ambulance waiting on the town-side of the bridge. Mrs. Russell, if Cole and I support you, do you think you can make it that far?"

"I'll try."

With Carrie's arms around Cole and Helen, the three made it just past halfway when Carrie's weakened body collapsed. "I'll carry her to the ambulance. It's not that much farther. You take care of clearing the bridge."

As Cole passed his father holding Mrs. Russell in his arms, Eddie, who was still inside Big Red, called out, "Do you need help, son?"

"I can manage, thanks." And he did manage to carry Mrs. Russell to safety where medics quickly placed her on a gurney and then inside the ambulance.

"I'm scared, Cole. Please don't leave me," Carrie pleaded.

Cole held Mrs. Russell's hand and comforted her, "I'll contact your husband, so he can meet you at the hospital, but I will have to hop out as soon as this ambulance has a clear path to the hospital. The Sheriff is asking folks to move off the road, so you should be on your way soon."

Relieved that the pile-up of cars was finally moving, Deputy Ward approached the two remaining vehicles stuck on the bridge to let the drivers know they could begin to back up. Sheriff Ken Stewart stood by as the pickup made it off the bridge to safety. "Okay, Deputy, let Eddie know that there's room for him to back up and get that dump truck off the bridge."

But as Deputy Ward neared Eddie's cab, the bridge began to shake violently. "Get out of your truck and off this bridge!" she yelled to Eddie as she began to feel the bridge collapsing. With fierce vibrations underfoot, Deputy Ward sprinted towards the town. With only a couple of steps to go, Sheriff Stewart and her husband grabbed her arms and pulled her to safety, just as the east side of the bridge fell into the stream below, taking Eddie and Big Red with it.

"Pop!" Cole jumped out of the ambulance and was immediately stopped by Sheriff Stewart.

“Cole, I know you want to climb down that embankment to be by your father, but you must let the firemen rescue Eddie. They’re all here and have trained for these emergencies. I need you get back in that ambulance and stay with Miss Carrie. I’ll ask Deputy Ward to fetch your mother and meet you at the hospital.”

Cole knew Sheriff Stewart was right, so he stepped up into the ambulance and watched as the sheriff closed the door. He called his brother, who said he and Angela would walk the few blocks to the hospital so they could all be together as family.

Eddie and Sheriff Stewart were close friends, so seeing Eddie fall from the bridge made the incident more horrifying. Just before the bridge collapsed, the sheriff noticed that Eddie must have released his seat belt because he noticed that Eddie had one leg outside the door and on the truck’s running board.

CHAPTER FORTY-NINE

Hospital Visitors

As paramedics transported Eddie into the emergency room. Roy, Angela, and Cole sat huddled in the family waiting area, clutching one another's hands. The voices of hurried medical staff echoed down the hall and over the sound system which gave Roy and Cole a glimmer of hope that their father was still alive. They knew their mother would arrive shortly, but they had no idea when they'd receive a doctor's initial report on Eddie's condition.

Larry and Cathy Dunn, who also lived in town, learned that the bridge had collapsed, and were shocked to learn that Eddie was one of the casualties. They, too, dashed to the hospital where they met up with the family. No words needed to be expressed as their hugs of compassion said it all. Long-time friend Cathy was like a sister to Jenna, so this accident was most heartfelt.

Moments later Deputy Ward and Jenna arrived. "Any word yet?" Jenna asked.

"No," Roy said, "But we believe Dad's still with us."

Jenna took a deep breath and grabbed Cathy's hand. "Thank you for being here with me."

Twenty then forty minutes passed before the emergency physician on duty entered the room. "Mrs. Dorman, Eddie has multiple injuries, and he's covered with mud. Those who rescued Eddie said he was thrown from his truck as it tumbled down from the bridge. We've given him something for pain, but he's alive, and he has mumbled a few words—though nothing coherent. We will need x-rays and an MRI to know the full extent of his injuries. Time is not on our side until we know what we are dealing with, so may I suggest that you use this afternoon to get something to eat and get the personal items you may need for tonight. It's almost eleven now. Perhaps if you come back at two, say after lunch, we can discuss the full extent of his injuries. Now, if you'll excuse me, I must get back to the patient."

Cathy put her arms around Jenna. "I'll make sure the staff puts a sleeping chair in Eddie's room for you."

Larry took Jenna's hand and chimed in, "Cathy and I have agreed to take care of all the legal work for you—pro bono. We want you to focus on Eddie and let us handle all the insurance and liability issues so that you're not overwhelmed by paperwork during Eddie's recovery."

Cathy put her arms around her longtime friend. "Jenna, we are like sisters, and this is something Larry and I want do for you."

Jenna became weepy-eyed. "Thank you for your generosity and care."

"Dry your eyes, sweetie, and be grateful that I'm only handling your legal matters rather than making you a meal." Both ladies giggled. "Courtrooms I can handle, but I need to stay out of the kitchen."

"Oh, Cathy, you and Larry are simply wonderful friends."

Mrs. Russell, while lying in her hospital bed, watched Reverend Hayworth enter her room. She had suffered a mild heart attack and one black eye from her car's airbag and would be hospitalized for a few days. She looked into the minister's eyes. "Reverend, is Martin here?"

"He is, Carrie, but he wants to compose himself before seeing you. By chance, I met him in the hospital parking lot. He's a broken man, tearful and full of remorse, so I suggested to him that we first go to the hospital chapel and talk."

"Reverend, it wasn't by chance that the two of you met. It was an answer to my countless prayers."

"I believe you're right, Carrie, because in the chapel he shared his guilt with me, and he wants to share his shame with the county. He now realizes how wrong and selfish he had been regarding the condition of the bridge. Then the two of us got down on our knees, and Matin prayed the sinner's prayer. I believe his spiritual eyes have been opened. With you in the hospital and Eddie Dorman's life hanging in the balance, Martin is broken and will need time so his emotional pain can heal, but he's here, waiting in the hall, and he has some important things to tell you."

That afternoon Jenna, Cole and Roy returned to the hospital to sit with the emergency physician and learn about Eddie's extensive injuries.

"He has a broken pelvis, collar bone, and femur that will need to be pinned. He has had a concussion, and a severe laceration that will also need surgery. The good news is, we've cleaned him up and his injuries are all fixable, but he'll be hospitalized for some time."

"How long?" Jenna asked.

"Let's take it one day at a time. But first, give your husband twenty-four hours because his body has suffered a great deal. We will know more tomorrow."

CHAPTER FIFTY

The Homecoming Mid-June

As the weeks passed and after the winter wheat had been harvested, the vast fields on the Johnson and Dorman farms displayed acres of gray-brown stubble. Though the yield was not as successful as the previous year, their crop proved to be profitable, and now the land was ready for planting corn and soybeans.

Inside the Dorman kitchen the women were busy preparing a grand luncheon to welcome Eddie home. With the house overflowing with love, it was about to be a glorious welcoming. Guests included all the Johnsons and the Dormans, Cathy and Larry Dunn, Reverend Hayworth, Martin and Carrie Russell, Sheriff Stewart, Helen and Darryl Ward, and all their neighbors.

Outside, Walter, Darcy and Joe were busy putting the final touches on the flowerbeds. Walter paused for a moment and leaned on his hoe while admiring his work. "Miss Jenna wants the gardens to be beautiful when Mr. Eddie comes home, and she's gonna get her wish."

Their work was interrupted by the rumble of a new John Deere combine driving up their lane by their neighbor Mr. Stevenson. Darcy stood in the driveway and directed him where to park it—next to the new, shiny red Mack six-wheel dump truck which was parked on the lawn in front of the house.

Mr. Stevenson climbed down from the combine. "Eddie is sure gonna be surprised when he pulls into his driveway."

"That's what we all expect," Joe said. "And he should be here soon. Cole and Roy went to get him, and we should wash up and join the party."

The new farm vehicles slowly came into view as Cole, Roy and Eddie approached their house. Completely flabbergasted by the new truck and combine in his front yard, Eddie said, "What's this all about?"

"We promised Mom that we'd let her explain," Roy said as he and Cole helped their father out of the SUV and into a wheelchair. "This ramp we're going up was built by Chip, Joe, Darcy and Walter, and it's coming down as soon as you're able to toss this wheelchair."

Hudson and Jake held open the screen and front doors as the men entered. "Welcome home, Grandpa," Hudson said.

Jake took Eddie's hand. "We missed you, Grandpa."

The main hall was lined with guests to greet Eddie, who followed him into the living room. Jenna leaned over and kissed Eddie.

Eddie took Jenna's hand and placed it on his heart. "Okay, love, now tell me about that dump truck and combine on our front yard."

"While I was spending most of my time with you at the hospital, Cathy and Larry took it upon themselves to handle all the legal work for us. That truck and combine represents the fruits of their labor, but that's not all. Mr. and Mrs. Russell bought you three platforms for the combine."

Martin stood next to Eddie. "It doesn't assuage my guilt for not getting the bridge inspected, but I felt it was the least I could do, and I hope you can forgive my negligence."

"Of course, I can! Forgiveness is what life is all about."

Rob said, "While Chip was away at school getting certified to work on the latest John Deere machines and tractors, Clyde Stevenson pitched in and helped us harvest our wheat. Clyde only asked that he could drive the new combine from the dealership to Corinth."

"Well, Clyde, you certainly deserved that pleasure. And my old combine?"

Chip chimed in, "Uncle Eddie, I was having so much trouble finding parts for it, Dad and I decided to sell it."

"A wise decision," Eddie smiled.

Jo Lynn tapped a glass with a spoon. "Lunch is ready and laid out buffet-style on the dining table. Cole, would you please say the blessing, and then we can start. Please help yourselves after our guest of honor."

While dozens of friends and family members enjoyed the luncheon, Rob walked over to his brother-in-law. "It really is great to see you back home, and I'm counting on you to be fully recovered in time for deer season."

"You won't have to worry about that. I'll be up and around long before the leaves turn colors."

"One other thing, Eddie," Rob said. "Sis and I decided to use our reserve money to stock the front of Roy and Jasper's store with made in America gifts with a special section for items manufactured on Delmarva. We did that knowing that we'd have a profitable harvest on our wheat. I hope you don't mind that Jenna and I made this decision without you. We also stocked their market with organic produce."

"That's very generous of you to do that for my boy, but, Rob, how and where on earth did you source all of this merchandise?"

"Well, Roy and Jasper's friend from Mapledale, Mr. Gordon, hooked the fellas up with an organic produce wholesaler, and Jasper hired a professional buyer to find all the gifts. She's also a wonderful display artist. You need to stop by the store and see how good it looks. Pamela has been doing a great job running the coffee bar and keeping the shelves stocked. In fact," Rob looked across the room. "Jasper, Pamela come over here and tell Eddie your good news."

Eddie looked at Pamela. "What's this diamond I see on your hand?"

Jasper smiled proudly. "Pamela and I are engaged."

"Well, I'll be! Congratulations. I away from home for several weeks, and all sorts of wonderful things happen."

Jenna looked at Dave and noticed how tired he looked. "Are you okay, Daddy? Would you like to lie down?"

"Oh no. It's just with so many people in the house, the air feels a bit close. I think I'll go out on the front porch and sit in my rocker for a spell. Don't you worry about me, Jenna. I'll be back for dessert."

Dave walked outside, sat on his porch rocker, and reached down to pet his dog Samson. As he looked out onto his freshly harvested land, the gray-brown stubble instantly turned a verdant green. It was his favorite site, a vast field of young winter wheat that had recently poked up from the ground. "Did you see that, Audrey? Our field turned green before our eyes."

"Yes, I saw that."

Dave turned his head towards Audrey's rocker and saw his wife as beautiful as she was on their wedding day—his fondest memory of her. She was even wearing her long, white bridal gown.

"And, David, if you look around, you'll notice blooms on the magnolia trees. And look at the wisteria, the forsythia, tulips, roses, day lilies, and dahlias are all in bloom."

"Audrey, there's so much color! I've never seen all the plants flowering at the same time, even our redbud tree is shedding its crimson petals. Your father called it the Passover tree because when we sit under the redbud tree as its petals flutter down, it should remind us that we are under the grace of God. Let's go sit on our bench under that tree for old time's sake."

The two walked across the lawn and sat facing the house. "David, look at the front porch. Your daughter Jenna has just discovered that you have passed, and now she's going back in the house for help."

"But she's not just my daughter. Jenna is *our* daughter."

"No, David, I'm not Audrey, only your favorite memory of her. I'm an angel sent by God. He knows how you struggled in this life. Things weren't always easy for you."

"No, they weren't."

"When your father died of a heart attack in his early fifties, you had to take on the work of two men to keep the farm going. It was several weeks before Audrey's father could find and hire extra help for you. Do you remember how you cried alone in the barn because you hadn't slept for days, and how you worried about saving the farm? However, you weren't alone because God saw your tears and heard your pleas for help. He recognized your deep desire to provide for your two toddlers, a wife, and a mother."

"Recalling those days is very painful for me."

"But I have some good news that will give you joy. Chip and Sandy will welcome into this world a beautiful little boy on Thanksgiving Day."

"A son!"

"Yes, and they'll name him in honor of you, David William Johnson. But that's not all. They will eventually have two more boys—Robert David and Charles David Johnson."

"Three Johnson great-grandsons when I only asked God for one! My cup runneth over!"

"David, before you leave this life, God wanted you to have one last glimpse at the blessings you received here on earth. They are standing on your front porch—most of your friends and family. We don't always see our friends and family members as gifts from God, but they truly are, including Timothy who will return to Corinth for your funeral. He will be anxious to see his brother and sister again along with his Aunt Millie. All their relationships will continue to grow. David, love is the greatest blessing, and the people on your porch represent the love you shared with them, and they with you."

"You said one last glimpse? Are you saying I won't remember my life here on earth?"

"That's right, but heaven is a most glorious place. Audrey is waiting for you, and most of all, you will be in the presence of God, which is the most magnificent gift one could have."

Dave watched as they carried his limp body inside the house, and after the last person was indoors, rather than feeling sad, Dave was satisfied.

The angel said in a soft tone, "In a few moments Jesus will escort you to paradise—your eternal home."

David stood, faced the heavens, and placed his hands over his heart. "For Thine is the kingdom and the glory forever, amen."

STUDY GUIDE

PROLOGUE:

Romans 8:28 - "All things work together for good to them that love God, to them who are call according to his purpose." Serious mistakes in judgement are common, especially when we are young. However, if we confess our sin to God and turn away from that bad behavior, God promises to work things out for us, even if it's in an unexpected way or takes longer than we would like. Monica admitted her sin, turned to God for help, and the Lord delivered on his promise.

Do you turn to God in your time of need? How has God helped you through a serious struggle in your life?

Chapters 1 – 2

Proverbs 22:6 – "Train up a child in the way he should go: and when he is old, he will not depart from it." Dave is in his eighties, and although he is not an active farmer, he has an important role in the farm operation by teaching his family to walk with God.

How have your parents, grandparents, teacher, or neighbor helped you in your walk with the Lord?

Chapters 3 – 6

Geroge Washington Carver - "Ninety-nine percent of the failures come from people who have the habit of making excuses." Roy's drinking habit was due to his excuse-making and his refusal to admit he had a problem. He had turned away from the Lord, and in doing so, became an alcoholic.

Have you been making excuses for laziness, overeating, tardiness, gossiping, or other bad habits?

Chapter 7

Matthew 12:30a – "He that is not with Me is against Me." In this verse, Jesus makes it clear that you are either a follower of Jesus Christ or a follower of Satan. To lure you away from God, the Devil wants you to believe that there is a vast area of gray and that it is okay to dip your toe in sinfulness. However, evil never does good. Chip knew that Sandy would not be comfortable at Rodney's Roadhouse, so he rescued her.

Do you have a discerning heart when selecting which book to read or what movie or concert to attend?

Chapters 8

Prayer is how we communicate with God. Often, we experience new emotional situations as Roy with self-pity, anger and fear; Chip with anxiety, the fear of getting hurt, and self-consciousness. Like these two characters we find ourselves in over our heads.

When you face similar situations, do you pray? If so, how has God helped you process these feelings? If not, why not?

Chapter 10

John 7:24 – "Do not judge by appearances, but judge with right judgement." Roy's first impression of Jasper was not favorable. His facial tattoo, blue hair, and crazy clothes at first seemed abhorrent to Roy, yet in the end, they became best friends.

Have you had an experience of wrongly pre-judging someone?

Chapters 11 & 29

Psalm 147:3 – "God heals the brokenhearted and binds up their wounds." When we rely on God, He acknowledges our pain and mends our broken hearts. In Chapter 11, Tim grieved the loss of his wife, and in Chapter 29, Jenna grieved as her son clung to life. In both instances God healed their brokenness. Tim found his lost family and discovered that they were full of love. Jenna's son received a chance to live.

Have you experienced the loss of a loved one? If so, did you turn to God for comfort?

Chapter 12

Romans 12:4-6 "For just as each of us has one body with many members, and these members do not all have the same function, so in Christ we, though many, form one body, and each member belongs to all the others. We have different gifts, according to the grace given to each of us…" There are many chores and responsibilities in a home, and there are many responsibilities to the operation of a farm and a church.

What are your gifts/responsibilities that you have shared at home, work, in your church, and community?

Chapters 13 – 15

Proverbs 27:9 - "A sweet friendship refreshes the soul." Jasper and Roy are both believers, and as their friendship grows, so does their faith in God. It is important to have friends who are supportive and share a common belief in our Lord and Savior Jesus Christ.

Where is the best place to meet friends who are also believers? What places should you avoid?

Chapter 16

Christianity is most accurately seen as a relationship with God through Jesus Christ that transforms the way a person thinks, speaks and acts rather than a religious system of rules someone keeps to please God. As a believer invests in their relationship with God, the more visible God's transforming work will be. Cole's capacity and sincerity in caring for others is an expression of God's work in his life.

In what ways is God's transformative work visible in your life? What might someone who knows you say is evidence of God's transforming work in your life?

Chapter 18

Proverbs 16:16 – "How much better to get wisdom than gold, to get insight rather than silver?" Dave is the wise grandfather who guides his family in many ways.

Do you have a grandparent or a mentor who passed down their wisdom to you? What words of wisdom will you pass on to your children?

Chapter 19

Matthew 19:4 "Haven't you read, he replied, that at the beginning the Creator made them male and female, and said, for this reason a man will leave his father and mother and be united to his wife, and the two will become one flesh." God created only two genders: male and female. He also declared that marriage is between one man and one woman. God does not make mistakes. He knows there are sexual attractions between men and women because that's the way He made us. However, God also expressed limits on our sexual conduct—He wants us to be married first. In this story, Dave observed that his grandson Chip was getting too sexual with Sandy, so he guided their relationship in a Godly way by having a frank discussion with Chip.

What tricks does Satan use to discourage young men and women from marrying?

Chapter 20

C. S. Lewis – "What draws people to be friends is that they see the same truth. They share it." Jasper is eager to share his faith, and he insists on knowing that his good friend Roy truly loves the Lord. His baptism also allows him to share his Christian faith with his fellow residents at Mapledale. God wants us to associate with other Christians, but He also wants us to tell others about our Savior Jesus Christ.

What can you do to share your Christian faith with others?

Chapter 21

Matthew 5:4 "Blessed are those who mourn, for they shall be comforted." Tim lost his father, mother and more recently his wife. As he looked at his mother's ring, he realized there was a chance to connect with his biological father and perhaps discover additional family members. It is often said when a door closes, God will open a window.

Have you experienced a blessing after a sad period in your life?

Chapter 22

Martin Luther King, Jr. - "Faith is taking the first step even when you can't see the whole staircase."

Many people shy away from heavy decisions, but Angela stepped out on faith and gathered the courage to insist that Roy go to Johns Hopkins. She realized that she had to take control of the situation or Roy could die. Are you willing to step out on faith when important decisions must be made, or are you a person who wants others to decide for you?

Chapters 24 – 26

Elizabeth Gaskell - "God has made us so that we must be mutually dependent…The most proudly independent man depends on others around him…" We should count it a joy to help others.

In each of these chapters there are many ways that the characters help others. Can you find them?

Chapter 27

Galatians 6:9 - "Let us not grow weary while doing good, for in due season, we shall reap if we do not lose heart."

Psalm 133:1 – "Behold how good and pleasant it is when brothers dwell in unity!" Teamwork makes the dream work, and in this chapter, teamwork was essential in order to beat out the impending storm. Chip also did not hesitate to help his neighbor in the wee hours of the morning.

How supportive are you with friends and neighbors?"

Chapter 29

Colossians 3:12 – "As God's chosen people, holy and dearly loved, clothe yourselves with compassion, kindness, humility, gentleness, and patience." The Dormans and the Johnsons invited several friends and neighbors to join them in an Independence Day celebration.

Why are community gatherings important?

Chapter 31

Titus 2:7 - Show yourself in all respect to be a model of good works, and in your teaching show integrity and dignity." Good character is something we are born with, and it goes downhill fast if we fail to protect this precious gift. Mr. Stevenson gave up half of his award money, which demonstrated his good character. Honesty, kindness, and sincerity are important virtues in this regard.

Can you think of others?

Chapter 32

Proverbs 3:6 - "Trust in the Lord with all your heart and lean not on your own understanding. In all things acknowledge Him and He will direct your paths." Tim ministers to Angela and Roy by quoting from Zephaniah to assure them that God will create calm in their lives.

When you need direction in life, do you pray and trust in the Lord?

Chapter 33

Proverbs 19:17 – "Whoever is generous to the poor lends to the Lord, and He will repay him for his deed."

We do not give to get. We give because it is what God wants us to do—to help others in need.

Do you think this is the first time the Johnson-Dorman family helped a homeless person or others in desperate need?

Chapter 34

I Timothy 5:8 - "But if anyone does not provide for his relatives, especially for members of his household, he has denied the faith and is worse than an unbeliever." Providing for a family is not just with monetary means; it's also providing them with God's Word. The Johnsons and the Dormans are believers in Jesus Christ and his Word, which is why they were so accepting of their new family member Tim Higgins. Tim provided for his nephew by donating a kidney.

How often should a family pray together? Read the Bible?

Chapter 35

God puts people in our lives to help us. Monica met Tim at a critical point in her life. Roy met Jasper who helped him cement his relationship with the Lord. Chip met Sandy who proved to be a great match for both. Tim met Dave at a critical time in Roy's life.

Is there someone in your life you feel God has placed?

Chapter 36

Matthew 22:37-39 "Jesus said to him: You shall love the Lord God with all your heart, with all your soul, and with all your mind. This is *the* first and great commandment. And *the* second *is* like it: You shall love your neighbor as yourself." Love and unity play an important part throughout this novel. Dave honorably demonstrated his role as the family patriarch.

Do you see the Johnsons and the Dormans as role models for raising a Godly family?

Chapter 37

Ephesians 4:32 Blended families are becoming more commonplace, even in Christian homes. Nevertheless, love should be our guiding principle in order to live peaceably with step or half brothers and sisters. Here Jenna and Rob embraced their new half-brother, and ignored their father's past indiscretions as it wasn't for them to judge him.

Chapters 38 – 39

Psalm 25: 16-21 Loneliness affects all of us at some point in our lives. Dave missed his wife and deals with his lonesomeness by reaching out to friends. Actions rather than isolation is the cure for loneliness.

What do you do when you're feeling lonely?

Chapter 40

Proverbs 28:27 and Luke 12:15 Greed vs. Generosity. The miserly Martin Russell didn't want for anything and wasn't willing to share his wealth. His kindhearted wife Carrie was the exact opposite. She took pleasure in looking out for the needs of others.

Her priority was to serve God. Whereas Russell's was to make money.

What are your priorities?

Chapter 42

II Thessalonians 1:9 Non-believers or atheists don't care what happens to them when they die because they don't believe in an afterlife. Their goal is to get as much out of this world as possible which is an attitude that fosters greed and a lack of compassion. Martin exemplifies a godless mindset.

Chapter 43

Luke 2:14 This chapter embraces the spirit of Christmas—good will toward men. The Johnson and the Dormans want those who must work on Christmas Eve know that they are loved and appreciated. Here, God is glorified and generosity abounds.

Chapter 44

Matthew 19:4-6 The ungodly world has its own ideas of marriage. However, God ordained marriage to be one man and one woman until they are separated by death. He states that the two shall become one. This means that the families of both the bride and groom are also related by law—God's law. That's why we use the terms: father or mother-in-law, sister or brother-in-law, etc. Sandy and Chip's families are committed Christians, and in this chapter, we see the beauty of the two families united by their Christian faith.

Chapter 45

II Corinthians 6:14-18 God tells us not to be unevenly yoked with unbelievers. The partnership of Jasper and Roy is a good example of two men with the same religious beliefs going into business. But then Pamela comes on the scene. She's from a broken home, has no concept of Jesus and Salvation, but God directs her to a place where she can hear the Good News, also known as the Gospel Message. God uses believers to spread his Word, and as believers, we have a duty to teach others of God's love. John 3:16

Chapters 47

Hebrews 10:24-24 A huge pre-dawn warehouse by fire spurred Pamela on to make sure the first responders had plenty of coffee and donuts, however she spent all her money to make it happen. Jasper was impressed by her generous spirit and compared her to the widow in the Bible who gave up her last two mites for the offering plate. The Holy Spirit seemed to be leading Pamela to salvation as she revealed that she wants to be baptized.

Chapters 49

Ephesians 1:18 The opening of one's spiritual eyes often comes late in life, as demonstrated by Martin Russell. The thief on the cross is the best Biblical example of a last-minute conversion. We only know that it was God's will that the thief should meet Jesus before he died, so he could be saved. Tragedies often brings people to the saving knowledge of grace, as it is often said, "There are no atheists in foxholes."

Chapter 50

Isaiah 65:17 We often wonder what heaven will be like. In this verse God declares that he will "create a new heaven and a new earth; and the former shall not be remembered, nor come to mind." But we do know that our eternal home is called paradise, and that it will be glorious.

The Lord's Prayer

Our Father which art in heaven,

Hallowed be thy name.

Thy kingdom come,

Thy will be done in earth, as it is in heaven.

Give us this day our daily bread.

And forgive us our trespasses,
as we forgive those who trespass against us.

And lead us not into temptation,
but deliver us from evil:

For thine is the kingdom, and the power,
and the glory, forever.

Amen.

Made in the USA
Middletown, DE
02 May 2024